MY BROTHER'S KEEPER

JEREMY AKERMAN

A Marc LeBlanc Mystery

Cover art and interior drawings by the author
Cover design: Rebekah Wetmore
Editor: Andrew Wetmore

ISBN: 978-1-998149-71-1
First edition February 2025

Moose House Publications
2475 Perotte Road
Annapolis County, NS
B0S 1A0
moosehousepress.com
info@moosehousepress.com

Moose House Publications recognizes the support of the Province of Nova Scotia. We are pleased to work in partnership with the Department of Communities, Culture and Heritage to develop and promote our cultural resources for all Nova Scotians.

We live and work in Mi'kma'ki, the ancestral and unceded territory of the Mi'kmaw people. This territory is covered by the "Treaties of Peace and Friendship" which Mi'kmaw and Wolastoqiyik (Maliseet) people first signed with the British Crown in 1725. The treaties did not deal with surrender of lands and resources but in fact recognized Mi'kmaq and Wolastoqiyik (Maliseet) title and established the rules for what was to be an ongoing relationship between nations. We are all Treaty people.

Also by Jeremy Akerman

and available from Moose House Publications

Memoir
Outsider

Politics
What Have You Done for Me Lately? - revised edition

The Marc LeBlanc Mysteries
Holy Grail, Sacred Gold
Unspeakable Evil
The Plot to Kill the Premier
Best Served Cold

Fiction
Black Around the Eyes – revised edition
The Affair at Lime Hill
The Premier's Daughter
In Search of Dr. Dee
Explosion
The Rise and Fall of a Premier (due in 2025)

This book is dedicated to the memory of
Leslie Alcock, OBE, FSA, FRSE, FSA Scot,
who was senior lecturer in archaeology at Cardiff University when
he was my friend and mentor. I excavated with him on a number of
occasions and learned a great deal from him. Later he was
Professor of Archaeology at University of Glasgow, where I last saw
him. He was one of the leading experts in medieval archaeology,
and especially in the Early Christian Period (Dark Ages).
His most famous excavation was at South Cadbury castle, the site
reputed to be Camelot of the Arthurian legends.
He died in 2006.

This is a work of fiction. The author has created the characters, conversations, interactions, and events; and any resemblance of any character to any real person is coincidental.

My Brother's Keeper

My Brother's Keeper

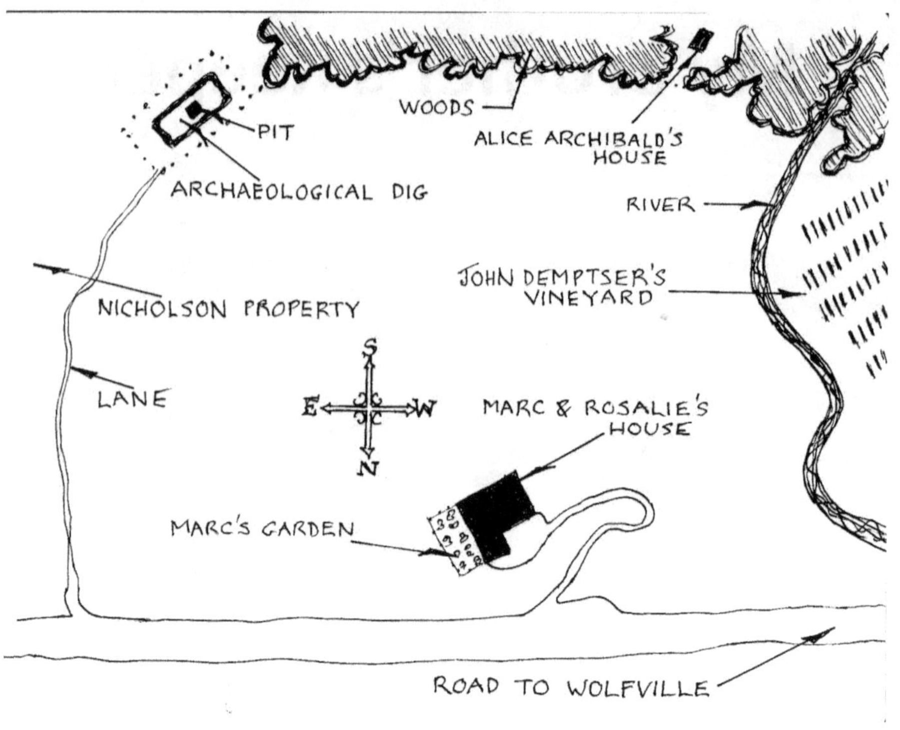
PIT
WOODS
ALICE ARCHIBALD'S HOUSE
ARCHAEOLOGICAL DIG
RIVER
NICHOLSON PROPERTY
JOHN DEMPTSER'S VINEYARD
LANE
S
E
W
N
MARC & ROSALIE'S HOUSE
MARC'S GARDEN
ROAD TO WOLFVILLE

1

It was another of those wonderful early-summer mornings, full of bird song and golden clouds streaking across the horizon. The sun had just risen on fields of bright, new growth, pale yellow-green leaves on trees and rows of carefully trained vegetation in the vineyards.

All was right with the world. At least it was with my world, because I had recently received excellent news about my investments, learning that they had earned me almost a million dollars in the previous twelve months.

I had made an immense amount of money when I was a merchant banker in London, speculating in bank shares in the depth of the recession in 2008, and had then inherited well over a million on the death of my father.

In addition to handsome returns on my regular investments, I had finally realized a surprising amount of income from my shares in John Dempster's winery. John had once been my best friend, but we had experienced a serious falling out which I have described in *Holy Grail, Sacred Gold*, the book I wrote about my first adventure as a private detective.

Two other pieces of news had lifted my spirits. The first came from Sheik Abdul Aziz, a friend I had made in London but had not seen since I returned to Canada in 2018. He informed me that he could obtain for me a mint-condition, second-hand 2012 Bugatti Veyron L'Or Blanc, a car I had long coveted but had not been able to afford new at the going price of $2.4 million. While my own Bugatti Veyron Sports Vitesse was also in its twelfth year and was running perfectly, I knew I would not be able to resist Sheik Aziz's offer if I could persuade my wife, Rosalie, to agree to my accepting it.

A piece of news, scarcely of the same magnitude but nonetheless very welcome, came in the form of a telephone call from our friend Bill Jolly, a fisherman and boat owner in Kingsport, to the effect that he had just docked at the wharf and had some very fresh mackerel for me. Rosalie and I are devoted to mackerel in all its manifestations, but we especially enjoy it for breakfast, which explained my speeding over the Habitant River at 6:20 am.

The Bugatti maintained a throaty roar as it negotiated the twisting road through Canning, past the Blomidon Winery and to the Kingsport wharf. Bill did not often dock here, usually using other harbours around the coast for his small fleet, but today all three of his vessels were awkwardly tied up here, and he was standing alongside the first of his Cape Islanders, *Bill and Jenny*, a cigarette in his mouth and a sack slung over his shoulder.

"'Mornin', Marc!" He called as I gently eased the Bugatti to a halt. "I got your fish ready."

"Lord, Bill, how many are in that sack?" I asked in amazement.

"If you don't want 'em, I'll take 'em back."

"Oh, no, you won't! What I don't eat today, I'll clean and freeze."

"Good idea," he said, stubbing out his cigarette. "I likes a bit o' mackerel meself, but there's not that many that do."

"Yes, even if it was more available, it seems to have gone out of fashion."

"Well, you enjoy 'em." He flung the sack on the ground in front of me. "I got work to do. So you won't mind if I git goin'?"

"No, not at all, Bill. I'm very grateful for this. How much do I owe you?"

"Not a thing, Marc. Friends don't charge friends."

"That's very kind of you. You'll let me know if I can return the favour."

"Sure will. See you around," he said as he clambered back on board and disappeared into the wheelhouse.

It had just turned 7 am as I pulled into our yard at Grand Pre. Ours was a large, modern house, consisting of more glass than any other material apart from the roof, with a large deck and patio at the rear, a vegetable and herb garden to one side and a long, grassy hill heading toward woods at the summit. To the west we could just see vines at the tail end of John Dempster's winery and, to the east, the many twists and turns of the Gaspereau River, and the sea beyond.

An older, more-traditional Annapolis Valley house would have been my preference, but when I arrived back from Britain there was nothing suitable on the market, and this property was going for a good price because most potential buyers regarded it as "weird." It had been built in an ultra-modern style by a local businessman who had subsequently gone bankrupt and left the area, and while it took some getting used to, we were glad of its up-to-date conveniences, especially its top notch security system and its bunker-like garage for the Bugatti.

Rosalie was starting to stir when I got in, so I prepared for breakfast by laying the table, setting out pans, bread, butter and grinding some of our favourite Blue Mountain coffee beans. We liked our mackerel simply fried and served with bread and butter without any other accompaniments, except for a tiny dab of horseradish.

I met my wife during my first foray into the world of private detection, and we have been blissfully happy ever since. Rosalie is a part-time Associate Professor of History at nearby Acadia University, and is a vital and invaluable collaborator on my investigations. She comes from a poor fishing family with antecedents in Wales and Scotland, some details of which may be found in my book *Best Served Cold*.

I, on the other hand, am of French Acadian stock, son of a Wolfville book seller who, alarmingly, turned out to be the head of an international crime syndicate, murdered by a mysterious Russian who left the country before he could be apprehended.

When not pursuing an investigation, Rosalie and I live quite quietly, walking on our hill, reading, talking, cooking and enjoying the contents of my extensive collection of very fine wine. We have a small circle of friends in the area, chief among them being Ray Bland, a car dealer and his wife Rachel; Walter Bryson, my lawyer, and his wife Joyce; and Gary and Jane Marshall, local business people. From further afield our friends are limited to Frank Wilberforce, a large and encyclopedic agent for the Canadian Agency for the Prevention of Art Theft and Forgery; and Patrick Kennedy, a superintendent in the Royal Canadian Mounted Police, and his wife Ruth. Rosalie and I are not involved in any local societies or projects, chiefly because should an investigation arise it would command all our attention and we should be unable to meet our commitments to the community.

The mackerel was superb and we both overindulged, each devouring three fish and most of a loaf of freshly made sourdough bread. As we were draining the last of the coffee, the telephone rang.

"It's for you," said Rosalie.

"Who is it?"

"I don't know. A man with a strange accent."

"What kind of accent?"

"Hard to tell. Maybe British."

"Okay. Thanks."

I searched my brain to think of anyone I met during my years at the bank in London, but could think of none who might be calling me here. "Hello. Marc LeBlanc speaking."

"Good morning, Mr. LeBlanc." The accent seemed like a strange mixture of English and American.

"Good morning."

"My name is Outerbridge. Nicholas Outerbridge."

"What can I do for you Mr. Outerbridge?"

"I am a solicitor in Hamilton."

"Ontario?"

"No, Hamilton, Bermuda."

"Yes, go on."

"Well, more by default than anything I am representing a client who has been detained on certain charges and requires someone of substance to stand bail for him."

"What on earth has that got to do with me?"

"The, er, client is a Mr. Lawrence LeBlanc."

"*Larry?*" I saw Rosalie's head snap up. She hurried over to stand beside me.

"Yes, your brother, I believe," Outerbridge said.

"Good God! What is he charged with?"

"It is a rather obscure charge under the Banking Amendment Order of 2014. It would take some time to explain it to a layman."

"But what does he want me to do, and why?"

"You would have to come to Hamilton and put up the bail money or otherwise stand surety." Outerbridge sounded apologetic.

"How much is the bail?"

"Not much as these things go. Two thousand Bermudian dollars."

"How much is that in real money?"

"Bermudian currency is real money, Mr. LeBlanc." Outerbridge said, sounding aggrieved.

"Yes, of course, I'm sorry."

"That would be $2,790.50 in Canadian funds."

"I would have to bring cash. A cheque would be no good?"

"If it were certified."

"And why can't Larry take care of it himself?"

"That is something to which I am not privy, Mr. LeBlanc."

"Well, why have I got to be there in person? Can't I email the money?"

"It would seem not."

"Why not?"

"Again, I cannot say. I am just carrying out the instructions of my client."

"Very well, Mr. Outerbridge." I sighed deeply. "I shall come as soon as I can. Where do I find you?"

"My office is at 23a Front Street in Hamilton."

"Okay. Goodbye."

"What on earth was that all about?" Rosalie asked, her eyes wide with expectation.

"Pack your bags, girl. We're off to Bermuda."

"Oh, goody!"

2

Rosalie had to be at the University for most of the day, so we did not have a chance to discuss recent events until we sat down to dinner. I cooked a rare rack of lamb with roast potatoes, buttered cabbage and mashed turnip.

To accompany the meal, I selected a Chateau Pichon LaLonde 1982 which I had first tasted in Bordeaux in 2009, but which at the time had been too closed and tannic. I suspected it would be one of those wines which never "came around" and ended life as a tannic shell, but was amazed to find it vibrant and almost flamboyant. It was rich, and big-bodied, redolent of blackcurrant with hints of chocolate and a long, cedar-like finish, a perfect example of how patience can be richly rewarded.

"That was very weird, that man calling you like that," Rosalie said. "What was his name again?"

"Outerbridge," I replied.

"Outerbridge. That's not a name you come across every day of the week."

"No it's not, but I checked and it is a fairly common family name in Bermuda."

"Really?"

"Yes. There are a few family names which are distinct to Bermuda, like Trimmingham, Woolridge, Tucker, Butterfield, Swan, Gibbons and Pearman."

"Yes, you don't hear those names around here."

"But, Rosalie, it's not the name which bothers me."

"What does bother you?

"The man's voice."

"What about it?"

"It sounded vaguely familiar."

"In what way?"

"I can't put my finger on it. It may be my imagination."

"Probably is. You have a very vivid imagination."

"Thank you. This wine is spectacular. I'm not imagining that," I said as we sniffed our wine glasses, appreciating the remarkable work of both vintner and time.

"No, it's quite wonderful. It's hard to believe it's over 40 years old."

"Can you get the time off work?" I asked.

"That depends upon how long we would be gone for."

"If I went on my own, I would only take two days at the most, but if you can come we can take a week."

"I think I can swing that," she said. "Have you been to Bermuda before?"

"Oh, yes, I used to go there for vacations when I lived in London. You'll love it. It is the most civilized place. The people are wonderful, very friendly and helpful."

"What's the climate like there?"

"Sort of a cross between the Southern states and the Caribbean. It only gets extremely hot there in the summer."

"How about the crime rate? I've heard it can be very high in Caribbean countries."

"Bermuda isn't in the Caribbean, and except for poor old Sharples, there has been comparatively little crime there."

"Who's Sharples? What happened to him?"

"Sir Richard Sharples was the Governor of Bermuda who was murdered by assassins back in 1973. His assistant, Hugh Sayers, was also killed"

"Good God, why?"

"It was done by a Bermudian Black Power group called the Black Beret Cadre. They were a very small, unrepresentative gang."

"Did they catch them?"

"Oh, yes. They were the last people to be hanged in the British Commonwealth."

"A sad story."

"Even sadder was what happened to Lady Sharples afterwards,"

I said. "The British government said she had to pay full death duties on their house because Sir Richard didn't lose his life in the line of duty."

"Mean bastards!"

"Indeed. She had to sell the house to pay the taxes."

"What happened to her?"

"She was made a baroness, had two more husbands and died a few years ago, a month short of her 100th birthday."

"Wow!" Rosalie took a sip of wine. "Do you have any idea what sort of trouble Larry is in and why he chose to contact you?"

"Outerbridge, the solicitor—"

"What's a solicitor?"

"Same as a lawyer. Except under their system solicitors do not appear in court."

"Then who does?"

"Barristers. But you're getting me sidetracked."

"Sorry."

"Apparently it has something to do with banking regulations, but I don't know any more than that."

"Seems very strange. Given Larry's power and connections, why would he need your help?"

On a previous investigation, which I have described in my book *The Plot to Kill the Premier*, I was obliged by circumstances to break my resolve never to tell Rosalie about Larry. Suffice it to say she was shocked to learn that he was a highly-dubious character who had inherited the leadership of my father's crime syndicate, and even more shocked to discover that Larry was officially dead, having "died" so I could benefit from my father's will.

"I can't imagine why he would need my help," I said, "or why he would be using his own name."

"A name of someone who is supposed to be dead."

"Exactly. Well, there's only one way to find out. Can you leave at any time?"

"Whenever you can get flights."

3

The next morning, after a breakfast of more mackerel, fresh bread and farmhouse butter, I saw Rosalie off to the university and got down to the business of booking our trip. To my intense annoyance, while I was able to obtain direct flights to Bermuda and back, I could not get them for four more days.

I called the number on Nicholas Outerbridge's card but got an answering machine, so I left a message indicating that our arrival would be delayed. I then secured rooms for us at the Hamilton Princess which, even though cost was no object to us, struck me as being inordinately expensive.

Our stay in Bermuda was dictated by the date of our return flights, so we would have five full days on the island, which would give me a chance to show Rosalie most of the better sights.

Then I sat out on the deck reading a magazine for about an hour, when something I had not noticed before caught my eye. Up on the left, at the top of our grassy hill before it meets the woods, and between our property and the adjoining Nicholson farm, two features puzzled me. The first was that there appeared to be a kind of no-man's land between the properties, each of them fenced off. The second was that, while on each side the grass was a rich green, in the intervening space it was shorter, paler and browner.

I sat staring at it for several minutes, wondering if the no-man's land portion belonged to us or to old man Nicholson. Further, I couldn't figure out why it was fenced on both sides if it belonged to either of us. There was no point in calling old Nicholson because he was in his late nineties and was as deaf a post.

Finally, my curiosity got the better of me and I ambled up the hill to get a closer look. I had seen this area before but it had not registered on me until today that there was anything unusual about it. Sure enough, the fences were intact, although more secure on his side than on ours, and the area enclosed by them was about 35 feet wide by approximately 80 feet long.

I hopped over the fence, tearing my pants in the process, and shuffled around, staring at the ground. It took me some time to ascertain what was under my feet, but there seemed to be a bank, possibly a slight ditch, a level stretch and then a much larger bank. I thought there might have been some kind of structure, maybe a building, on the site at some stage in the distant past.

Since old Nicholson lived alone, there was little point in taking my inquiries there, so I thought my lawyer, Walter Bryson, might be able to supply some answers. I went back down the hill, rather surprised to find myself running, jumped into the Bugatti, and drove into Wolfville.

Walter was with a client, so I had to wait until he was free, during which time Wanda, his secretary, noticed my torn trouser leg, hastily produced a needle and some thread and offered to undertake a temporary repair.

"Give me your pants and hop into the washroom." She told me. "I'll give you a shout when they are ready."

Very reluctantly, I agreed because Wanda, a huge, ferocious woman, is not the sort you want to upset. I waited in the washroom for about ten minutes and then I heard her call out.

As I exited into the waiting room, Walter and his client emerged from the inner office. They stared at me, with amazement on Walter's part and disgust on the client's. Wanda's waving the pants around in the air did nothing to reduce my embarrassment.

While Walter saw the client out, I unsteadily struggled to get back into the pants, and was zipping them up when he re-entered.

"I won't ask what you and Wanda have been up to, Marc, but I assume you want to see me."

"Mr. Bryson, you've got the wrong end of the stick—" Wanda began to protest.

"Your business is your business," said Walter, throwing me a wink, "but please in future do not do it on the firm's time. Come in, Marc."

After I had outlined the nature of my inquiry, Walter went to one end of the office where there was a large cabinet containing a number of very wide drawers. In these he kept plans and other large documents, one of which he withdrew and spread out on his desk. He took off his glasses and held them at arm's length while he examined the plan.

"It belongs to you, Marc. That little bit of land is yours. It's been part of your property for at least 210 years." He pushed the plan aside and pulled another over. "This is dated 1815 and look: there it is."

I looked carefully. There was no doubt about it. In the earliest plan, and in all successive plans, the little bump at the top of my hill was included in my land, not Nicholson's.

"Was there ever any building on it?"

"Shouldn't think so." Walter replied. "It'd be a strange place to build. Let me have a look at town maps prior to 1815."

He returned to the cabinet, rifled through the papers, finally producing a map dated 1802. He placed it in front of me.

"This is a copy, of course. The original is in the provincial archives. Now, let's see." He repeated his strange routine with his glasses. "No building, Marc, but there is a small annotation which might refer to your site or it might not. The scale of the map is questionable."

"What does it say? It's much too small for me to read."

"It looks like *Domi et foraminis*. I'm guessing that would be Latin."

"Why would they use Latin?"

"Mapmaker's conceit maybe. I don't know, but there are a few other notes in Latin."

"What does it mean?"

"What does what mean?"

"*Domi et foraminis*."

"Oh. Not a clue. Let's Google it and see." Walter turned his computer to face him and tapped out the question. "It says the translation is: At home and in the hole."

"What the hell?"

"It sounds rather like a reference to someone who is in serious debt." Walter chuckled, "But since that hardly applies to you, Marc, I think that is the extent of the assistance I can render on this occasion."

"Well, thanks anyway, Walter. I assume you'll be billing me for this consultation?"

"Most assuredly. Good bye, Marc."

4

The next day I was expectant, for what I could not say, but some sense of excitement was in the air.

When I got home from seeing Walter Bryson the previous day, I had called an old associate, Akerman, a former archaeologist living in Halifax. Now in his 80s, he had followed a number of callings during his life, one of which was as an archaeologist on excavations at the Fortress of Louisbourg in Cape Breton. I explained what I had found and asked him to speculate on what it might be.

"It's impossible to say without actually seeing the site," he said, "and maybe not even then."

"Would you take a look? I could shoot up and fetch you."

"That would mean you'd have to bring me back, too. No, I'll come down. My wife, Caroll Anne, is not working, so I'll bring her with me."

"Could you stay over? We have lots of spare rooms and we'd give you a good dinner."

"In that case, I accept. We'll see you in about an hour and a half."

When I told Rosalie we would have overnight guests, she was surprised, and when I told her who they were, she looked askance at me.

"Are you sure it's a good idea, getting involved with that guy again? He crops up in every investigation."

"I like him, but I know a lot of people don't think much of him."

"The Premier for one. Wendell dismisses him as a crank."

"I know, but he was crucial in getting Wendell's would-be assassin. And he's been quite helpful in the past."

"Alright. What shall we have for dinner?"

"We have an excellent prime rib of beef in the pantry. Let's have that with some Brussels sprouts and Yorkshire pudding."

"Lovely. Will you take care of the wine?"

"Sure. I have a few bottles of 2005 Arcadian Pinot Noir from California."

"Which one? They have a number in their stable."

"The Dierberg Vineyard in Santa Maria Valley."

"I'm not familiar with that. Are you sure it won't be over the hill?"

"We'll find out tonight!"

~

I was pulling some weeds out of my vegetable and herb garden when I heard the crunch of tires on the gravel of our forecourt. I walked around and saw a little red Hyundai pulling up in front of the door. My friend got out and opened the door for his wife, a short, blonde, attractive woman many years his junior.

I took her inside to meet Rosalie, and invited them to join us on the hill, to which they agreed with alacrity.

We were all chatting away like a cageful of monkeys, so I did not notice until we were half-way up the hill that there was somebody at the site ahead of us. It was a middle-aged, bearded man, moving around taking photographs.

Rosalie said, "Oh, it's Ralph. Ralph Giffin, from the university. He's an archaeologist, or anthropologist. I forget which."

At the sound of our approach he stopped and walked toward the fence. "Hello, Rosalie. Fancy seeing you. Do you live around here?"

"Yes, this is our property," she replied with a laugh, "and you're trespassing."

"Oh, I'm sorry. I didn't know who owned the land, so I couldn't ask permission. In any case, I didn't think anyone would mind if I took a look."

After introductions had been made all around, I asked Giffin what he was doing there and why he was taking pictures.

"Ah. I ran into Walter Bryson in the supermarket and he said there was—a structural anomaly, he called it—at the top of this field."

"That was nice of Walter to betray lawyer/client confidentiality!" I said, and seeing the look of dismay on his face, added, "It's quite alright. I have no objection."

"Oh, good."

"Now you've seen it, what do you make of it?"

"I'm not at all sure. Clearly there has been some kind of structure here, but I haven't seen anything like it."

"How about you?" I turned to ask Akerman, but he had already climbed the fence and was pacing up and down in the stunted grass. I called out to him, "What have you found?"

"The discoloration of the grass indicates where some kind of walls have been, and the slightly darker patches show where there might have been ditches or gullies." He moved down the site. "You see here at the bottom, this darker line could have been a ditch or gully, and these lighter lines the outline of a building."

"What about that dark feature in the middle?" Giffin asked. "What do you think that was?"

"That looks like a pit. It's too big to have been a well. But what it was doing right in the middle of the house I have no idea."

"House? You said 'house'. What made you say that?"

"The site is almost identical with platform houses in the uplands of Wales." He pulled out a notebook and pen and drew a diagram. "What they did was to dig into a hillside, scoop out the earth and deposit some at the bottom, but most at the top. The earth at the top end was a kind of hood, to protect against the weather. So you had a flat platform with a bank at each end and, usually, a slight ditch cut around the hood and running down the sides to divert groundwater away from the living quarters."

"Yes, I see," muttered Giffin, studying the diagram, "what date were these Welsh platform houses?"

"The ones I dug with Professor Alcock were thirteenth century."

"Thirteenth century!"

"Ralph," Caroll Anne piped up. "Who would have been here in the thirteenth century?"

"No Welsh, that's for sure, and no Europeans. John Cabot didn't swing past these parts until 200 years later, and the French didn't come for 100 years after that."

"Someone must have been here," I said.

"The Wabanaki Confederacy," said Rosalie, "which would have included Maliseet, Passamaquoddy, Penobscot, and Abenaki tribes. They were primarily hunters and gatherers, but also skilled saltwater fishers. In this area, the Mi'kmaq held sway."

"Did any of those tribes leave behind anything like this platform house?" Caroll Anne asked.

"Not that I'm aware of," said Giffin.

"Did any of the Welsh platform houses have a central feature like this?" Rosalie asked Akerman.

"No. The central area was always laid with beaten earth or stone to make a livable floor."

"Then what the hell is it?" I exclaimed.

"That's something we can't ever know."

"Maybe not," Giffin said quietly. "Marc. You're sure you own this piece of land?"

"Quite sure. Walter Bryson confirmed it yesterday."

"In that case, do I have your permission to conduct an excavation here?"

"Certainly!"

"Thank you. If you don't mind, my assistants and I will come up tomorrow to survey the site, then we will lay out lines for trenches. Is there any way we could get vehicles up here?"

"Well, I'd rather not have an Armada churning up the grass on the field, but there's a narrow lane running between the properties. It's overrun with brambles and only goes so far. It ends about sixty meters from here."

"That'd be fine. I can find a crew of six or eight to start with. The university and the schools will be out next month, so I can recruit more volunteers then."

"You plan a full scale excavation?" Caroll Anne asked.

"Half measures won't be good enough," said Giffin. "I have a feeling this is a very important site. I'll talk to the university bigwigs tomorrow to see if I can get funding."

"You know what intrigues me the most?" Akerman said.

"What's that?" I asked.
"This pit in the middle. I wonder how deep it is."

5

I awoke early, so, rather than get up and possibly wake the others, I lay in bed and cast my mind over the events of the previous evening. We had experienced a surprisingly enjoyable and riotous time. At the last minute we decided to invite our friends Gary and Jane Marshall to join us for dinner. Gary was a local lawyer in his mid-forties whom both Rosalie and I liked. Neither of us cared much for Jane, because she was an inveterate gossip, and was quite bigoted on some matters, but we could not have one without the other.

Jane was particularly loquacious, regaling us with a succession of jokes, not all of them appropriate for the occasion. Akerman treated us to a host of stories about his days as a politician and later as a newspaper editor. Caroll Anne described growing up in a Cape Breton mining community and Rosalie responded with an account of her poor childhood in a Digby fishing village. Gary and I sat back, sipping our wine and laughing at the many anecdotes.

The food was very good. We started with a seafood soup, which I made by julienning onions, carrots, celery and tomatoes, sweating them in olive oil and then adding fish stock. Then, just before serving, I added shrimp, scallops and pieces of haddock. With that I served an excellent 2009 Chateau Haut Brion Blanc. The prime rib was beautiful, and I was lucky that the Yorkshire pudding rose perfectly.

I had frequently had trouble with getting Yorkshire pudding to rise and, while it still tasted good, often we had to eat a fairly flat product. I discovered the secret which has ensured success ever since, namely adding a teaspoon of baking powder, using water instead of milk, and pouring the mixture into a fiercely bubbling pan of hot oil.

Rosalie had made an exquisite lemon tart, requiring the use of an enormous number of lemons, which we enjoyed with a Billecart-Salmon Demi-Sec Champagne.

After about two hours of brightly-buzzing conversation, a lull prompted Gary to lean over towards me.

"What's this I hear about digging up on the hill?"

"Yes, Ralph Giffin from the university is to conduct excavations."

"Where, exactly?"

"At the top of the hill on the left there's a small piece of scrub land which has some strange features. Giffin wanted to investigate, so I told him to go ahead."

"But the land is not yours," Gary said. "It belongs to Adam Nicholson."

"No, it doesn't. Walter checked it out on the old deeds."

Gary did not seem to like my answer. He frowned, looked at his wife who nodded.

"You'd better tell them, Gary."

"Tell us what?" Rosalie asked.

"There's a curse on the place."

"A what?"

"A curse. When I was a little boy I lived just beyond your woods, where the Clarks live now. We were constantly told there was a curse on the place."

"You're joking?"

"No, I'm not. My brothers and I stayed away from that spot, but others who didn't all had bad things happen to them."

"What kind of things?" Caroll Anne asked.

"Couple of kids died young—"

"That could have been due to any number of unconnected diseases," Akerman interrupted.

"Maybe. Others had broken arms and legs. Then there was Mary Callaghan."

"Who was Mary Callaghan, and what happened to her?" I demanded.

"She went walking over the hill one day and came back mad."

"Mad?"

"A gibbering idiot." Gary's face was serious. "She never recovered. She was like that for the rest of her life."

"Coincidence," I said.

"You think? Years ago, both your field and the adjoining Nicholson field used to grow crops." Gary said. "Cabbages, I think. Maybe turnips. Anyway, for some distance on either side of that place, the crops were stunted and died."

"I've never heard such bunk in my life!' I exclaimed. "What about you Mr. Akerman?"

"You know what Shakespeare said?"

"What did he say?"

"'There are more things in Heaven and earth than are dreamt of in your philosophies.' I wouldn't rule anything out, out of hand, but in these cases there is almost always a logical explanation for apparently inexplicable occurrences."

"That may well be," Gary said, "but why take a chance? If I were you, Marc, I'd tell Giffin to go dig someplace else."

"Gary, you can't be serious." Rosalie said. "This is the twenty-first century."

"Do what you want," Gary said peevishly, "but don't blame me for the consequences. Come on, Jane, it's time we were heading home."

~

The sun was now well up and filling the bedroom with a lambent glow. I was astonished to see it was already after nine o'clock.

Rosalie woke, stretched and went to the bathroom. I wandered over to the window and threw it wide open, breathing deeply the cool air, in which a mixture of the sea and grass could be detected.

My attention was attracted first by a faint noise of crashing and threshing, and I quickly saw it came from people clearing brambles and other growth from the small lane. Ralph Giffin had wasted no time in getting on with his task.

Then I noticed a flashing light at the bottom of the lane, where it meets the road. Since this was partially obscured by two maple trees, I could not identify the source, so I dressed, pulled on my shoes, went downstairs and out into the field. I was not sure why, but I was running hard towards the flashing light, only to discover it was an ambulance just leaving.

Giffin was watching it depart so I went up to him. "What's going on, Ralph?"

"Oh, hi, Marc. Poor Sandy, one of my helpers lopped some of her fingers off hacking at these old brambles."

"Good God. Is it serious?"

"I'm not sure. They have the fingertips on ice and are rushing her to Halifax. I guess they'll try to stitch them back on."

"Well, let's hope for the best. Not the most auspicious start to your project."

"I guess not, although I was up with the birds and have already laid out lines for trenches up above." He nodded in the direction of several students who were attacking the overgrowth on the lane. "These guys should have cut their way through by lunch, so then we can get the jeep up there with all our tools and equipment."

"Sounds like you have everything under control. Look, around ten, if you come over to the house, I'll have several thermoses full of coffee for you, and some bacon sandwiches."

"Wonderful! We didn't have time for breakfast because we wanted to get a head start on the work. Thanks, Marc; I'll see you around ten."

"Oh, Ralph?"

"Yes, Marc?"

"Was there anything unusual about the injury?"

"Unusual?"

"Yes, anything unexplained?"

"I don't think so. Jeff—that's the tall fellow in the yellow shirt—said one of the brambles sprang back and caused Sandy to cut herself with her billhook. Why did you ask?"

"No reason. I'll see you later."

When I got back, the Akermans were sitting down to breakfast. Rosalie had laid out bagels, butter, smoked salmon and a huge pot of coffee, and was in the course of making lashings of scrambled eggs.

"Where have you been?" she asked.

"Over to the lane. Giffin's crew have already cleared a good stretch of it. He thinks he may be able to get the jeep up to the site after lunch."

"He's a quick worker," said Caroll Anne.

"Yes, he's already laid out the trenches. Oh, Rosalie, I told him I would have a few thermoses of coffee and some bacon sandwiches for them about ten o'clock."

"They'll be lucky! We're out of bacon. Will sausages be okay?"

"I'm sure they will be."

"What's wrong, Marc? You have that look on your face."

"It's nothing. One of Ralph's helpers chopped some fingers off. There was an ambulance moving off as I arrived. They've taken her to Halifax."

"Ouch. What happened?"

"Apparently a bramble jumped the wrong way and caused her to cut herself."

"Vegetation is often like that," said Akerman. "At least it's not an M.R. James case."

"What's that when it's at home?"

"M.R. James was a mystery and horror writer. He died in 1936. He was an English medieval scholar who was provost of King's and Eton colleges as well as being Vice Chancellor of Cambridge University."

"What's that got to do with anything?" Caroll Anne interjected.

"James wrote a story called 'The Malice of Inanimate Objects', in which a man was convinced he was being attacked by the objects around his house. He thought the ghost of a guy who had committed suicide was moving the objects."

"Why would you bring that up now?"

"Because of the curse." Akerman laughed loudly.

"Not that again! I thought we'd dispensed with that nonsense." I said. "Anyway, Rosalie and I are off to Bermuda tomorrow. Even if there is a curse, I'm sure it never leaves home."

6

Arriving by air at most Caribbean locations, when you step out of the aircraft onto the top of the gangway it is like being enveloped in a hot, wet towel. It is nowhere as hot or humid as that in Bermuda, although in August temperatures can exceed 30°C. In early summer it hovers around 25°C, so our short walk from the plane to the terminal was pleasant. As it was already dark, the plane having landed at 8:30, the sounds of exotic birds could be heard in nearby trees.

Bermuda is a strange, thin island, shaped rather like a shrimp with its tail curled up behind it. It lies about 1400 km due south of Nova Scotia, roughly on a level with southern South Carolina and northern Georgia. Only 78,000 people live there permanently, although as many as 450,000 tourists may visit the island in a year.

Somebody had spilled water all over the floor of the terminal, so we had to wait while staff mopped it up. This meant that the Hamilton Princess transport had left without us and we had to get a taxi.

Most streets and roads in Bermuda are very narrow, extremely serpentine or highly congested, and the speed limit is 35 mph, so it takes a long time to get anywhere. A trip from one end of the island to the other, about 24 miles, usually takes an hour and a half by road, but only 45 minutes by ferry.

From the airport, near St. Georges, our taxi took a little over 30 minutes to get to our hotel, an impressive, pink six-story complex on Pitts Bay Road, an extension of Front Street which, in turn, springs from Middle Road, on which we had entered the city.

The Princess was luxurious (which it should be, for between $600 and $1300 a night) and we were speedily checked in and conducted to our room overlooking the harbour. We had not had dinner on the flight so were very hungry, but did not want to get changed for dinner, so had snacks and drinks at the beach club.

We sat listening to the waves and the sounds of birds for about an hour then went up to our room. I was very pleased to be back in Bermuda, where I had spent some very happy times, but was not looking forward to seeing Larry and sorting out his problem.

From what Outerbridge had told me, Larry's offence had something to do with an obscure infringement of the Island's banking regulations, but it would not surprise me if his visit to Bermuda was connected with a variety of more serious crimes. Whatever they happened to be, I wanted to stay as far as possible away from them, and I particularly wanted Rosalie not to be tainted by association.

As I had previously indicated to Rosalie, crime in Bermuda was a lot lower than in the United States and in most Caribbean countries. In fact, Bermuda's crime rate was at its lowest in 2019, which was a considerable decline from previous years. However, gang violence had increased since then, the government having formed a Gang Violence Reduction Team with particular reference to combating gun crime.

Worse, the Bermuda Police had to investigate two murders, and then the bodies of four people, including two children, who were found dead in an apartment complex. The police did not say how the four people were killed, but it was speculated that they were murdered. I saw from the *Royal Gazette*, which I picked up in the lobby, that Deputy Police Commissioner Antoine Daniels had said that Bermuda was navigating through an unprecedented and difficult period, having recently experienced seven murders. He said the violence in the community was a real concern and that police would be increasing operations in a bid to tackle the problem.

I did not think that Larry had anything to do with these crimes —at least I devoutly hoped not-- but it made me extremely uneasy and I did not sleep well.

7

We awoke next morning to find the sun streaming through the blinds, making bright patterns on the thick carpet. Clearly it was going to be a beautiful day, so we hurriedly conducted our ablutions and went out onto the waterfront in search of breakfast.

We found it at a lovely place called The Cloud, where Rosalie had a Florentine omelette with shallots, spinach, mushrooms and Hollandaise sauce, and I had two poached organic eggs, *jamon ibérico*, arugula, and mustard Hollandaise on johnny bread.

Then we strolled along the harbour to the ferry terminal, noticing a posted schedule which featured five different ferry routes to various locations around the island. In conversation with a friendly official we learned that Bermuda had a remarkable public transit system, and that we could buy special passes which could be used innumerable times on both ferries and buses. He told us we could never get lost in Bermuda because bus stops were indicated by coloured poles, pink meaning that the bus would be travelling toward Hamilton, and blue poles signalling that the bus would be travelling away from the capital.

"Well," I finally said to Rosalie, "I guess we can't put it off any longer. We should go and see Outerbridge."

"Yes, I think so. Let's find out the worst."

"Why do you put it like that?"

"You know that nothing connected with your brother will be straightforward. There are bound to be complications."

"Yes, you're right. And likely unpleasant ones."

We wandered along Front Street, admiring the brightly-painted buildings and equally brightly-clad people.

At one point Rosalie stopped me. "Look over there and tell me what you see."

"What?"

"Those men are dressed in shirts and ties, but are wearing shorts."

"Ah yes, Bermuda shorts. Very sensible in this climate."

"Look, there's number 23."

We crossed the street and stood outside an ornate, four-story building, the ground floor being occupied by a clothing store. We searched, but could find no number 23A.

"It can't have disappeared. Maybe it's round the back."

"We'd better go and ask."

A very large, smiling black woman was behind the counter. "Hello. Wopnin?"

I later learned this was the local abbreviation of 'what's happening?'

"Good morning." I said. "We were looking for number 23A, but couldn't find it."

"That 'cos it don't exist." She laughed loudly.

"Really?"

"You be wantin' Ole Nicky, I bet."

"We were looking for Nicholas Outerbridge. Is he Old Nicky?"

"That him!" She laughed again. "He used to have an office on the top floor many moons ago."

"He doesn't have one now?"

"Hell, no. Leastways not here. These days his office is at the Astwood." She laughed uproariously. "That where you'll find him, I guess."

"Where is that?"

"Just up the street here. You can't miss it."

She was right. A little way up Front Street there was a sign: The Astwood Arms. It was a bar.

Rosalie looked at me and frowned. "What now?"

"We go in, I guess."

The place had an old fashioned, rather elegant bar but the rest was in standard pub furnishings, with barrels spotted around the floor. In the farthest corner, alone at a table, sat a very old, very small man of indeterminate ethnicity, nursing a glass of almost black liquor. He was immaculately dressed, but in a fashion that had long since gone out of fashion. He wore a white, three-piece suit, a striped shirt and a bow tie, with a silk handkerchief spilling out of his breast pocket.

When he saw us approaching he gripped the table and unsteadily stood up. "Mr. and Mrs. LeBlanc I presume." He said. His voice was mellifluous with a slight tremor. It was definitely not the voice I had heard on the telephone a few days ago.

"Mr. Outerbridge?"

"For my sins, I am he. Please be seated."

As we sat down I studied him more carefully and judged him to be at least in his late eighties, of obviously mixed racial parentage, and to be extremely fastidious. In particular I took note of the fact that, despite his suit being very old, the lapels were hand pricked and the jacket had a nipped-in waist, signs of expensive bespoke tailoring.

"You have brought the money?" He asked quietly.

"Yes, a certified cheque."

"May I see it?"

"Certainly,"

I took it out of my wallet and passed it to him. To my surprise, he glanced at it and passed it back.

"Don't you want it?"

"Not I. You will need it later. I ascertain that you went in search of me at my old address."

"Yes. Don't you have an office now?"

"I do not. I have little need of one."

"Do you still practice law?"

"No."

"But—"

"I never did."

"What?"

"Pray do not alarm yourself, Mr. LeBlanc. A certain amount of deception was necessary to obtain your attention. All will be revealed to you in the fullness of time."

"I don't like being deceived, Mr. Outerbridge."

"None of us do." He took a sip of what appeared to be very dark rum. "We have several hours to wait."

"For what?"

"To conduct our business. I suggest we make the best of things, relax, have a drink or two and then have lunch at a little restaurant up the road. The rock fish there is excellent."

Rosalie looked at me and shrugged, a gesture I knew meant I should not lose my temper, but should accept the situation until I better understood it. She was, of course, right and, after all, we were on a vacation of sorts.

As it turned out those few hours were highly enjoyable, Outerbridge being a kind and hugely entertaining host. As well as informing us on a great many aspects of Bermuda's history, he revealed that he was 95 and sprang from a black mother and a father who was half English and half Portuguese. He had been born at the beginning of the Great Depression, long before Bermuda became self-governing, and had succeeded to his father's import-export business, although he was at great pains to point out that he was in no way related to the Outerbridge family which manufactured Bermuda's famous sherry peppers. He had, he told us, sat in parliament for a number of years and had been an intimate of Sir Henry Tucker, the island's first premier.

It seemed likely to Rosalie and me that Outerbridge could no longer obtain an audience for his reminiscences either because everybody had heard them so many times, or because he could only open up to strangers. Whatever the reason, once he had started there was no stopping him and he talked almost non-stop until lunch time.

He reeled off names which meant nothing to Rosalie, and very little to me, their being politicians from many years ago. He talked of Jim Woolridge riding his horse along Front Street, of Honeybee Vesey, of Shorty Trimmingham, David Wilkinson and Harry Viera. This last, apparently, was an inveterate womanizer who opened a fake real estate office for the express purpose of meeting and seducing women. Outerbridge described at length his part in a successful plot to overthrow Premier Jack Sharpe in the 1970s when he and Senators Stan Rattray and John Stubbs forced Sharpe to resign in favour of their man, David Gibbons.

During this extraordinary monologue I observed that our host had consumed five glasses of rum, I had put away three beers and a whiskey and Rosalie had drunk several glasses of wine.

At one o'clock he led us up the street and round the corner to a restaurant called Barracuda, where we settled, Outerbridge ordering a bottle of Roserock Chardonnay by Drouhin 2018, from the Dundee Hills in Oregon. Since he had made a point of recommending it, Rosalie and both had rock fish while Outerbridge took the yellow fin tuna. The rock fish was superb, reminding me that it is in the same league as turbot and John Dory, and in my experience sometimes surpassing them for quality and flavour.

Rosalie and I were astounded at the enormous appetite this frail old man possessed as, in addition to his yellow fin, he had Bermuda fish chowder (with sherry peppers), and gingerbread toffee pudding for dessert.

After a coffee and brandy he sat back and with a satisfied sigh, wiped his mouth, looked at his pocket watch and beamed at us. "I think the time has come when we must do what has to be done."

8

Rosalie and I waited out on the street while Outerbridge went to the toilet. As we watched the small trucks, cars and scooters go by, she turned to me.

"Marc, who paid the bill in there?"

"I did."

"And at the Astwood Arms?"

"Yes, that one, too."

"Why? I thought we were his guests."

"It's obvious he doesn't have a cent to his name, poor old guy."

"Then what the hell is Larry doing with him?"

"Don't know. Why don't we ask him?"

After a few minutes, Outerbridge shuffled out of the restaurant and stood unsteadily on the sidewalk. When he noticed we were looking at him quizzically he asked what was wrong.

"Nothing." I said. "We were just wondering what the connection is between you and my brother."

"Ah," he said ruminatively, clearly wondering if we were capable of hearing the truth. "Let us just say that many years ago your brother did me a great favour, which I never forgot."

"What was the favour?"

"That is neither here nor there," he said, a little irritably, "but I told him then that if I could ever return that favour, I would do so. You can imagine my surprise when after all this time I got a message from Daphne that he was here in Bermuda, at the Westgate."

"Who's Daphne?"

"The lady you talked to at the clothing store."

"And what's the Westgate? Is that a hotel?" Rosalie asked.

"No, m'dear, that's the jail. The Westgate Correctional Facility.

It's out near the Dockyard."

"Are we going there?"

"Yes, but we have to go somewhere else first."

"Where?"

"Follow me."

Proceeding at a painfully slow pace we followed Outerbridge back down to Front Street and along to Church Street. This was a pleasant road full of handsome buildings, but was on a hill which required him to come to a stop and ask for my arm.

Supporting him in this fashion, we crawled along until we came to a modern block called the Dame Lois Browne Evans Building.

"Who was the Dame?" Rosalie asked.

"Ah." Outerbridge smiled. "She was a very feisty lady who was Leader of the Opposition back in the 70s. Inside the parliament she used to attack me viciously."

"And outside parliament?" I asked, sensing a mystery.

"Ask me no questions and I'll tell you no lies," he said with a shaky, but salacious laugh. "We go in here to pay the bail."

We approached a stout woman at the reception desk who wore the tightest fitting dress I have ever seen, had her glasses on a rope around her neck and a huge tortoiseshell comb in her gleaming black hair.

"Wopnin?" She said. "Hi, Nicky!"

"Hello, Lavinia. This gentleman has business with you."

"Yes, I've come to pay the bail for Lawrence—"

I was interrupted by a howl like a wounded animal from Outerbridge, who desperately dragged me to one side.

"No, no, no. He's not Lawrence LeBlanc here," he said in a whisper.

"Oh, right. What is his name here?"

"He said it was Edward Cornwallis."

"You're joking?"

"No, that's what he told Daphne."

"He must be mad. He must have lost his mind!"

When I gave the name Cornwallis to the woman at the desk, she did not bat an eyelid, accepted the cheque and gave me an order for Larry's conditional release pending his court appearance in a week's time. She explained that I had to present it to Mr. Benjamin, Commissioner of Corrections, or his designate, at the Westgate Correctional Facility on Pender Road.

I thanked her profusely.

"How you doin', Nicky?" she inquired of Outerbridge. "Not see you here for a while. Guess you must be keeping out of trouble."

"Oh yes, m'dear. You know me."

"Indeed we do," she said with a chuckle. "Nicky's a regular here."

Outerbridge pulled us towards the exit.

"That lady is a terrible chatterbox," he said on the stairs, "an awful gossip and rumour spreader."

"Do we go to the jail now?" I asked when we were back on the sidewalk.

"Yes."

"Shall we get a taxi?"

"If you want to pay over $120, we can. We should go by ferry. That will only be about $30."

"Oh, let's take the ferry," said Rosalie delightedly.

We made our way back down to Front Street and along to the ferry terminal where, after a short wait, we boarded the boat. At a much faster speed than I had expected, it headed out into what Rosalie said was the bluest water she had ever seen. I had been on these ferries some years before, but it was a special treat for Rosalie to be passing between the many islands in the Great Sound on her left and the brightly painted houses dotted along the shore of Pembroke Parish on her right.

In less than half an hour we pulled into the wharf near the Royal Naval Dockyards, and from there it was only another fifteen minutes to the correctional facility.

When we suggested Outerbridge come into the prison with us, I thought he was going to have a heart attack, so we left him sitting by the highway on a large rock.

Once inside, it took us another twenty minutes to jump through bureaucratic hoops. but eventually our papers were approved and soon Larry appeared, grinning from ear to ear.

"What the hell kept you?" he cried. "I was hoping you'd be here a lot sooner. It really buggered my plans."

"You ungrateful bastard!" Rosalie said. I had seldom seen her so annoyed.

"Hello, Rosalie. God, you're looking good. Too good for that useless little brother of mine."

"Good to see you too, Larry," I said sarcastically. "Let's get out of here. Outerbridge will have been cooked by now, sitting in the sun all this time."

"Nicky's here? Oh great. How is the old coot?"

"Very old. I was afraid he would croak on his way here."

"He'll live forever. If he stays out of jail."

"Yes, I got the impression his past is much more checkered than he let on."

"You don't know the half of it."

Larry paused, then took me in his arms. "Seriously, though, Little Brother, I am grateful you came."

We walked through the gates and towards the place where we left Outerbridge.

"Why did you come to Bermuda?" Rosalie asked. "Was it to straighten out your banking difficulty?"

"Hell, no. I wasn't even aware there was a difficulty with the bank until they nabbed me. I came to do some research on the Triangle."

"The Bermuda Triangle?" Rosalie sounded skeptical.

"Yeah. You know, Marc, how one of my sidelines is spreading lies and creating myths?"

"Yes, you told me when I saw you in London."

"Well, there might be something in this triangle shit, so I thought I should come and dig around a bit."

"Seems a trivial pursuit to take you away from your nefarious activities as head of an international crime organization."

"You say that as if you don't approve, Marc. Besides, there was another reason for my coming."

"What was that?"

"I heard that *he* would be here."

"Who's 'he'?"

"You know, *him*."

"No, I don't know."

"*Him*. The Russian."

"The Russian?"

"Yes, the one who killed our father!"

"Jesus! He's here?"

"I don't know for sure yet, but I got intelligence to that effect."

"What's this?" Rosalie asked. "Who are you talking about?"

"Nobody," I lied. "Rosalie, please go on ahead and make sure Outerbridge is okay."

"All right," she said, giving me a strange look.

"What are you going to do if he is here?" I demanded when Rosalie had moved off.

"What do you think?"

"If that means what I think it means, I want nothing to do with it. You understand? Nothing!"

"Message received. Don't worry, Little Brother, your hands will be as clean as the driven snow."

"You make sure they are. But why on earth was it necessary for you to drag us down here? Why couldn't you just pay the bail yourself?'

"I arrived with only credit cards. They took them from me when I was arrested, and in any case won't let you use them for bail. And my assets in the bank here, no matter how small they are, have been frozen until after my trial."

"How will that go? Do you have a good lawyer?"

Larry looked at me as if I were a simpleton, and shook his head. "You don't think I am going to hang around for that? Are you crazy? I'll be long gone."

"What do you mean 'gone'? You can't get a plane."

"There are other ways to leave. There are lots of boats in Bermuda."

"How will you pay for that?" I asked stupidly.

"That's where you come in, Little Brother," he said, smiling sweetly.

9

We spent most of the following three days in Larry's company, sometimes with Nicky tagging along to provide colour commentary about the places we visited. From these occasions Rosalie and I learned a great deal about Bermuda's history and particularly about the characters who inhabited it.

I sadly reflected that almost of all the politicians and women with whom Nicky had fought and romped were dead. According to him (although how he knew I could not fathom), apart from himself there were only eight Bermudians aged 95 or older. With a braying laugh, he told us that one of his favourite pastimes was attending the funerals of his few remaining contemporaries.

Larry and I had quickly come to an agreement that I would pay all his expenses until we parted and obtain $10,000 in cash for him from Butterfield's bank. Presumably, with that he would find his way to the United States where, he said, there were many members of his organization, including expert document forgers. When I asked him if the amount was sufficient, to my surprise he said it was more than enough for what he had in mind.

Getting the money was not easy, and I had to obtain a meeting with a senior executive, Mr. Rawlins, at the bank. He seemed a little uncomfortable over the vagueness of my reasons for the withdrawal, but I produced my bona fides and laboriously attended to all the necessary paperwork, so walked out with an attaché case full of money.

I had also managed to arrange a room for my brother at the Hamilton Princess on the same floor as us and, at his request, to slip Nicky a few hundred dollars. Larry said he would find a way to repay me within a month, although he did not say how he would accomplish that.

I realized that this was the first time I had spent more than fifteen minutes with my brother since he left home almost twenty years ago. It was strange to watch him interacting with Rosalie and Nicky. Although he was informal and easy-going with both, it was clear that, while he considered Rosalie an equal, Nicky was definitely a subordinate. In similar fashion, Nicky was uninhibited, almost garrulous, with us but deferential to Larry.

Many times, I wondered about the nature of the favour Larry had done for Nicky all those years ago, and just what he would have to do until the debt was repaid. That will remain a mystery because, no matter how much I probed, neither of them showed any inclination to provide details.

As our time together wore on, I noticed a complete transformation in Rosalie's attitude towards my brother. At first she had been hostile and angry, but slowly his charm and chummy manner won her over until, by noon on the second day, they were bosom pals. As I watched them laughing together and occasionally touching, I asked myself if Larry would have any scruples about seducing my wife, and regretfully concluded that he would not. It was not that I did not trust Rosalie implicitly, but I imagined that if he wanted to, Larry could invent all manner of highly compelling reasons and excuses for any of his actions.

He was four years my senior, but he seemed to be much older, not so much in his appearance, but in his manner and worldly demeanour. Where I was slim, Larry was broad and barrel chested, with rippling muscles. Certainly he had a little grey around his ears, but his eyes were a brighter blue than mine, and he had a dimple in his chin, which I lacked. Whereas I was fairly reserved, he was ebullient and ever ready with a clever comment or joke.

The more I thought about it the more I recognized that he was by far the more handsome, and I was jealous. It irked me that I was so willing to help an acknowledged criminal, who made me feel uncomfortable, called me "Little Brother" and flirted with my wife. While part of me enjoyed seeing the sights and learning new information, another part of me wanted it to be over, for Larry to be out of our lives, and for me to have my wife to myself in my own home.

"Say, Little Brother," Larry said as we were sipping exotic cocktails at a waterside bar, "do you still have that snazzy Bugatti?"

"Yes, I do."

"How's it running these days?"

"Beautifully. As smooth as silk."

"How old is it now?"

"Almost thirteen years old."

"And still going strong? That engineer was amazing. What was his name?"

"Wolfgang Schreiber."

"That's the guy. Of course, the whole caboodle was virtually put together by hand. You're a lucky man."

As he said this I noticed he flashed a quick glance at Rosalie.

"How many did they build?"

"Ninety-two. But I've been thinking of trading it in for a one-off."

"Another Bugatti?"

"Yes the L'Or Blanc." I said.

Larry whistled loudly.

"You never told me this," Rosalie interjected.

"I only got the offer just before we came here. It sort of slipped my mind."

"You heard from Sheik Abdul Aziz?"

"Yes."

"The Arabian prince?" Larry asked. "You know him?"

"Slightly. We're both Bugatti fanatics."

"He's a really nice fellow."

"Do *you* know him?"

"Oh yes, I've...er...done a bit of business with his family."

"What kind of business?"

"You know, a bit of this and a bit of that."

"Anyway, as well as owning L'Or Blanc, Aziz has the Voiture Noire."

"Holy catfish! What did he pay for that?"

"Nearly nineteen million."

"Way out of your league, darling." Rosalie said.

"Yes, and Larry's."

He fell quiet, putting his head to one side and looking at the sky. It annoyed me beyond measure that I was sure he was doing the mental arithmetic to calculate if his assets would cover the cost of the car.

"Hmm. Right now it would be tight," he said thoughtfully. Then he turned to me with a big smile. "So what does he want for the L'Or Blanc?

"Sheik Aziz said I could have it for half the original price."

"Which would be about $1.2 million?"

"Yes."

"Marc!" Rosalie cried, her eyes widening.

"But presumably you could get half a mill for yours?"

"About that. There are scores of buyers who want one."

"So the L'Or Blanc would set you back about three quarters of a mill?"

"More or less, yes."

"Could we afford that, Marc?" Rosalie asked.

"With a bit of juggling, yes. But nothing is settled yet. We have to talk it over and consider all the pros and cons."

"Right," she said firmly. "No hurry."

"No, he won't let it go to anyone else until he has heard from me."

"That's convenient," Larry said in a strange voice.

Suddenly it hit me. It was the voice on that first telephone call, pretending to be Nicky. Then I recalled that, in a previous investigation, Larry had fooled me by faking the voice of a character he invented called Babich. So, along with his many other talents, most of them of a dubious nature, Larry had a gift for impersonation.

But I could not figure out how and why he had employed it on this occasion, and why he had not got Nicky to make the call himself. This confusion irritated me even more, and I would have sulked had not Larry loudly made an announcement.

"Little Brother, Rosalie: I have a surprise for you. Tonight, I have arranged a lobster feast at Four Ways."

"That's no place for me," said Nicky, who had until then been sleeping happily. "Dinner there would cover my rent for a week."

"I'm paying, Nicky," Larry said, then, nodding to me, "or rather, Marc is paying."

"Thank you for the acknowledgement," I said, "but lobster season doesn't start for three months."

"I know, but these are flown in from...Nova Scotia!"

"Good God, Larry. We just came from there."

"I thought it would be a special treat for you." He looked genuinely crestfallen.

"Larry, we'll enjoy the lobsters," said Rosalie. "It was a lovely thought."

"What's so special about this Four Ways place?" I said, not pleased at the turn of events.

"It has the reputation of being the best place to eat on the island. A long time ago, Dad got some shares from one of the original partners in the restaurant. Nicky, you remember David Wilkinson?"

"I certainly do." Nicky was wide awake now. "He was Speaker of the House for some years when I was an MP. We were on the same side. The old United Bermuda Party, it was called in those days."

"Anyway, Dad got the shares from him and he gave the shares to me."

"So, we'll have the run of the place tonight?" Rosalie said with a laugh. "We'll be lording it over the common people."

"Ah, no. The shares are not in my name."

"You mean, not in the name of Edward Cornwallis?"

"Not him, either. They're in another name of someone who also doesn't look like me."

"We'll bite," I said. "Who is this other person?"

"Joshua Slocum."

"Good God, Larry, is no there no end to your idiot skulduggery and devilish deception?" I asked, thoroughly exasperated with my brother.

"Come to think of it, Little Brother, I don't believe there is."

10

On our final day in Bermuda, we were having breakfast at our hotel when an extraordinary thing happened. Larry had taken the best seat at the table, facing the sea and Rosalie had a side view, while I had my back to the sea, facing the door. Larry and I had each ordered three egg omelettes with mushrooms and smoked salmon (he had sausages added to his) and Rosalie had avocado on toasted bagel with tomato salsa and a poached egg.

I was tucking into my meal when I noticed a strange fluttering by the door. I stared intently for some seconds, but all I could make out was that it was a handkerchief being waved around the door lintel.

"What the hell is that?" I said.

"What?"

"Someone is waving a hanky by the door."

"Oh," said Larry, "that'll be Nicky."

"Nicky? Why in the blazes doesn't he come in?"

"He probably feels self-conscious in such a ritzy place," Larry said, not at all convincingly. "I'd better go out."

He got up and walked out to the corridor.

"What is that all about?" Rosalie asked. "It seems very strange."

"Everything connected with Larry is very strange, when you think about it."

After a few minutes both of them walked in and sat down at the table.

"Have some coffee, Nicky," Larry said.

"I don't mind if I do," Nicky said, reaching for the coffee pot.

"What was that funny performance all about?" Rosalie inquired.

"Oh, nothing."

"Nothing?" she said. "It didn't look like nothing."

I gently kicked Rosalie under the table because I noticed something different about Larry from when he had left us. Just protruding from his shirt pocket was a tiny mobile phone. His phone had been confiscated by the police to undergo a forensic examination, and he had been without one since he was released.

I confess I did not understand what this meant, if anything, and believed that Larry carried out many weird actions simply to increase his mystique. Of one thing I was sure, however, and that was that Nicky had used the money I had given him to buy the phone.

When he had finished his coffee Nicky rose and bowed to Rosalie. "Farewell."

"Leaving already?" Rosalie asked. "Aren't you going to spend the day with us?"

"Alas, no. I have things to do. I have promises to keep, and miles to go before I sleep."

"And debts to repay?" I asked pointedly.

Nicky shot me a hostile glare and shuffled out of the restaurant, moving decidedly faster than I had ever seen him. When he had gone Rosalie frowned at me as if to say we should pursue the mystery, but I shook my head.

"Where are we headed today, Larry?" I asked quickly.

"You should see St Georges, I think."

"Is that at the other end of the island from the Dockyard?"

"Yes, Rosalie. We'll get a bus."

"Can't we go by ferry?"

"Not unless we want to go all the way back to the Dockyard first."

"Oh. How long does the bus take?"

"About an hour. It makes dozens of stops."

"That might be interesting and fun," I said.

We boarded a bus, which at first only carried six other people. However, soon it was full, mostly with large black women cheerfully gossiping and laughing. A number of them took a shine to Larry, and a couple actually stroked his shoulders and upper arms, saying how handsome he was. It did not surprise me in the least that Larry lapped up this attention and flirted outrageously with the women, all of whom were in advanced middle aged.

The bus took us along the north shore and when Rosalie stood up and went to a window to see Bailey's Bay Island, Larry leaned over to me.

"It's been confirmed."

"What has?"

"He is here. His name is Dimitri Alexandrovich Boroskov."

"I don't want to know!" I said hurriedly, "and for God's sake, keep your voice down."

Rosalie returned to her seat and we journeyed on in silence. Just after we had passed a fork in the road, the bus stopped to take on more passengers.

"Gotta go," said Larry, jumping up. "If I don't catch up with you in St. Georges, I'll see you tonight."

He leapt off the bus and we saw him walking back, and taking the turning which said it was the Coney Island Road.

"What's going on, Marc?"

"I don't know. I'm getting tired of Larry's antics. I'll be glad to get home."

"I'm beginning to agree with you. Let's forget about Larry and enjoy our day. I've heard St. Georges is a lovely little town."

It *was* a lovely little town, if rather touristy, and we wandered hand in hand in the sun. The only excitement we experienced was when Rosalie shrieked that she had seen a red cockroach over two inches long, basking on one of the walls.

Larry did not appear, and in the late afternoon we caught a bus back to Hamilton.

Arriving at the Princess, we went up to our rooms to freshen up and change for dinner. While Rosalie was in the shower there was a knock on the door, so I opened it to find a young hotel employee standing there.

"This is for you, sir."

"What is it?"

"I don't know, sir. The front desk asked me to deliver it."

I gave him five dollars and opened the note. It said:

It's done. Paul LeBlanc can rest in peace.

If there was any doubt what it meant, the reference to our father dispelled it.

Hastily I ripped it up and threw the pieces in a waste bin. Then I stalked up the corridor to Larry's room and pounded on the door. When there was no answer I pushed on it and it opened.

There was no sign of human occupation. Larry was gone.

"Who was that, Marc?" Rosalie called from the bathroom when I returned to our room.

"Someone to tell us that Larry checked out."

"Checked out? Where did he go?"

"South Carolina or Georgia would be my guess."

"He couldn't fly there. How did he get a boat?" she asked, coming into the room wrapped in a huge, fluffy towel.

"I imagine Nicky arranged it."

"Of course. But, Marc, why did he leave so suddenly?"

There was absolutely nothing to be gained by telling Rosalie the truth. I should never have even told her about Larry's existence when we were in London, and only did so when compelled to by exigent conditions. I have described those circumstances in my book *The Plot to Kill the Premier*. Now, I could not take the risk of implicating her in a crime, no matter how indirectly the connection.

"I don't know, sweetheart, and, what's more, I don't care."

11

All my life I have been troubled by homecomings. I have never been able to explain why this should be so, but I have always had a sense of foreboding whenever I returned from a business trip or vacation.

In my early years, I feared untoward events that naturally revolved around my parents, but later I was never short of a list of catastrophes which might await me. Had the house burned down? Had something happened to the Bugatti? Had a flood destroyed my wine cellar? Was there an ominous piece of mail awaiting, advising me of an impending prosecution?

All these, at one time or another, had preyed on my mind as I approached home, but the worst fear was, when I had been away alone, that something had happened to Rosalie in my absence. On one occasion, which I have related in my book *Best Served Cold*, that fear was not groundless, but fortunately it occurred only once.

But this time I had no such worries, so overjoyed was I to be back in Grand Pre, to be away from Bermuda and, most of all, to be rid of my criminal sibling. Exasperation had turned into intense revulsion when I had bought a copy of the Royal Gazette at Bermuda airport. The story was on the third page:

RUSSIAN TOURIST FOUND DEAD AT CONEY ISLAND

The body of a man in his late twenties was discovered by a dog walker in the park at Coney Island, St. George's parish, early yesterday evening. The man, believed to be a tourist, carrying a Russian passport in the name of Dimitri Boroskov, was found bundled into some bushes. Apparently he had been dead for several hours. Bermuda Police said foul play is suspected, but as yet nobody has been detained in connection with the death.

I had almost thrown up on the airport floor, and it had taken a real effort to control myself as we boarded. Fortunately, Rosalie was some yards in front of me, so I was able to dispose of the Gazette before getting on the aircraft. I was still a little shaky when we got back to Halifax.

What he had done, or had somebody else do, could not be justified no matter how one looked at it. If I believed that Larry had acted as he did out of loyalty to our father, it would only slightly mitigate the deed, but I was convinced that he had done it to boost his reputation in the international underworld and enhance his business.

I admitted to myself that until now I had felt a sneaking admiration for Larry and his phenomenal chutzpah, never really facing up to the probability that he had been guilty of a good many heinous deeds in pursuit of his criminal activities. But all that had changed. I certainly had not the slightest intention of ever contacting him, and devoutly hoped that he would stay out of my life for good.

We landed in Halifax well before lunch, so we were back in Grand Pre within an hour and a half, using Rosalie's Fiat, an uncomfortable but convenient little vehicle.

There was a message on my answering machine from Bill Jolly, saying he hoped we'd had a good trip and that if I came over to Kingsport that afternoon he would have some good fish for us. I asked Rosalie if she wanted to come with me, but she said she would rather unpack, do some laundry and poke about in the house.

As I went to extract the Bugatti from the garage, I looked up the hill and could just make out Ralph Giffin and several other people working on the archaeological site. From a distance it appeared that they had already achieved a fair amount and, looking lower down, I could see that the lane had been completely cleared of its brambles and undergrowth, which was confirmed by the presence of two jeeps up at the site.

In the other direction, I could see that the lush vines were grow-ing apace in John Dempster's vineyard and, although I could not actually see them, I suspected they were covered with tiny grapes.

Bill Jolly was just about to put out to sea when I pulled onto the wharf and called out to him.

"Hey, Bill!"

"Hey, Marc. D'you have a good trip?"

"No, not really. Glad to be back. What've you got for me?"

"More mackerel—"

"Oh good!"

"But I also have some fine looking halibut if you want it."

"Sure would," I said. Halibut is not my favourite fish because I like flaky rather than solid fish flesh, but I knew Rosalie and most of our friends loved it.

"You fancy some lobster, too?"

"No thanks, Bill." I did not explain my refusal, but said I would take some scallops if he had any.

"We got a few," he said. "How many do you want?"

"Couple of pounds should do it."

"Okay." He shouted my requirements down to his mate, Ronnie. "Won't be a minute."

A little later he slung a sack over the side.

"How much?" I asked.

"Say fifty."

"That's not enough for all that fish."

"We're friends, Marc."

"Many thanks, Bill."

"See you. We gotta get out of here. Okay Ronnie, cast off."

I watched them go, thinking how lucky we were to have access to very fresh products and from such a friendly and obliging skip-per.

When I got home and laid out my prizes on the kitchen counter, Rosalie beamed. "You have been lucky. Good old Bill!"

"He's one of a kind."

"Marc, it would be a shame to freeze most this. Let's have some friends over for dinner tomorrow."

"I'm game. We haven't had Walter and Joyce over for a while. And we may as well invite Gary and Jane again as well."

"Alright. Is there anything in your garden that's ready to eat?"

"Only radishes and tiny little lettuces."

"I'll go into town tomorrow and get some scallions and tomatoes for a salad. What will you do with the fish?"

"They're not getting the mackerel. That's for us! I thought I would poach the halibut and have it with a creamy sauce with scallops in it."

"That sounds nice. What veg do you want me to pick up?"

"See if there is any asparagus, but only if it is thick. I can't stand that thin, wispy stuff."

"And if there isn't any thick asparagus?"

"How about little carrots and zucchini? And yellow potatoes."

"Fine. Will you call the Marshalls and Brysons, or shall I?"

"I'll do it. What do you want to eat tonight?"

"Mackerel."

"For breakfast tomorrow as well?"

"Why not?"

"Okay with me."

It was good to be back in familiar surroundings, and it would be even nicer to be dining with good friends the next day. Already, Bermuda seemed worlds away.

12

Bill Jolly's mackerel was absolutely delicious sautéed, and served with scrambled eggs, fresh bread and yellow butter. Rosalie and I had a long, inconclusive discussion as to why mackerel should be so rare these days, or at least rarely seen in the stores. Several times we had seen Spanish mackerel in supermarkets, but they were far from fresh and in any case did not have nearly as good a flavour as the local fish. We surmised that its infrequency resulted from a low demand for the product because it had acquired reputation for being a fish for "the poor" and therefore had fallen out of fashion.

As Rosalie headed off to the university in the Fiat, I cleared the table and put the dishes in the washer.

I was cleaning up in the kitchen when I heard an explosion. I ran outside into the yard and, seeing nothing, went around to the rear of the house. I could see smoke rising from the archaeological dig at the top of the hill, apparently emanating from one of the jeeps. Since there was a slight chill in the air, I went back inside to get sweater, then headed up to where I could see figures milling about.

When I got to the top, the first thing which struck me was not the vehicle which had caused the incident, but how much the diggers had accomplished in the week we had been away.

The entire area had been stripped of turf and scrub except for one vertical and three horizontal baulks which had been preserved to maintain walking areas and to provide sections for recording purposes. Two of the six rectangular trenches thus created had only a modicum of clearing done to them, two more had been excavated to a depth of about four feet, and the remaining two had been dug down almost six feet.

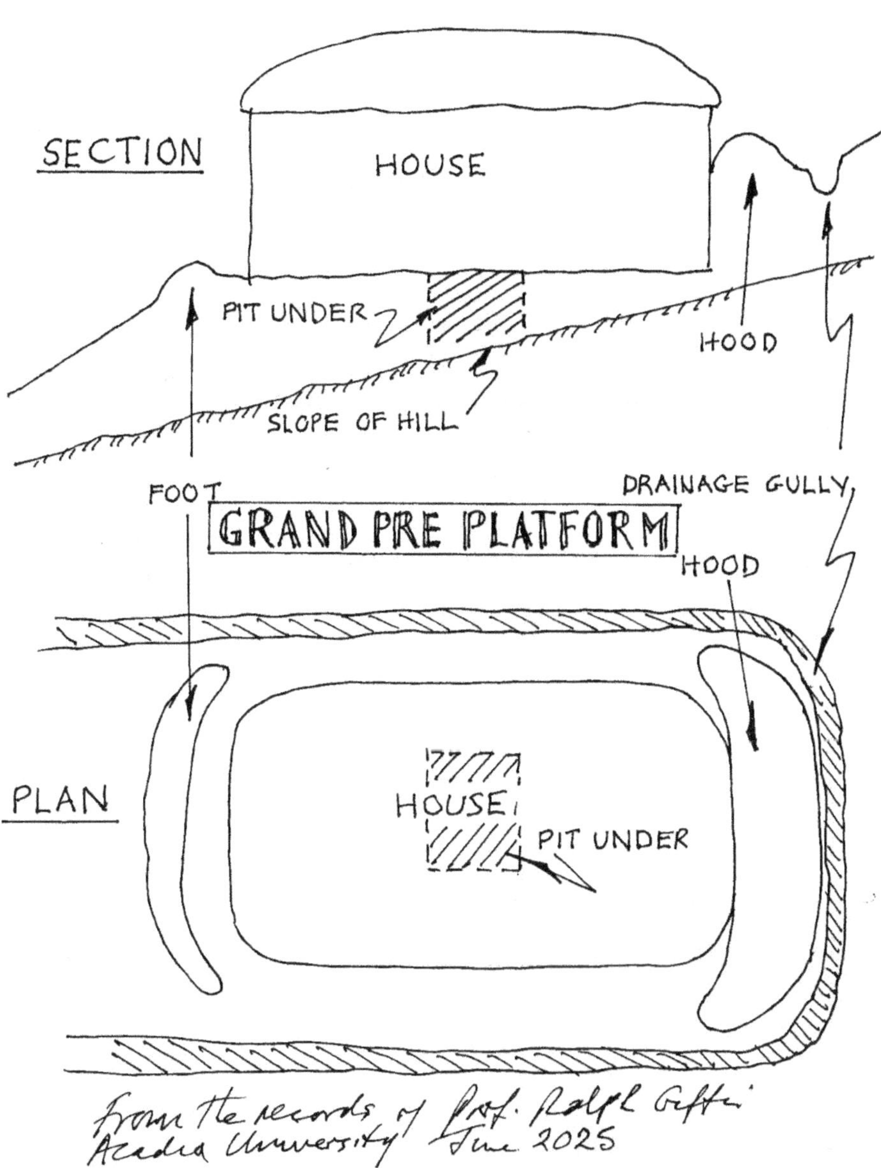

SECTION
HOUSE
PIT UNDER
HOOD
SLOPE OF HILL
FOOT
DRAINAGE GULLY
GRAND PRE PLATFORM
HOOD
PLAN
HOUSE
PIT UNDER
from the records of Prof. Ralph Gifts
Acadia University June 2025

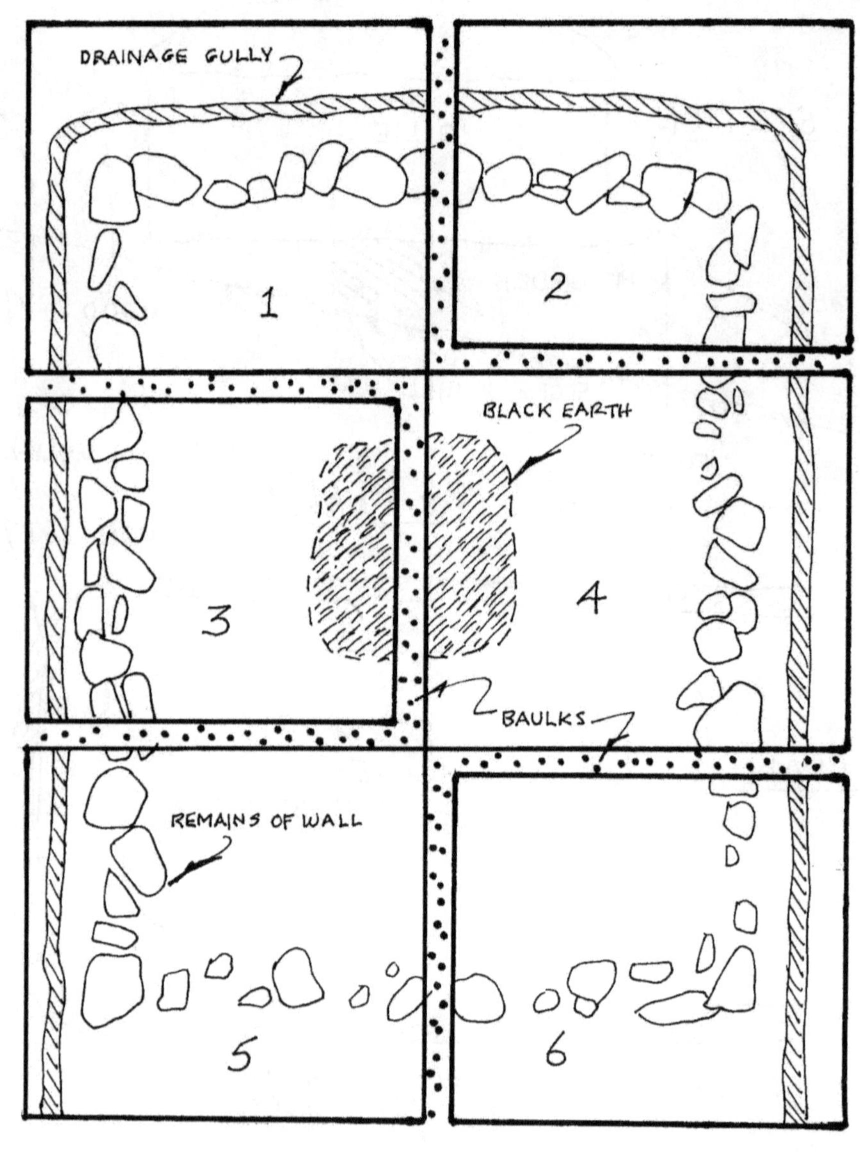

DRAINAGE GULLY
1
2
BLACK EARTH
3
4
BAULKS
REMAINS OF WALL
5
6

In the approximate centre of the site and bisected by the baulks was a large square of blackened earth, contrasting markedly with the light-brown soil of the surrounding area. The tops of the remains of rough stone walls had been uncovered, revealing an outline of what had once been a building, and a dark line indicating the presence of a ditch ran along the outer edges of the walls.

I was sufficiently familiar with archaeology to know that the rectangular patch of black soil more than likely indicated the presence of a hole of some sort, but how deep it might be was impossible to say at this stage. Littered around were stiff hand brushes and masons' trowels, together with plastic finds trays to hold any artifacts which might be discovered.

I quickly transferred my attention to Giffin and four others, who were clustered around the jeep parked furthest from them.

"Hey, Ralph. What's going on?"

"Oh, hello, Marc. You're back."

"Got in yesterday. What's all the smoke about?

"Don't know. A few minutes ago the engine blew up."

"Blew up?"

"Well, it seemed like that. There was a bit of a fire, but we managed to put it out. Fortunately, nobody was hurt."

"Did it blow when it was just sitting there?"

"No, Allan was starting it when it went. He was lucky no flying metal hit him."

I looked at the young man called Allen. He was grinning from ear to ear, but his face was blackened.

I drew Ralph over to the side. "Ralph. That sounds suspiciously like sabotage. The ignition must have triggered the explosion."

"Jesus! You mean like Apolonia Corleone in *The Godfather*?"

"It could be. If I were you, I'd take it to a garage and have them check it out."

"Allen, you okay to travel?" Ralph called.

"Sure. Just a bit shaken that's all."

"Hitch this up to the other jeep and tow it into town. Have one of the garage mechanics go over it."

"Okay, Prof. Will do."

We sauntered back to the site and I followed Ralph along the grass baulks. He stopped at the two furthest trenches, which were the deepest excavated so far.

"As you can see, we didn't waste any time. You probably noticed in a couple of the other trenches that there was a floor of beaten earth, but in these two you can see there was an earlier floor also."

"Where? I can't see it. You've already dug it up."

"Step down." Ralph laughed. "Careful where you tread."

I did as he instructed and he pointed to the side of the trench, which displayed a series of layers of soil of different sizes, textures and colours.

"This wall we call a 'section', and what you see here is stratification. Based on the principle that what appears lower down in the section has to have been deposited before what is seen higher up in the section."

"That makes sense."

"There are a few exceptions to this rule."

"What are they?"

"One, if somebody dug—say a hole—through a layer to a level below."

"Why would they do that?"

"Maybe to create a post hole for a roof support or possibly to hide something."

"Okay. What are the other exceptions?"

"If somehow worms had burrowed through a layer, or if water had permeated a lower level and taken higher deposits down with it. You understand?"

"Yes. I have a feeling you're telling me this for a specific reason. What is it?"

"We'll get to that in a minute. Look at the section again. Down here, we have a floor of beaten earth—that's the light brown layer with little stones in it."

"Got it. Go on."

"Then we have a layer of what I'll call debris, which is the occupation layer, containing animal bones and, if we're lucky, bits of pottery. Okay?"

"Yep."

"Then above that we have a layer of black with flecks of red in it. That indicates there was a fire. We can't really tell at this stage how bad it was, but the thickness of the layer suggests it certainly was not minor."

"I'm with you."

"Then sometime after that, we have another floor laid down. That's the other layer of beaten, light-brown earth."

"I see it."

"Now come over and look at trench 3. What do you see?"

"I see a fairly large area of blackened soil which suggests a large hole."

"Very good. But you'll notice that we've taken these trenches down –not as far as the ones we're standing in—but down about three feet."

"Yes."

"Now look at look at the section in those trenches."

"Ahh. I see the two layers of beaten earth. The floor levels."

"What else do you notice?"

"I don't know."

"The area of black earth—which we'll call the pit, for present purposes—preceded both occupations levels and the fire."

"Meaning?"

"Meaning that it is probably the earliest feature on the site, and probably that it was here before the building."

"So, the building was put here because of the pit?"

"Exactly. Now walk with me into the field, Marc. I have something to say I don't want anyone else to hear."

We climbed the fence and wandered over the brow of the hill. Ralph sat down and tugged at some grass which he proceeded to chew. I joined him, anxious to know what was bothering him.

"I'm telling you because I owe it to you as owner of the land. I don't want this going any further—at least not until I've had a chance to delve into the matter more deeply and get a second opinion. And even a third opinion."

"What is it, Ralph?"

"Have you heard of the Imago Mundi?"

"No."

"The Imago Mundi is a baked-clay tablet which was found in Iraq around 1882. It is believed to be 3,000 years old and depicts a circular map of the world, allegedly indicating the present whereabouts of Noah's Ark."

"What's that got to do with us?"

"Yesterday I found a small piece of fired clay which looks alarmingly like the Imago Mundi."

"Here?"

"Yes, I was clearing up after the students had left and, since the light was still strong, I took my trowel and started scraping."

"How for down was it?"

"About three feet down."

"Could it be a fake?"

"I don't think so. I'm not an expert in Babylonian art and archaeology, but it looks genuine to me."

"Could it be a plant? Could someone be having a joke on you?"

"It's possible, but I can't imagine who would have access to such an artifact, and it looks far too worn to have been manufactured recently."

"Now I see why you explained about the exceptions to stratification. Are you sure it wasn't taken to a lower level by worms or water?"

"Quite sure. The soil around it was very compact and similar in composition."

I looked out over the Minas Basin. Dark clouds were just beginning to gather on the horizon and the wind was getting stronger. Some crows were squabbling down by the house. A ripple ran through the grass, sweeping by us, upturning the daisies and buttercups.

"Ralph."

"Yes?"

"Where exactly did you find this thing?'"

"In the pit."

13

Next morning I was a little hung over from the previous night's revelries, so I was a little slow in preparing breakfast. Rosalie was not yet up, but I knew that once I put the coffee on, she would soon appear.

I decided to brew a pot using a coffee which was new to us and which I had just received from my supplier in Toronto. This was Kopi Luwak from the Gayo Highlands of Northern Sumatra in Indonesia. There, the civet, a cousin to the mongoose, lives freely in the jungles where the coffee grows. Along with ripe jungle fruits, the civet has a nose for only the best, ripest beans, and enjoys coffee beans as part of its general diet. Upon ingesting the beans, a natural process occurs which alters the bean's properties, removing its bitterness and introducing flavourful notes of exotic jungle fruits. Kopi Luwak is then collected from the jungle and processed by specially trained farmers.

After I had ground the beans and they had started to brew, I heard the sound of footsteps on the stairs, and a rather dishevelled Rosalie entered.

"My God, that was some dinner party!"

"It was. I don't think any of us were sober at the end of it, and Jane was pie-eyed."

"How much wine did we go through?"

"I haven't counted the empty bottles, but it must have been about eight or nine."

"What on earth were Gary and Walter arguing about?"

"I'm not absolutely sure. Are you hungry?"

"Ravenous. What's on offer?"

"How about an old-fashioned full English breakfast?"

"Lovely! But don't you dare put any black pudding on my plate."

"I won't. Do you want baked beans? As you know I'm not fussy about them."

"Alright, I won't bother with them either."

I poured her a cup of coffee, took out several pans and set about cooking the food. We had crispy bacon, homemade sausages, mushrooms, tomatoes, fried bread and fresh farm eggs.

"This coffee is amazing," said Rosalie. "Is it new?"

"Yes, Kopi Luwak. We just got it from Toronto yesterday."

"I think it might take over from Blue Mountain as my favourite."

"Close, but I think the Jamaicans still win."

I set out the food and we tucked in with relish. About half-way through the meal, we started to discuss some of the events of the previous evening. We were six people: Walter and Joyce Bryson, Gary and Jane Marshall and ourselves. Everybody was in a cheerful, chatty mood and we did not sit down to dinner until we had consumed several bottles of Krug Champagne.

To start, we had a simple salad of crispy, young romaine lettuce, little French Breakfast radishes from my garden, and cherry tomatoes lightly dressed with extra virgin olive oil and a sprinkle of lemon juice. I topped this with shaved, curly wafers of a good, aged Parmigiano.

With the salad I had chosen a *Chenin Blanc* from *Domaine Huet 2022 Haut Lieu Moelleux Premier Trie* from Touraine in France's Loire Valley, a rich but crisp, lively wine from one of my favourite producers.

For the main course I gently poached the halibut from Bill Jolly and served it with a creamy sauce in which I added halved scallops at the last minute so they would not be rubbery. With that I served some steamed zucchini and baby carrots, and potato bon-bons, which were grated yellow potatoes, squeezed, formed into balls and deep fried.

This course was quite rich, so it called for something really special as an accompaniment. I hesitated before choosing the 2005 *Domaine de la Romanee-Conti Montrachet Grand Cru* because I only had four bottles left in my cellar, but I decided the dish deserved this amazing wine.

For dessert we just had fruit and ice cream with more champagne.

"Tell me again about that weird idea of Walter's." Rosalie said.

"I'm not sure if it's his theory or even if he believes it, but it's been around for some time. I think they call it the 'Upward Percolation theory'."

"What does it entail? I was in the kitchen for some of the discussion."

"Basically, it's a notion that all events in history are connected, and all cultures and their products are linked through some amorphous underground stream."

"Of water?"

"No, not that kind of stream. Maybe a stream of consciousness. I don't pretend to understand it, and it sounds nuts to me, but the idea is that somewhere beneath our feet—God knows how far down—all these things are somehow tied."

"Where does the percolating come in?"

"The believers say that every now and then something—"

"Like what?"

"Oh, I don't know. A statue or a weapon, something like that. Anyway, they say these items can be brought to the surface from the underground 'stream'."

"How?"

"Heaven knows. It's not my theory, darling. I didn't invent it."

"Sounds insane to me."

"Precisely."

"I'm surprised Walter would be spouting something like that."

"Me too. But he did defend us about the dig."

Rosalie nodded. She knew I was referring to the argument between Walter and Gary about the archaeological site on top of our hill. Gary had continued with his apparent objection to the dig taking place, while Joyce, more than a little worse for wine, rattled on about the so-called "curse" which had been mentioned on their previous visit.

"Walter, are you absolutely sure Marc has title to the land up there?" Gary had asked.

"Positive. There was a dispute in the early part of the last century and since neither party would give in, the area was fenced off so nobody got to use it. Later, when the property changed hands it was re-surveyed and established as part of the Robson estate—that is the land Marc now owns."

"I heard someone was hurt there the other week," Jane interjected. "And that there was a bomb went off up there today."

"No, not a bomb, Jane. The jeep's engine caught fire."

"That's two bad things in as many weeks. Sounds to me like the curse is coming true."

"Don't be so ridiculous Jane!" Joyce was irritated. "This is the twenty-first century."

"Don't you be calling me ridiculous?" Jane cried.

"Alright," said Walter, "Joyce I think you should apologize."

"You're right, darling. Jane, I'm sorry."

But Jane had fallen asleep, so Gary quietly called a taxi, gently picked her up and, softly saying his thanks and goodbyes, padded out to the yard.

"We'd better be going too," said Joyce. "Thank you both for a lovely evening."

"It was a lovely evening until that point," said Rosalie.

"Yes, it was rather. I must say I think we give first rate dinner parties."

"Yes, we do! We must invite Rachel and Ray Bland over next time. They've not been here for a while."

"That's a good idea." I replied.

The Blands were very good friends of ours who lived over in Port Williams. Ray owned a large car business in New Minas and Rachel worked at the hospital. The extraordinary circumstances under which we got to know them are described in my book *Unspeakable Evil*.

"I think we might also ask Ralph Giffin. I have a feeling he is in need of friends these days."

"What makes you say that?"

"I'm not really sure. Maybe I'm wrong."

14

Two days later Rosalie returned from the university looking pale and nervous. I did not press her, but it was clear she had something on her mind.

As I laid the table for dinner I could hear her moving around upstairs, rather more noisily than usual. At one point I heard her say, "Bastards!" I could not imagine what was troubling her but I knew she would tell me when she was ready.

I was cooking Coq au vin. It is a fairly simple dish, in which you brown floured chicken pieces with small onions and button mushrooms, flame it with brandy, then add a bottle of wine, garlic, parsley and thyme. Normally, I use a bottle of dry Riesling, but others think a red wine gives the dish more body. Then you let it simmer gently for an hour and serve it with the starch of your choice. I was serving boiled potatoes, but many prefer it with rice or orzo.

To accompany the dish, I brought up some 1998 *Château Rayas*, a Rhone wine made from the Grenache, a grape I do not normally care for, but in *Ch. Rayas* it is very special.

Rosalie came downstairs and flopped down in the living room, staring out of the window. Then she got up, went to the sideboard and poured herself a brandy, something she very seldom does.

I poked my head around the doorway. "Coq au vin. That alright for you?"

"I guess so," she said flatly.

"Be ready in about half an hour."

"Okay."

I returned to the kitchen and stood there waiting. I guessed it would take her about five minutes to get ready to unburden herself. Sure enough, after she had time to imbibe several measures of brandy, she came in and sat at the counter.

"It's probably nothing," she said.

"What is?"

"It's likely someone playing the fool."

"What is it?"

"I think the best thing to do is to forget all about it."

"If you think that's best."

"You don't even know what I'm talking about."

"No I don't, and I never will unless you tell me."

She reached into the pocket of her jeans and pulled out a piece of crumpled paper, which she handed to me. I unfolded it and read:

mind youre own business leave things as they were
or you wont be happy

"Where did this come from?"

"It was on my desk when I went into my office."

"What does it mean?"

"I've no idea. Do you?"

"Have you antagonized anyone recently? A colleague maybe?"

"Not that I'm aware of. I don't get into fights or arguments."

"It's type-written, and not very elegantly done, as it has no punctuation, but that could be deliberate to make us think the person is less educated than they really are."

"Should I take it to the police?"

"I don't think so. There's nothing they could do."

"How about the campus police?"

"You might do that. They may pick something up on their rounds."

"Alright, I'll do that tomorrow. Let's eat."

Later, around two in the morning, I thought I heard gravel crunching from a vehicle pulling into our yard, then, after a few minutes, leaving. I got up and peered out the window, but could see nothing because our bedroom faces south, the opposite side of the house from the road.

When I awoke and went downstairs the next day I saw a letter on the mat by the front door. Even before I picked it up I guessed that it might be a missive similar to the one received by Rosalie. I was right.

*if you dont get those guys off the hill they mite
dig up something you wont like*

Whereas Rosalie's note had not been specific, this one explained what the writer (or writers) objected to, namely the presence of Ralph Giffin and his students on the archaeological site. Why they objected was as much a mystery as their identity. Again, I noted the lack of punctuation and the poor spelling, but was not fooled by it.

In neither note was there any direct threat other than a vague suggestion that unless we complied we would be unhappy. I doubted the notes constituted criminal acts and I was certain the police could do nothing.

As she descended the staircase, Rosalie saw the note in my hand and gasped. She rushed over and grabbed it from me.

"So *that's* what it's all about! The dig. But why, Marc? Why would somebody want to stop the dig?"

"Maybe it's somebody who wants to guard us against the curse."

"Aren't people like that supposed to sign themselves 'a well-wisher'?"

"Somehow I don't think the letter writer is a friend."

"What should we do?"

"I think, darling, that we should ignore this for the time being. If it continues, or the writer starts making specific threats, we can think about getting in touch with Patrick."

I was referring to our very good friend Chief Superintendent Patrick Kennedy of the RCMP, a man with whom I had shared a number of adventures in the past, most notably those described in my books *The Plot to Kill the Premier* and *Best Served Cold*.

"Should push come to shove," I said, "if nothing else, Patrick might be able to provide some measure of protection."

"Protection! My God, Marc, surely it won't come to that?"

"Probably not. I hope not."

"Do you think we should tell Ralph to wind up the work?"

"What? Give in to these bastards? Is that what you want?"

"No, I guess not."

"I might tell him about the notes...just to warn him."

"Yes, that's a good idea. What's for breakfast?"

"Homemade sausages and scrambled eggs. Sound alright?"

"Sounds wonderful. Can we have some more of that Cupe Lowak coffee?"

"You mean Kopi Luwak?" I laughed. "Of course we can."

Despite our tribulations we both had good appetites and soon demolished the breakfast and several pots of coffee.

Rosalie was putting on her jacket to go to work, when suddenly she turned to me. "Marc, you don't suppose that student getting hurt and the jeep catching fire are connected to these notes, do you?"

"No, of course not."

It was pure coincidence, I told myself as I watched Rosalie's Fiat disappear down the lane. Or was it?

15

The following two days I spent in Halifax. I had to go there to talk to the people at Butterfield's Bank who wanted to iron out some technicalities associated with my withdrawals in Hamilton for Larry. When I got there, they assured me there was not a problem if I just signed some papers.

When I had completed these formalities I thought I would look up Patrick Kennedy, but when I called H-Division I found he would not be available until the late afternoon, so I made an appointment and then booked a room in a hotel.

Reckoning that I might find my old friend Akerman in residence, I walked up to the north end and found him watering the plants on his balcony. He seemed glad to see me and invited me to go up.

I gave him a brief progress report on the excavations, albeit in layman's language, indicating as best I could what had appeared in each of the trenches.

"So I was right. It is a platform house."

"Yes, it looks like that."

"It is isn't all that unusual. They had them in Europe in the Bronze Age, as well as in the medieval and post-medieval periods, and they've been recorded in other places in the world."

"In North America?"

"I believe some of the Mohawk longhouses were built on hill platforms."

"How about in Nova Scotia?"

"Not that I'm aware of. There may be sites possessing certain features of a hill-platform house, but not all of them. Your site seems to have them all."

"I think Ralph has established that, although they have all summer to find out more. He'll be getting more volunteers now the university term is over."

"They've already done a lot in such a small space of time," he said. "Usually it's very slow going at the beginning, when you're not sure what you're dealing with. This pit sounds very intriguing."

"Yes, I wonder what it could be."

"It's not likely to be a refuse pit or midden. Who would want that in the middle of the house? Or if, as you say, it was the original feature, why would someone want to build on top of it?"

"That wouldn't make sense."

"No, it wouldn't. Originally it could have been somewhere to store or hide something, or even somewhere to bury people."

"I hadn't thought of that. Would they want to live on top of corpses?"

"I wouldn't, but I'm sure it would be acceptable in some forms of ancestor worship."

"You're suggesting an early native origin?"

"At this stage, almost anything is possible. Have they found any resistance in the pit, or is it uniformly soft?"

"Soft. Or rather softer than the surrounding soils, some of which are packed and beaten to form floors."

"But no barriers?"

"Barriers?"

"Floors for example. Or any sealed level. If you like, a lid?"

"No. Not yet."

Akerman got up and went to the kitchen to get a glass of water. "Want one?"

"No, thank you. Tell me, what kind of artifacts would you expect to find in this pit?"

"Pottery. Maybe coins." He took a sip from his glass and placed it on a pile of books. "Possibly weapons."

"How old?"

"We don't know by how many years the pit predates the structure, so the finds could be any age. The finds at the Paleo-Indian site in Debert were 11,000 years old, and Debert is only about 40 miles from your place, as the crow flies."

"I won't keep you any longer, but there is one more thing I want to ask." I had to word my question carefully because Ralph had sworn me to secrecy on the Babylonian inscription. "In your experience have you ever come across a find which was...out of place?"

"You mean inapposite? Something from another place entirely?"

"Yes."

"There is a great deal archaeology can't answer." He stared at me intently. "For example, some people of the Amazon basin have the same DNA as Pacific Islanders, so if an artifact associated with the culture of one showed up in the other place we would be puzzled, but would have to assume that long ago one or the other was capable of making long sea journeys."

He emptied his water glass and set it down. "But the direct answer is that I have had some personal experience of this phenomenon, and have heard of it happening elsewhere. In most cases they turned out to be practical jokes. An Egyptologist who dropped a scarab at Stonehenge; that sort of thing."

"I see. Thank you."

"Why did you ask me that question?"

"No reason. I was just curious."

"I suspect you are curious because you have a very good reason for asking it, but I won't press you for an explanation."

~

In Dartmouth at H-Division, Patrick Kennedy was in his corner office overlooking the parking lot. Only the Chief Super, Patrick's boss, had an office with two good views, one of Bedford Basin and the other of miles of woodlands.

Patrick and I had known each other for five or six years, during which he had risen rapidly in the ranks of the RCMP and our relationship had progressed from veiled hostility to the warmest possible friendship.

When I first met him at the time of my father's murder, I guessed he saw me as a hostile witness, if not a suspect. That had been a difficult time, discovering the unwelcome news that my dad had been a shady character at best, and an out-and-out criminal at worst. As time went on I got to know and like Patrick extremely well, as he became involved in the various cases I undertook as a private investigator. Now, he and his wonderful wife, Ruth, were among Rosalie's and my fondest acquaintances.

"Marc, please sit down. It's extraordinary you should come by today, of all days."

"Why's that?"

"We've just had a report from the Royal Bermuda Police that the body of a man was recently found who might have been your dad's killer."

"Really!" I had to feign astonishment. I could not dare let him think I had the slightest inkling of the demise of Dimitri Alexandrovich Boroskov. "So, if it is him, justice has finally been done."

"Justice?" Patrick stared at me strangely. "I should have thought that justice only comes after a trial and a conviction."

"Yes, yes. You're right." I was flustered, "what I meant was that in the absence of the law taking its proper course, his death would be the next best thing. Do we know who killed him?"

"Who says he was killed?"

"I thought you did." I was digging a deeper hole for myself. "Maybe I figured that a man like that would meet his end the way he had lived."

"I haven't read all the details yet, but it appears that foul play was involved." He gave me another penetrating look, then said: "But that's not why you came to see me. What's on your mind?"

I told him of our receipt of threatening letters and their possible association with incidents at the dig, and asked his advice on what, if anything, we should do.

"That's a pretty tenuous link, if you ask me, but if it becomes substantial let me know. As for the letters, it's dubious if they are criminal. No specific and direct threat was made. 'You'll be sorry' is not much of a menacing ultimatum, and no money was demanded, so I doubt if a charge of blackmail would stick. That is, even if you could find out who sent them."

"If there are more incidents, will you get involved?"

"Certainly, if the law has been broken. And should push come to shove, we could arrange a modicum of protection."

"A modicum? That doesn't sound very encouraging."

"Maybe not, but we are undermanned in the rural areas, so what we could do is limited."

"I understand."

"Sorry I can't promise anything further. Is there anything else? I have a meeting with my chief."

"If you get any time off in the near future, let me know, and you and Ruth can come down for dinner and stay the night."

"That sounds wonderful. Then I can see your mysterious site, and set all your fears and concerns to rest."

As I walked over to the Bugatti, I considered that Patrick was certainly more complacent than I was, and I reflected on how content we had been a few weeks ago, when our hill was still undisturbed.

16

When I got back to Grand Pre the next morning, Rosalie had already gone to work, so I went down to the cellar to rearrange some of my wine. Empty spaces on some of the shelves told me it was time for me to restock.

I noticed that I was particularly low on white Bordeaux and was reduced to only a handful of bottles of *Chateau Haut Brion*, *Château la Mission*, and *Domaine de Chevalier.* To replenish these with wine which was ready to drink would be an extremely expensive proposition, even if I could find them.

I decided to put the matter in the hands of my very capable business partner, Louise, who I knew would scour the auction houses and get the best deals available. To fill the spaces, I brought some wine from the back of the cellar where it had been patiently aging for some years, still in its original cases.

Having nothing special to do, I thought I would wander up to the dig to see how they were progressing. I spent some minutes in my garden pulling up weeds and crunching radishes, then I climbed over our wall and into the field. The grass on the hill was covered with wildflowers, including seapea, trillium, and bluets as well as the more common dandelions, daisies and buttercups. The scent thrown up by this colourful conglomeration of blossoms was intoxicating and made me feel almost guilty for disturbing them with my clumsy feet.

As I approached the crest of the hill I saw Ralph coming down to meet me. When he came closer I thought he looked slightly greyer and older than usual, and his mannerisms seemed quite nervous.

"Hey, Marc. I was just coming down to see if you were home."

"Hello, Ralph. Why what's up?"

"We've uncovered a floor, or maybe a ceiling, in the pit. We don't yet know which."

"Really?"

"Yeah. We were about to penetrate the layer and thought you might like to be there."

"Yes, I would. Thanks, Ralph."

"Of course, there may be nothing underneath the layer except more black earth."

"Either way, it will be interesting."

As we walked up the hill, our feet brushing through the lush growth, Ralph drew closer to me; at one point our shoulders were touching.

"Marc?"

"Yes?"

"How shall I put this? Has anything...weird happened to you recently?"

"Weird?" My senses were alerted, but I wanted to hear what he had to unfold before I said anything."

"Out of the ordinary?"

"Why are you asking?"

"Last evening I had to go into college for something and I bumped into the Head of our department."

"Yes?"

"And he...well, he didn't exactly tell me to stop the dig, but he didn't exactly tell me to continue."

"That is weird."

"Yeah, that's what I thought. And then he said something even weirder."

"Oh?"

"He said it in a cheery way, but he made it sound sinister." Ralph paused and licked his lips. "He said he'd heard that the University President had been overheard saying something to the effect: 'We're here to advance learning, not to be digging up the backyards of every Tom, Dick and Harry.'"

I then told him about the letters we had received and my consultation with Patrick Kennedy.

He whistled. "So, the powers that be want to stop us."

"We shouldn't jump to any conclusions, but it is beginning to look rather as if someone wants us to stop."

"Is that what you want, Marc?"

"God, no. Fuck them, whoever they are."

"I was hoping you'd say that." He held out his hand for me to shake and I took it. "Let's go and do some archaeology."

The site looked very different from when I had last seen it some days ago. Trenches 1, 2, 5, and 6—the most northerly and southerly trenches—had been taken down to what appeared to be the same very compact, reddish-brown material, at a depth of six feet at the south end and three feet at the opposite end.

"That's the natural." Ralph said.

"The natural?"

"Yes, natural clay. Material which has never been ploughed or affected by humans or animals. That represents the original slope of the hill."

Then we looked at trenches 3 and 4, those in the centre of the site. The grass baulks had been removed so the whole area was exposed. Even though the natural had been everywhere exposed in these trenches, the area of the pit was still clearly visible.

Ralph jumped down and pulled out his trowel. "This means that everything else we have discovered here, the house, main occupation levels and subsequent activity all came later, maybe much later, than the pit."

"We're still calling it 'the pit'?"

"For want of a more precise term, yes. We may be able to get a better definition as we go down."

He started to trowel the area, producing a rasping sound.

"This is no longer soft material," he said, "This is a hard surface."

"What is it composed of?"

"It looks like hundreds of tiny stones which have been beaten into a receiving earth or clay, which then may have been subjected to intense heat."

With considerable difficulty he prized out a small amount of the material and handed it up to me. "You see that smooth, blue-green which looks like glazing?"

"Yes. What does it mean?"

"That has been vitrified."

"What's that?"

"The original material, whatever it was, has been transformed by heat and fusion into hard, non-crystalline glass."

"Is that something you find often?"

"Quite frequently. In Scotland and Ireland entire forts were vitrified. The walls must have been exposed to fire for an extended period until all the stones were bonded or fused."

"Why was it done in this case?"

"We don't know. Of course, if it was accidental there would not have been a purpose. But if it was intentional it would have to have been done to provide a hard surface."

"As a floor?"

"I think not. You see, vitrification, while it fuses the material, tends to make it more brittle. I would say this would have been in the nature of a seal."

He clambered out of the trench and joined me on the grass, cleaning his trowel on the seat of his pants. As we stood there, it occurred to me that I had been very remiss in not asking after the student who had been badly injured by a billhook in the lane some weeks ago.

"How's Sammy? Is that her name?"

"You mean Sandy?"

"Yes. Sorry, Sandy."

"She's on the mend. She's been out of hospital for some time, but she has to go in to be checked on a regular basis. I'm afraid she lost one of the fingers. They managed to sew the other two on successfully. I've no clue how they did it, but they did. It's amazing really."

"Too bad she can't come back to work. She seemed very enthusiastic,"

"She's one of my better students. She says she will be back next week."

"Wow! That's determination! Good for her."

I looked out across the big field. A murmuration of starlings created an amazing aerobatic display overhead. As I watched this synchronized, shape-shifting phenomenon, the sound of hundreds of tiny wings dominated the air around us.

When the birds had moved off, I turned back to Ralph. "What happens now?"

"I'll get my assistant, Stefan, to go through the vitreous layer while we stand here and watch."

"Like observers at a delicate medical operation?"

"Something like that."

"Will Stefan be able to trowel his way through?"

"He'll attempt that first and, if it doesn't work, he'll use a mattock."

Stefan climbed down into the trench and carefully placed a bucket, a tray and a thick doormat on the ground next to the feature. He knelt on the mat and started to scrape with his trowel.

After a few minutes he sat back on his haunches. "It's no good. It's solid."

"Try the mattock."

"Okay, Prof."

The mattock was a trenching tool developed for the United States Army in World War II, having a small, collapsible shovel on one side of the haft and a small pick on the other. Stefan wielded this gently at first, but then with force, but we could see it was having no effect.

"Alright, Stefan, try the pick axe, but go slowly."

Stefan stood up and walked over to the edge of the trench.

"What is it, Stefan?" Ralph inquired.

"Prof, I was figuring that if I go at it with only moderate force, it could shatter the whole surface whereas a quick, hard blow might just give us a clean hole. Then we can insert a borescope and take a look before we go any further."

"Good idea. Let's do that."

Stefan returned to his position, carrying the pick axe. He raised it above his head and swiftly brought it down.

It is hard for me to describe what happened next, except to say that, as the pick penetrated the surface, it released the most horrible, repulsive, sickening odour I have ever smelled in my life.

Stefan immediately collapsed, apparently unconscious, and the rest of us violently vomited. All over the site, people were on their knees, coughing and retching. Most, like me, crawled as far away as we could get. I managed to wriggle under the fence and dragged myself into the field.

When I had finally recovered some kind of composure I looked about me and saw Ralph gagging a few yards away.

"What the hell was that?" I gasped.

"God knows," he choked. "But if it left any traces I'm going to have it analyzed at the lab."

"That was far, far worse than disgusting," I said.

"Yeah." He appeared frightened, in addition to looking ill. "Evil is the word which came to my mind."

17

I felt so sick for the next two days, I did not dare leave the house because the headache and diarrhea were so severe. I was not in direct contact with Ralph, but looking at the hill out of my window it seemed that everyone else who was present when Stefan had wielded the pick axe had been similarly affected. The site was completely deserted.

From a distance, I could not tell if the foul odour had dissipated or continued to emanate from that small hole, but I did notice that for at least a day birds and animals seemed to be avoiding the area.

On the morning of the third day I felt a great deal better and was able to eat some scrambled eggs and a piece of toast. It was my first food of any kind since the appalling incident.

The day after that, being physically much stronger, I was planning on going out and was gingerly approaching the site when the phone rang. It was Ralph.

"Marc. How are you feeling?

"Much better, but the past few days have been rough."

"Yeah, me, too. I thought you should know that we're going to start work again tomorrow."

"Is it safe?"

"I had a guy in first responder's gear go up and test for noxious gas and he said it was clear."

"What the hell was it?"

"Ah. The lab was only able to find faint traces on my clothes— which have since been burned by the way—of three substances. I'll show you the full report tomorrow."

"Look, Ralph, why don't you come to dinner tonight? I see from Rosalie's day timer that my friends, the Blands, are coming. You can show me the report then."

"That sounds good, but I'm not sure anything too spicy would be a good idea. Unless it's Italian."

"Why Italian?"

"I'm Italian. You didn't know? My real name is Raphaele Giffoni. My father changed it when they emigrated to Canada."

"No. I had no idea. Well, that's something else for us to talk about tonight."

"What time should I come?"

"Come about six." Then I added, "Ralph, what were the three substances you mentioned?"

"Melthylbutanoic acid, thiocetone and dimethyl disulfide. These were all they could identify."

"Wow! I sure will look forward to hearing the details."

In honour of Ralph's ancestry, I decided to attempt Italian food for dinner. As an appetizer I would make angel hair pasta with an anchovy carbonara sauce but omitting the pancetta because Rachel is an observant Jew. I had two dozen lamb shanks in the freezer, but they were frozen together and I knew they would be too much for five people.

Then I had an idea which would easily solve the problem: I would invite our old friend Frank Wilberforce to join us. Frank was an agent for the Canadian Prevention of Art Theft and Fraud Agency whom I had involved in a number of my investigations. He was a huge man with an appetite to match his size and girth, and he seldom turned down an invitation to dine.

He did not disappoint me, and promised to come, adding that he was particularly hungry today!

Before proceeding, I called Ray Bland to make sure the dish was something Rachel could eat and, on getting his clearance, I put the lamb in cold water to thaw, gathered my ingredients and laid them out on the kitchen counter. I had onions, carrots, celery, tomatoes, olive oil, red wine and kosher chicken stock, and would get herbs from my garden later. Then I went down to the cellar and, after some poking around, came up with several bottles of *Biondi Santi Brunello di Montalcino* 1999 to go with the lamb, *Enrico Serafino Gavi di Gavi* 2007 to accompany the starter, and some 2011

Franciacorta as an aperitif and to go with dessert. The latter was a sparkling wine from north-western Italy made from chardonnay and pinot noir grapes.

When I came up from the cellar I carefully put the bottles on the table and called Rosalie at work to ask her to pick up some fresh fruit on her way home. I am lousy at making desserts and she can usually do magical things with a few fruits and some ice cream.

I went out into the garden to see what herbs were sufficiently advanced to pick. The rosemary was small but abundant, so I cut a fair amount of it, together with a handful of thyme. From force of habit I looked up the hill to the dig, at first noting that the site was deserted, but as I turned back to the house I thought I saw something out of the corner of my eye.

I swivelled again quickly and could just make out a very small, hunched, black figure flitting across the trenches. It was there for less than a second and, although I stood watching for quite some time, it did not return.

Later, when the lamb had thawed, I browned the shanks on all sides, and then put them into three large, oval roasting pans along with finely chopped onions, carrots, celery, tomatoes, rosemary, bay leaves, thyme, bisected heads of garlic, dried oregano and the wine. Although I am a believer in the notion that you cannot make good food with bad wine, and that ideally it is better to cook with the same wine you are serving to drink, I could not bring myself to pour the 1999 *Brunello* in with the meat. Instead I used some fairly decent *Chianti Classico* from the 2014 vintage.

I firmly replaced the lids on the roasting pans and put them to cook in the oven for four hours at a very low temperature. When they were ready I would serve the shanks with plain boiled potatoes, baked butternut squash, and green beans.

Ralph arrived first, in fact some thirty minutes early. Rosalie was upstairs changing and I was attending to various pots and pans.

"I came early because I thought you might not want to discuss this matter in front of your other friends."

"Why on earth wouldn't I? They're not children." I was annoyed that he wanted my attention when I still had a number of tasks to perform for dinner.

"I thought it might spoil their appetites."

"I guess that's a fair point," I conceded. "Tell me what was in the report from the lab."

"They isolated four substances."

"I thought you said there were three."

"Yes, I'll come to that in a moment." He fished some papers out of his briefcase and riffled through them. "Okay. The first was methylbutanoic acid, otherwise known as isovaleric acid. It is classified as a short-chain fatty acid. Like other low-molecular-weight carboxylic acids, it has an unpleasant odour."

"They can say that again!"

"It is found in the flowering plant valerian, in many essential oils, in cheese, soy milk, apple juice, dairy and beef products, dry-cured meats, and fermented foods. Also in the human gut, produced by gut bacteria through fermentation of amino acids, such as leucine."

"In other words, it tells us nothing, unless there is a cheese factory in the pit." I ran to the stove to turn down a burner.

"Marc, please don't shoot the messenger."

"Sorry."

"The next one is thioacetone, which is an unstable, orange compound known for its extremely foul odour, which can cause people to stagger, clutch their stomachs and run away—"

"That much we already knew!"

"Please don't interrupt. It can normally be produced only by treating acetone with hydrogen sulphide—that's bad-egg gas to you—in the presence of a Lewis acid."

"What the hell is a Lewis acid?"

"There's a scientific explanation here, but I don't understand it. Apparently it is an electron-pair donor, whatever that is."

"Search me. What's the next one?"

"That is the product of the Rafflesia arnoldii, or stinking corpse lily, which is found in primary and secondary rain forests."

"Which begs the question: How did it get here?"

"Precisely."

"And the fourth substance you mentioned. What was that?"

"They don't know."

"What?"

"This is what the report says: This is an unknown, apparently hitherto-unrecorded substance, likely partially of chemical origin, partially organic. Further comment should be withheld until submitted to either the Chinese Academy of Sciences or the French National Centre for Scientific Research, but it should be noted that the material, which is vestigial, is deteriorating at a rapid rate."

"Meaning: Forget it. We will never know."

"Afraid so. But even if we knew exactly what it was, it wouldn't necessarily tell us how it got there."

"Or why."

"Or why. Yes."

"Thanks Ralph. Why don't you go and sit in the lounge until Rosalie comes down. I'll get you a glass of bubble to keep you company."

A few minutes later Rosalie descended, looking extremely attractive and sporting her best jewellery. I suspected she had gone to extra effort so as not to be eclipsed by Rachel, who was stunningly-beautiful in addition to being extraordinarily vivacious.

Soon, the Blands arrived, and Rachel's quicksilver voice rang through the house, accompanied by Ray's jovial bass. Shortly afterwards, heavy footfalls in the porch heralded Frank Wilberforce and the Marshalls, and the party was complete.

From the beginning, Frank and Rachel showered Ralph with questions about the dig. For a long time they pursued inquiries about what the diggers had found, the anomalies in the excavations, the smell which had made us all sick, and the misfortunes associated with the site, such as Sandy's accident and the explosion of the jeep. Then Rosalie told them about the threatening letters she and I had received.

"Hard to say if that means anything," said Frank. "Could be cranks. I see lots of those in my business."

"Rosalie, you take care," said Rachel softly. "You don't want to take any chances. As you know, I have had my share of those kinds of letters."

We knew she was referring to her receipt of anti-Semitic communications a few years ago when I was conducting an investigation for her husband, an adventure I have described in my book *Unspeakable Evil*.

"Then of course there's—" I broke off, because I realized that I had told nobody about the figure I had seen, or thought I had seen, when I was in the garden.

"What is it, Marc?" Rosalie seemed concerned. The look on my face must have told her that I was quite uncomfortable.

"It's probably nothing."

"Don't hold out on us," Frank said.

"It's just that earlier I thought I saw someone moving about the dig."

"When was this?" Ralph asked, sitting forward.

"A few hours ago."

"What do you mean when you say 'moving about' the dig?" Rachel intervened.

"Well, not exactly walking. More like darting."

"Darting?" Ray said.

"That's what it looked like. Flitting rapidly."

"What was this person like? Male or female?" Rosalie demanded.

"I couldn't tell. I only got the merest glimpse out of the corner of my eye. It was—"

"Why do you say *it*?" Ralph asked.

"I don't know. I guess because I couldn't tell the gender. It was very short, all in black and sort of humped."

"Humped?"

"Did I say humped? I guess I meant hunched. As I say I got only a flash. It's quite possible I imagined it. Anyway, friends, it's time to eat. Ralph, did you enjoy the *Franciacorta*?"

"Yes, very much. It doesn't come from my part of Italy, but it is *molto gradito* none the less."

"Are you Italian?" Rachel asked.

"Yes. Well, my family is from Italy."

"Really? What part?"

"From Trentino-Alto-Adige. Up in the north east corner of the country. My people came from a little village near Mezzocorona in the Rotaliano Valley."

"I don't have any wine from there tonight," I said, "but in your honour I have some fabulous Brunello from Toscana."

"Wonderful."

"Please go to the table," said Rosalie. "Sit anywhere you like."

18

It had been a remarkable evening. The conversation was wide-ranging, often scintillating, and frequently illuminating. I certainly learned a great deal of what I had not previously been aware.

Ray was his usual jovial, but thoughtful, self, only getting really excited when talking about the cars which provided his livelihood. Rachel, though slightly more subdued than on previous occasions, still glittered like a bright star, entrancing all of us. As always, Frank was as expansive as his waistline, regaling us with details of art none of us had known, all the while shovelling vast amounts of food into his insatiable gullet. Rosalie and I, for the most part, were listeners.

But it was Ralph who was the centre of attention, explaining details of the excavation, enlightening us on modern archaeological thinking, and giving us the benefit of his views on the Upward Percolation Theory, which we had discussed when the Brysons and Marshalls had recently been our guests. It was fascinating to listen to him, but as the night wore on he became more agitated ("frazzled" was the word Rosalie used) and more disjointed, and by the time he came to leave, he was barely conscious. The Blands had taken him home in their taxi.

"Was he drunk?" Rosalie asked me at breakfast.

"He certainly consumed twice as much as any of the rest of us—including Frank—and I remember going down to get several more bottles. But I got the impression there was much more at play."

"How do you mean?"

"I think he may be sick. Sometimes I've seen him in the daytime when he looks like an old man."

"Hmm. I think he's only in his mid-forties."

"That's my understanding."

"Frank was in fine form, too. Your little 'humped' woman—"

"I never said it was a woman. I said I couldn't tell the gender."

"Your little black person then. That got him going."

It had been while we were eating the pasta that Frank raised the subject of things, objects, and people rising or escaping from the underworld. Ralph glared at me, but I shook my head to indicate that I had said nothing to anybody about the Mesopotamian clay inscription, *Imago Mundi*.

"You know, artists have always been obsessed with depictions of hell, and many paintings of it are pretty horrendous. Such pictures span centuries and styles, beliefs and countries. Some are inspired by descriptions from Dante, some from the Bible, and others from the blackest corners of the imagination." He reached for another helping of pasta. "This is awfully good, Marc. I never knew eggs and anchovies could taste like this."

"Yes." Rachel said. "I confessed I wasn't sure what to expect, but this is delicious."

"Where was I? Ah yes. Some of the earliest come from the Limbourg brothers in 1411, Fra Angelico in about 1430, Hans Memling in around 1460, and Jacob Swaneburg about 1620. Then there are Pieter Breughel, Gustav Doré, Blake, and many others. The most famous is, of course, our old friend Hieronymus Bosch and his *Garden of Earthly Delights*. All these have one thing in common. What is it?"

"They're all scary," said Jane.

"They're all very dark canvasses," Rosalie ventured.

"They all show humans in hideous circumstances," Rachel suggested.

"All that's true, but it's not what I'm looking for. Ralph?"

"They all depict a descent into Hell. None shows anyone escaping."

"Right! The only one I can think of off the top of my head which is not a descent is Tissot's *Rich Man in Hell*, which seems to show a man either rising from Hell or waiting for God to help him out. Now, Marc, the question is: Was your black humped figure coming out of the trenches or being sucked in?"

"I...er...I never thought of it in those terms."

"Maybe you saw the figures escaping at first, but then when you looked again he, she or it had been drawn back down into Hades."

"All this weird stuff only reinforces my belief that you shouldn't fool around with that site, and that you should wind up your excavation as soon as possible," Gary said with emphasis.

We served the lamb shanks, which were beautifully tender and were complemented perfectly by the vegetables and rich sauce. Despite being 25 years old, the *Brunello* was magnificent, deep, brooding, and redolent of cherries with floral notes intermingling and a slightly sweet finish that seemed to go on forever.

"You're not really going to stop the dig, are you?" Ray asked.

"No, we have a way to go yet," said Ralph.

"You might live to regret it." Gary spoke quietly. "With so many strange events, it would be crazy to continue."

"Ugh," said Jane. "Can we please change the subject?"

"I would like to stay on the general subject for a while yet, Jane, if you don't mind," Rachel said. "Ralph what are your general impressions of this seemingly insane theory of upward percolation?"

"It is only a theory, Rachel, but I'm tempted not to entirely dismiss anything unless it is scientifically discredited."

"But that would mean some theories or beliefs could never be discredited. Like the existence of God," Rosalie said.

"Yes, I guess so. Take archaeology, which is constantly evolving. For instance, in almost every culture we are pushing back the time boundaries."

"What do you mean?" asked Ray.

"To take just two examples: we used to think the Neolithic period in Britain started around 3500 BC. Now we know—through more sophisticated carbon dating—that it began at least 1000 years earlier; Columbian rock paintings which were thought to have been made 13,000 years ago are now believed to be 25,000 years old. A similar readjustment has taken place all over the world."

"The same for cataclysmic events?" I asked.

"Yes, indeed. Take the Younger Dryas, which was a period of extreme climate change that occurred around 12,900–11,700 years ago was previously thought to have occurred later."

"What was the Younger Dryas?"

"A period when temperatures plummeted, vast numbers of fires raged, and massive floods took place. Or so we think."

"Think?"

"Like all such postulations, it is disputed."

"Ralph, I know this will be a difficult question, but what, in your opinion, is the most amazing archaeological discovery of our times?" Frank asked.

"I would have to say the Amazon Basin."

"What about it?"

"We look at it today, especially from the air, and what do we see? An immense carpet of forest stretching for thousands of miles, containing very few, isolated peoples."

"So?"

"It wasn't always like that. Something like 20,000 years ago, the land was clear and populated by thousands of highly-skilled people."

"You're kidding?"

"No, with special cameras which can see through the forest canopy, we know there are many thousands of vast earthworks of banks and ditches, like large forts, where we previously thought there was nothing. Each of these geoglyphs would have required a multitude of men to construct. From that we can extrapolate, there was a very large population." He sprawled back in his chair, knocking his napkin to the floor.

"What happened to these people?" Jane inquired.

"Nobody knows. Maybe the Younger Dryas wiped them out."

"Amazing!" I intervened, trying to wrap up the discussion.

"Also, polychromatic pottery approximately 10,000 years old has been found in South America." Ralph was beginning to slur his words. "Previously, we thought the earliest came from Greece about 8500 years ago."

"That's remarkable," said Rosalie. "Now for dessert. Who's for kiddingfresh fruit and ice cream?"

There being no dissenters from the proposition, she apportioned dessert into bowls while I poured more of the *Francicorta*. I could see that Ralph could barely lift his spoon to his mouth. He seemed to fall asleep, but not before he demanded and downed another glass of wine.

"How much longer do you think they will be digging up there?" Ray asked me as they were leaving.

"They don't know how deep the pit is yet," I replied. "They have to keep digging to find out what it's all about. It might go down for many metres."

"Or forever," said Frank ominously.

19

Somewhere around 3 am—I am not sure, because I did not look at the clock—I heard the sound of a vehicle at the front of the house. Before I could pull myself together and investigate, it had driven away down the lane. Being only semi-conscious, I drifted back to sleep, not realizing its significance.

As I came downstairs the next morning, I was relishing the thought of a long, relaxed breakfast with my wife since Rosalie did not have to going to the university today. As I rounded the corner of the staircase, my good mood left me because, facing me on the floor by the front door, was an envelope.

Rosalie came trotting down behind me so quickly she bumped into me. "What is it, Marc?"

"Another poison pen letter, I guess."

"Oh, no!"

"We'll soon find out," I said as I picked it up and opened it.

youd better lissen soon Leblanc or yor pretty wife
could get her face mesed about stop the digging now

"Damn! You'd better not look at it, darling."

"Like hell I won't!" said Rosalie, as she snatched it from me hand. "The bastard! I wish I could get my hands on him."

"How do you know it's a him?"

"What?"

"It could be a woman."

"You think? Why?"

"I'm just stating a possibility."

"Not very helpful," she said with a snort. "What are we going to do now?"

"Clearly this is now criminal because an actual threat of physical violence has been made, so I'll call Patrick right after breakfast."

"Do it now!"

I knew better than to argue with Rosalie when her temper was up, so I called Patrick at his home. Ruth answered and I had to indulge in a little backchat with her first, much to my wife's annoyance.

When Patrick took the phone, I read him the letter and he promised me he would arrange for a Staff Sergeant Lomas to come up from the Wolfville office.

"Don't expect too much, Marc."

"I don't, but at least we can get a file opened now."

"You know the chances of identifying the printer are infinitesimal unless we first have a lead on the perpetrator."

"Yes, I'm aware of that."

"What time of night was it?"

"I can't be specific, but in the early hours. After midnight."

"You didn't see anything?"

"No. Wrong side of the house to see the vehicle."

"There was a vehicle?"

"Yes."

"Why didn't you say so? What kind was it?"

"I'm not sure, but it sounded like a truck."

"A pickup truck?"

"Yes."

"I'll pass all this on to Lomas and ask him to come and see you later in the day, after he's made some inquiries."

"Thanks. Tell him that if I'm not at the house, I'll be up the hill at the dig."

"The dig?"

"Yes, the archaeological excavation I told you about."

"Oh, that. Okay, will do. Gotta go."

After breakfast I sauntered up the hill. It was a fine, but blustery, day with the wind blowing the long grass of the field almost flat. The thousands of little wild flowers seemed to have been engulfed by the restless sea of herbaceous greenery, and birds were being tossed around in the air like shuttlecocks.

When I was about two-thirds the way up I saw Ralph coming towards me. He looked terrible. I realize that a massive hangover does not do any favours to one's appearance, but he resembled a ghost who had been on a starvation diet, not one who had overindulged on food and drink.

"'Morning, Marc. I hope I wasn't too badly behaved last night."

"Well, you did put away a lot of wine."

"Very good wine it was, too. My apologies if I offended anyone."

"Apology accepted. What's new?"

"I wanted to see you before you got on the site."

"Oh?"

"I arrived early. We haven't yet put the borescope into the hole in that layer."

"Will you be doing that today?"

"Yes, yes, as soon as we go up there. But before the others got here I just had a little probe with my trowel and a large chunk of that hard covering material came away. What do you think I found emerging from that black soil?"

"There's the same black soil underneath that layer?"

"Yes, yes. Pay attention to what I'm saying, Marc!"

"Sorry, Ralph."

"I'll ask you again. What do you think I found emerging from that black soil?"

"I've no idea. What?"

"A replica or facsimile of the Dispilio Tablet." He was breathing heavily.

"What on earth is the Dispilio Tablet?"

"It's a piece of wood which was found in a Greek bog in 1993. Carbon-14 dated it to 7,000 years old."

"A piece of wood?"

"Not just any piece of wood, man"—Ralph sounded cross—"but one which carries a cryptic inscription that dates to 5,000 BC."

"So?"

"Before this was discovered, writing was not supposed to have been invented until about 3,500 BC, in Sumeria ."

"Wow!"

"Keep this to yourself."

"Yes, of course. How do you account for this?"

"I can't. Just as I couldn't account for the *Imago Mundi* turning up."

"Maybe the Upward Percolation Theory has more to it than we thought."

"That's what I was wondering."

"But it's too far-fetched."

"Maybe not."

"Can we go up now and do the borescope?"

"Yes, let's. But there won't be much need for it, now the crust has been penetrated."

"But it could tell you if there are more artifacts in the soil, so you can approach them with care."

"Yes, that's true. Remember to keep quiet about the tablet."

As we arrived at the site, I noticed many more people working, most of them students whose classes were now over for the summer. I recognized two of them and walked over.

"Hello, Jennifer. Hello, Tracey."

"Hello Mr. LeBlanc."

Jennifer was the daughter of my lawyer, Walter Bryson, and Tracey was her best friend. I had come to know them when investigating an accusation of sexual assault by a young priest who was a friend of Rosalie's and mine. These events I have described in my book *The Plot to Kill the Premier*.

After chatting with the girls, I moved over to where Ralph and Stefan had set up the borescope. Stefan guided it into the hole Ralph had made earlier, while we watched a small screen. He moved it this way and that for fifteen minutes or so, but found nothing.

"Doesn't look like there's much here, Prof."

"Go a little deeper, Stefan."

"Roger that."

He lowered the probe to about five feet below the hard surface he had tried to break days ago. Suddenly he threw himself flat and, reaching down, moved it laterally across the trench.

"Looks like we have another floor...or ceiling," he called out. "But the intermediate fill seems to be sterile of finds. What do you want done, Prof?"

"Hack up the surface and clean off to the next level."

"Okay, but it's five feet down, so it'll take some time to clear out the spoil."

"Well, get on with it. Do you think you'll have it done today?"

"Not likely. Maybe noon tomorrow."

"Alright," Ralph said, moving to the surrounding fence. "Are you in trouble with the law, Marc?"

He pointed down the hill to where a uniformed officer was slowly heading towards us.

"Ah, I know what that's about. I'll go down and meet him. Thanks, Ralph."

I shook hands with Staff Sergeant Lomas and we walked back down to the house, where he had left his cruiser.

"You're in luck, Mr. LeBlanc."

"Am I? Why?"

"We have three different witnesses on the nights in question. On each night we have two of them, independent of the other."

"Witnesses to what?"

"To seeing Alaric Balser's truck going up or coming down your lane."

"Good God, already?"

"Yes, sir. We can move fast sometimes, you know."

"Especially when you've been called by a superintendent."

"That wasn't very kind, Mr. LeBlanc."

"I know. I apologize. Who is Alaric Balser?"

"A well-known local eccentric, sir. Do you know him?"

He took out his phone and showed me a photograph of a scruffy-looking man in his late fifties.

"No, I don't. Do we know why he did it?"

"He lives just over the hill from the site. I gather he thought a bunch of students and other diggers would disturb his peace."

"I guess I can understand how he might feel that way, but he should have come to see me at the very beginning. What happens now?"

"If we can go inside, I get you and Mrs. LeBlanc to make official statements."

"Yes, of course."

"Then we'll take the evidence of the notes. You kept them?"

"Yes."

"Good. Then we will take Mr. Balser into custody and he will be charged. Then the law will take its majestic course." He grinned broadly. "Although between you and me, sir, I wouldn't be optimistic about a severe sentence if he's found guilty."

"Oh, why not?"

"I shouldn't say this, Mr. LeBlanc, but by all accounts Alaric Balser is a few cents short of a dollar."

"Ah."

"Apparently, he's always taking umbrage at something or other. I imagine he'll get a lecture from the magistrate and a suspended sentence."

"And if he should do it again?"

"Well, that would be a different matter."

20

While Rosalie and I were unsure of the final disposition of the charge against Alaric Balser, we were nonetheless greatly relieved that the person responsible for the nasty notes had been apprehended. Therefore I was in a good mood for several days, made even better by an early call on the third morning from Bill Jolly, advising me that he had more fresh fish waiting for me at the Kingsport wharf.

I was glad of this opportunity to talk to Bill, because I had heard some news reports on the radio to the effect that hundreds of millions of dollars' worth of lobster were being caught in Atlantic Canadian waters each year, but not reported to authorities, causing severe problems with tax evasion and conservation. One news report said that the Federal Government estimated that as much as 30 percent of lobster landings in the region were unreported, and was investigating the criminal networks believed to be responsible, and their associated money laundering.

Although I had been living in the area for over six years, this was the first I had heard of this problem and had always assumed that most catches were legitimate. Obviously, some fishermen were involved, and I presumed there must be many dealers and plant owners who were flouting the law. But I wondered what other pockets were being lined. Did the Mafia or some other arm of organized crime have a presence here?

After I arrived at the wharf and took delivery of some beautiful mackerel and cod, I asked Bill about what I had heard. He jerked his head, indicating that we should step away from the boat so his crew could not hear us.

"Yeah, it goes on. There's no doubt about that."

"Do you know anyone involved?

He looked at me as if I were a naïve child, which told me I would not get an answer even if he had one.

"Got to be careful," he said in a low voice. "Feller could get himself beat up or killed."

"Surely not?"

"Oh yeah. I heard the Mounties have laid over fifty charges in the past two years. Quite a few of them cases have involved violence.'"

"What kind of violence?"

"Fires set in fish houses. Homes being shot up. Trucks being overturned."

"I had no idea. How is it supposed to work? You know, for honest people like you?"

"All commercial fishermen like me have to fill out logbooks every day with all the dates, boat and licence numbers, where we fished, how many traps we hauled and what the lobster we caught weighed when we sold it to the plants."

"So, when you sell me fish over the side, are we breaking the law?"

"Officially, yes. But what you buy is just chicken feed. I don't think it'll bring down the government."

"I hope none of your crew turns me in to the cops."

"If they do, they won't be working for me very long."

I put the fish on the passenger seat of the Bugatti and drove off.

Bill had told me that, in recent years, the value of reported lobster landings had seen a low of $1 billion and a high of $2 billion annually. If the report was true, it would mean that as much as $600 million a year was being illegally obtained, so I could see why the government was concerned. I could also see why it might present a lucrative opportunity for organized crime.

After a delicious breakfast of mackerel, fried potatoes, locally-made honey and Blue Mountain coffee, I strolled up to the dig site. I had not been up there since the operation of the borescope because I supposed most of the work being carried out would just be shovelling earth out of the pit.

When I got there, it appeared I had been correct, because there was an enormous pile of black spoil on the edge of the central trench and the pit was now down to a depth of nine feet or so. As I got closer, I could see that Stefan, Jennifer, Tracey and Sandy, her hand bandaged, were on their hands and knees in the pit, trowelling and brushing the new surface.

When I saw Ralph, I was shocked by his appearance. In addition to the greyish pallor I had noted the last time I saw him, one side of his face seemed to be sagging and his arm was twitching slightly. Also, I could not help noting that he had a number of unpleasant facial sores.

"Good morning, Ralph. Is the new layer similar to the last one? Hard and pebbly?"

"Hi, Marc. No, if anything it seems to be harder. I think it might be metal. There is a small hole in it which might be caused by rust. We're scraping it down now. In a little while, we'll attempt to penetrate it on a larger scale."

He called down to Stefan. "Stefan, you should board up the walls of the trenches before we go any lower. We don't want any collapses. It could slow down our progress."

"Good point, Prof. I'll get on to it as soon as we've cleaned off this surface."

"Okay. Good," Ralph said. He looked around, then lowered his voice. "Take a walk with me, Marc."

We strolled down towards the old lane which his crew had cleared early on in the excavation. As we passed the pit, I could see that Stefan and the three women all had nasty sores on their faces. So did the two students drawing sections in the lower trenches, and the young man who was washing the jeep.

"Ralph, what's with the sores you all seem to have?"

"What? Oh, it's nothing. Probably some substance in the soil. Either that or some insect which lives in the ground here."

"You should see a doctor."

"Yeah maybe." He glanced over his shoulder. "Look, Mark, I thought you should know that early this morning, before the others came to work I found a piece of a Judean coin."

"From Israel?"

"Kind of. From Judea. That's what some call the West Bank."

"How do you know it's from Judea?"

"It has a menorah on the obverse and part of an inscription which is illegible."

"How about the reverse?"

"That's too worn to see anything."

"How old is it?"

"As far as I can tell it dates from about 40BC."

"Do you know what was going on in Judea in those days?"

"There was a civil war and an invasion by the Parthians. Herod the Great was put on the throne by the Romans and had to flee to Rome to escape. A few years later he came back with an army and re-established himself."

"Was he the guy who was responsible for Christ's death?"

"No, that was his son Herod Antipas."

"Oh. Where did you find the coin?"

"In the hole in the new level."

"Just like the Dispilio Tablet?"

"I guess so," he replied in a tone which suggested he thought my question impertinent.

"Let's go back. I want to see the penetration of the new level."

"We won't be doing that now because we have to shore up the trenches first. Come back tomorrow. Mid-morning should do it."

As I climbed the fence I thought I heard a 'crack', but put it out of my mind and meandered back down the hill, collecting a bunch of wildflowers for Rosalie as I went.

There was not a single cloud in the sky and I could see for miles, Cape Blomidon appearing to be much closer than its forty kilometres. In the other direction, John Dempster's vines looked vigorous and healthy, indicating a good crop of grapes unless the weather turned bad.

When I was about halfway down the field, I saw Rosalie come running out of the house and through the garden in my direction. She seemed extremely agitated and was waving furiously and shouting.

When we were nearer she ran into my arms, sobbing hysterically. "Marc, oh Marc, they're trying to kill us."

"Who is? What are you talking about?"

"Come see. They were shooting at us!"

"Shooting?"

"Yes. Right through the window."

"Widow? What window?"

"The living room window. Come and see!"

We ran down, into the house, and through to the lounge. There, about two thirds the way from the floor, was a small hole with a slight web pattern around it.

I immediately went to the wall on the opposite side of the room and hunted around. There I found another hole in which an object, presumably a bullet, was deeply embedded. It was clear that, at the very least, somebody was trying to frighten us and, if Rosalie was right, actually trying to kill us.

I gave Rosalie a large glass of brandy and called Staff Sergeant Lomas at the RCMP detachment. He told me that he and other officers, including a forensic expert, would be with us within an hour and, true to his word, they soon came.

We were asked to step out of the room while they went to work. They stretched a line from the hole in the window to the one in the wall to determine the angle of fire, then a man in a white plastic suit probed for the bullet.

"Excuse me, miss," he called to Rosalie. "How many shots were there?"

"It seemed like just one, but it might have been two."

"Thank you, miss."

We went and sat at the kitchen table while we were waiting for the Mounties to do their work. I made a pot of coffee and gave Rosalie a cup, then asked Lomas if they wanted some and was told they did not.

After what seemed like an eternity, Lomas came in. "Sorry for taking so long."

"That's alright. You have to do your job. What can you tell us?"

"This is only preliminary, you understand. Our technical guy says the shooter was almost certainly up on the ridge, likely in those woods. He says he thinks the weapon was a Barrett M82, which he says is highly unusual, so maybe easier to trace than a more common one. He found two bullets in your wall, so Mrs. LeBlanc was correct about that. They would have been fired in very rapid succession."

"What happens now?"

"I will leave Constable Hawkins here tonight and we'll be back tomorrow."

"Thank you."

"Stay away from the windows, and don't hang about in the garden or on the patio."

"Right."

"I have ordered the woods searched, but the shooter is probably long gone. Tomorrow some of my people may be crawling about, but I hope they won't inconvenience you. I imagine Superintendent Kennedy will have a special interest in this case, so I'll call him as soon as I get back to base."

"Thank you, Staff Sergeant."

"Thank you, sir. Try to get some rest, if you can."

21

At breakfast the next morning, Rosalie suggested that we invite the diggers from the site to come down to lunch. She told me she took pity on them eating sandwiches with dirty hands in filthy trenches.

If she was prepared to do the necessary preparation I had no objection. She asked me how many people would be involved and I said I seen as many as seven on the site, but that there might be more.

"I'll plan for ten. Will you go up and tell them?"

"Sure, I'm aiming to look in on them this morning anyway."

"What shall I provide for them to drink?"

"Coffee should do it. But not the Blue Mountain."

"Okay. How about wine?"

"If you like, but for heaven's sake don't give them Chateau Lafite or anything like that."

"I see what I can find."

"No, I'll go down and get you a few bottles of Beaujolais."

"You're such a snob."

About an hour later, when I made the invitation, Ralph said they couldn't spare the time, but he was overruled by a loud and immediate chorus of disapproval.

"Oh alright then," he said. "But only an hour. We've got a lot of work to do because I want to expand the trenches to explore some of the surrounding area. I want to be all back- filled and out of here by the end of August."

The news that they would eating lunch at the house seemed to raise the diggers' spirits and they bent to their work with fresh enthusiasm.

I wandered around, observing various diggers studiously drawing plans and sections, had a few words with Jennifer and Tracey, and then went and sat on the fence until they were ready to proceed on the next stage of the pit.

The excavation of the pit was now about ten feet deep, with the walls covered by planks secured by plastic rope. The surface of the new level, which had a strange, mottled, red-black appearance, was now completely cleared and brushed down. Except for the one small opening which Ralph had made, it was untouched.

Ralph and Sandy walked around the edges of the trench, taking photographs while the others watched.

"Stefan, down you go," said Ralph when he had put his camera away.

"Okay, Prof."

Stefan took his pick axe and gently pecked at the edge of the existing hole. He succeeded only in moving small pieces of material, which, when released from the surroundings, resembled asphalt.

"Give it some muscle, Stefan," Ralph ordered. "We don't have all day."

"Will do. Here goes." He lifted the instrument to shoulder level and brought it swiftly down.

We heard a crack and saw a flash, then suddenly a huge gush of flame came roaring out of the aperture the pickaxe had made. Stefan was sent reeling backwards, hitting his head on the planks. Foul-smelling black smoke hung over the trench for a few seconds, then dissipated.

"Jesus!" Ralph cried. "Stefan, are you okay?"

"Cut the back of my head, but apart from that I'm only shaken up."

Stefan, his face now blackened like a chimney sweep, and blood trickling down the back of his neck, clambered out of the trench.

"What the hell was that?" he asked.

"The fires of Hell," Ralph said quietly.

"Come to the house, Stefan," I said. "Rosalie can see to your wound. In fact, why don't we all go? Let's take an early lunch."

The other diggers all murmured their assent, but Ralph was standing, swaying slightly, and just staring silently into the pit.

"Ralph," I called. "Ralph!"

He did not move. So I told the others to go on to the house. Then I gently put my arm around his shoulders and guided him away. Being this close to him, I could see that his skin was like slimy grey plastic and the sores were now red and pustulated.

I slowly led him down the hill and, when we were about halfway to the house, he turned and grabbed my arm so tightly it hurt.

"Marc, I wasn't sure at first but now I believe."

"Believe what?"

"The Theory of Upward Percolation."

"Oh, Ralph! Surely, you can't buy that foolishness. You're a man of science, for God's sake!"

"I didn't want to, but I do now. It's happened again."

"What has happened?"

"Last night when the crew had gone home, I looked in the trench and there it was."

"What was there?"

"A Neolithic stone ball."

"A what?"

"An elaborately-carved stone ball. They've been found mostly in Scotland, dating from about 3,000 BC."

"You're joking?"

"No, no. Over 400 of these balls have been found, but never here. Their surfaces are sculpted, sometimes into raised circular discs and sometimes with deep incisions defining lobes in high relief."

"What did this one look like?"

"It had decorations in the form of spirals, similar to those found on pottery and monumental stones of the era. Some have been found in burials, others in settlements."

"What were they used for?"

"The original use of these stone balls has been a source of much debate for over a hundred years, but nobody knows. Did they hurl them at predators and pests? Were they weapons? Some have even suggested that they were used as rollers to move megaliths."

"That is extraordinary!"

"Not a word to anyone."

"Why not?"

"Could be used against me."

"What on earth are you talking about?"

"Shh!" He looked over his shoulder. "You saw the fire."

"Yes, but surely that was some methane previously trapped in the earth which was ignited by a spark from Stefan's pick axe striking the surface."

"You can believe that if you want," he said sulkily, and walked on ahead of me.

Rosalie had put on quite a spread for the diggers, considering how little time she had to prepare. There was a huge tureen of pea soup; ham, egg and cold beef sandwiches; a variety of cheeses; fresh fruit; cookies and cakes and several bubbling pots of coffee.

Jennifer and Tracey were laughing and chattering, Sandy was gaily manipulating a soup spoon with her injured hand, Stefan was shovelling in sandwiches like a starving man, and the others were digging into the food and maintaining a steady hum of conversation.

Ralph sat to one side, neither eating nor talking; but he had seen the Beaujolais, grabbed it, and was drinking heavily. The bottle in front of him was already at a low level and he had another lined up.

I went over to him, sat down and tried to reason with him, but he brushed me aside, saying that he wanted to be left alone.

After an hour had passed, Stefan, now adorned with a head bandage, rallied the troops and urged them back to work. They thanked Rosalie and filed out, dragging Ralph with them.

When they had gone I helped my wife clear up and noticed that two of the Beaujolais bottles were empty.

"What's wrong with him?" she asked.

"I wish I knew. Right now he's mad at me."

"Why?"

"Because I won't buy this Upward Percolation nonsense."

"Not that again! I thought he was a skeptic."

"He was, but apparently no longer."

"Oh dear. That's too bad." She loaded some plates into the dishwasher. "I have to go to the office for an hour or two. What will you do?"

"I imagine I'll wander back up to the dig. See you later. What do you fancy for dinner?"

"Do we have any of Bill Jolly's fish left?"

"Yes, we do."

"Then let's have fish and chips with mushy peas and your secret home-made tartar sauce."

"At your service, madame."

I peeled some potatoes, cut the chips and put them in cold water to soak. Then I made the batter with equal amounts of flour and water, a teaspoon each of salt and sugar and two spoonfuls of baking soda. This I put in the fridge, along with some beautiful fillets of cod. Then I headed back up the hill to the dig.

I could not see Ralph anywhere, but Stefan had taken charge and had ordered the removal of the red/black level. The fill underneath it appeared to consist of thousands of tiny pebbles mixed with a darkish soil, which Stefan said was rotted plant material. Since trowelling this was impractical he said they were going to "plough on down" with picks and shovels.

I left them to it and wandered the field along the line of the woods. Fairly soon I saw yellow tape where the RCMP had roped off the area from which I assumed the shots had been fired. I peered around but could see nothing, so I continued along the edge of the woods until I came to the beginning of the vineyards in which I owned a twenty-five percent share.

John Dempster, the principal shareholder, had once been my best friend; but we had a falling out which I have described in my book *Holy Grail, Sacred Gold*. John and I no longer spoke, but I maintained a lively interest in the vineyard and its wine.

The vine leaves were a lustrous dark green and showed little sign of attack by insect or mould. The grapes were still quite small, but I reached over, plucked some and tasted them. They had a very slight degree of sweetness which I took as a sign of good things to come later in the year.

I was aimlessly meandering back when my phone buzzed.

"Marc? It's me."

"Hi, darling. What's up?"

"I've had an accident."

"What? When? Are you hurt?"

"No. I was only going about twenty kilometres an hour when it happened."

"You were in the car?"

"Yes. Don't panic. I ran into a van on Main Street."

"Were you tailgating?"

"No! I was a fair way back but just couldn't stop."

"Where are you now?"

"At Ron's garage. I called them and they towed it here."

"Okay I'll come and get you. I won't be long."

I ran down the hill, hopped into the Bugatti and drove into Wolfville. It only took me three minutes to get to the garage, where I found Rosalie chatting with Cletus, Ron's assistant.

"Hey, Cletus. Will Rosalie's Fiat take long to fix?"

"The boss said you could probably have her back tomorrow or the next day."

"Good. Where is he?"

"Inside, working on it."

"I'll nip in and see him."

I found Ron with his head in the engine and had to tap him on the shoulder to get his attention.

"Hey, Marc. Close one eh?"

"Can you fix it, alright?"

"Sure." He looked around, then quietly pulled the door across. "Marc, I didn't say anything to your missus, but come here and look at this."

I bent over into the engine until our heads were almost touching. He moved his caged light closer.

"What am I looking at?"

"This. The connection between the brake pedal and the piston lever which pushes fluid from the master cylinder into the brake lines."

"What about it."

"It's separated."

"Separated?"

"Yeah. And if you ask me, I'd say it had been cut."

22

The previous day I had gone to see Staff Sergeant Lomas and told him what Ron had reported to me. He said he would speak to Ron and Cletus, commence investigations and let me know if and when they made progress.

"Should I call Patrick Kennedy, or would you rather do it?" I asked. "You know he is a good friend and he would never forgive me if he were kept in ignorance of something like this."

"Yes, I'm well aware of that, but I'd rather report this to him myself, if you don't mind."

"No, go ahead. Best keep it official."

Now, at breakfast the following day, Rosalie and I had the conversation I knew could not be put off any longer.

"Marc," she said looking over her coffee cup, "isn't it time to get serious."'

"How do you mean?"

"You know exactly what I mean."

"Do I?"

"Don't be an asshole! I'm talking about that calamity up on the hill."

"Ah."

"Don't you think it's time to pull the plug?"

"How? Just tell Ralph, Stefan, Jennifer, Tracey and the rest of them to go home?"

"Maybe not as crudely as that, but basically, yes."

"What words would you have me use, then?"

"I don't know. How about we give them a date? Give them a few days to clear up."

"Okay, I'll agree to that if you tell them."

"Me? Oh, no. I couldn't."

"How about I say that if it were left to me they could stay as long as they liked, but my wife is panicking and wants to evict them right away?"

"You bastard!"

"Be fair, Rosalie. Why should I have to do your dirty work?"

"I wish you wouldn't put it like that."

"How should I put it?"

She stood up and stomped off into the other room. I could hear her pulling curtains and punching cushions.

After a while she came back. "I can see why you wouldn't want these people—whoever they are—to win, so I'll compromise. Why don't we ask them to wind up the dig in a week's time?"

"That's not enough notice. How about a month?"

"Two weeks."

"Okay," I said reluctantly. I did not like letting Ralph down, but the prospect of war with my wife was even less appealing. "I'll let Ralph know when I go up tomorrow."

"Why not today?"

"Because I'm going to be in town all day. At the wine store."

"Oh, right. Will you give me a lift? I have to get my Fiat from Ron. He called earlier to say it's been fixed."

I spent most of that day at my wine store in Wolfville, going over the books and stock lists with my partner Louise. I had left all but a few business decisions to her and she had done a superb job turning an empty space into a tasteful, well-stocked, thriving concern.

I was particularly grateful to her for relieving me of the trouble of following wine auctions around the world in search of my favourite rare wines. Since the advent of Louise, I simply told her what I wanted and she found it for me.

The most successful of these requests resulted in Louise finding me two bottles of 1934, and four bottles of 1945 *La Romanee Conti* from the *domaine* of the same name. 1945 was a stupendous vintage with perfect growing conditions and a hot summer and fall, but World War Two had only just ended and the lack of manpower meant that only 608 bottles were made of the wine from that year. Rosalie and I had drunk one on our last anniversary and we found it to be in almost mint condition, offering an intoxicating bouquet of wild strawberries, cherries, and truffles, layered with subtle notes of cedar, tobacco, and spice. Each sip was a discovery of depth and complexity that lingered long after it was gone.

I sauntered around the shop, running my hands over the contents of the shelves and feeling very satisfied that I had made the decision to start this venture. I was even more satisfied that we were carrying a sensible selection of quality products and to discover that, after a shaky start, the business was now showing a healthy profit.

I was about to suggest to Louise that we open some champagne to celebrate when I looked up and saw a red truck heading straight towards the front window. One second it was driving down Main Street and the next it was hurtling from the sidewalk toward the store. I rapidly looked around and, noticing an alcove where Louise keeps her coat and umbrella, I pushed her toward it as hard as I could.

We barely attained this shallow refuge when the truck thundered past us in a shower of glass, smashing all in its wake. The noise of the engine and the breaking of hundreds of bottles was deafening until the truck piled against the back wall and stalled.

Louise had fainted so I gently laid her down, using her raincoat as a pillow, and extricated myself from the wreckage. Literally wading through glass, I got to the truck and peered into the cab.

The driver's face and neck were pouring blood, and the way his head was twisted left me in no doubt he was dead.

It was Alaric Balser.

I called Staff Sergeant Lomas, and within minutes he, several officers and an ambulance arrived.

"You're like a magnet for trouble, Mr. LeBlanc," he said, a little sourly. "Half my time seems to be spent on your problems these days."

"I sincerely hope you will actually do something this time."

"Now, now, sir. Calm down until we know what we're dealing with. This could just be an accident, coincidental with your other difficulties."

"You won't say that when you see who the driver is."

"Why, who is it?"

"Alaric Balser. The man you described as being a few cents short of a dollar."

He stared at me in what seemed like a hostile manner, then gave an enormous sigh. "Oh God. Maybe you could take the young lady to the hospital to make sure she's not injured in any way. We'll carry on here and throw a cordon around the place when we're through. You should call your insurance agent and have him or her come here as soon as possible."

"Yes. Thank you, Staff Sergeant."

It turned out that Louise did not have a scratch on her and was most indignant at the suggestion she should seek medical attention. She told me she would wait until the police were finished so she could make a complete inventory of all the lost wine and calculate its cost. I thanked her for her bravery and devotion to duty and walked to the car, which I had parked on the next street.

As I turned the corner, I almost bumped into Bill Jolly coming towards me. "Marc, are you alright? I just heard."

"Word travels fast in this town. Yes, thanks, I'm alright, although I've lost a lot of stock."

"I'm sorry to hear that."

He took out a cigarette and lit in cupped hands to protect the flame from the wind. "I also heard you had some other trouble too."

"You did?"

"Yeah, with your wife's car."

"Where did you hear that?"

"Cletus at the garage. He's told half the town."

"I guess it was inevitable, but I'd rather he didn't go blurting my business all over the place."

"Can't stop people talking," he said with a knowing look.

"What else are they talking about?"

"They're saying all this trouble comes from letting them university types go diggin' up your hill."

"They're not digging up my hill, they're digging a small part on my hill."

"Same difference. They say folks shouldn't' go disturbin' the past."

"Bill, there have been thousands of archaeological excavations all over the world in the last two hundred years, It's a perfectly usual thing."

"'Cept them as is cursed."

"Oh, not that old nonsense again! Curses are all bullshit!"

"What about that one where they dug up the Pharisee's tomb in Egypt?"

"The Pharaoh's tomb. Tutankhamun."

"That's the one."

"Bill, I happen to know quite a bit about that, and it's all baloney. That curse nonsense was created by the newspapers. They started it because Lord Caernarvon died of pneumonia five months after they found the tomb. He was a frail, old man who was already in a weak state."

"There were others that died."

"Oh were there? Who told you that? Of the 60 people who were present when the tomb was opened, only eight died within ten years, and Howard Carter, the director of the excavation, died in 1939, seventeen years later!"

"I dunno. That's why I spends most of me time on the boat. You don't run into as many problems at sea."

"Oh no? What about the *Marie Celeste*?"

"I heard about that. That crew could've been taken off there by a big wave. They happen. I've seen plenty myself."

"Or the *Flying Dutchman*?"

"That's just a whatyamacallit, a legend."

"Exactly! Just like this is a legend. A fairy story."

"Well, you just watch yourself, Marc. It ain't a good idea to be fooling around with things we don't understand. That's my opinion. And just remember…"

"Remember what?"

"Things could get a whole lot worse."

23

Most of the next morning was spent with the insurance people, answering questions and filling out forms. This arduous procedure would have been much worse were it not for Louise's diligence in keeping records of the stock, and of the cost of renovations carried out on the premises when we first took it over.

I had lunch with Rosalie and Rachel Bland in Wolfville, then, leaving them talking about the history of Islamic subjugation of women, I came home and meandered up to the site.

The first thing I saw when I reached the brow of the hill was the huge spoil heap, which had greatly increased in size in the short time I had been away. On reaching the sides of the trench, I could see the reason for this was that the diggers had reached a depth of more than twice the height of Stefan, who was scraping the bottom of the pit. I figured the depth must have been about fourteen feet, because the top ten feet were shored by planking, leaving approximately four unsecured feet below that.

I looked around and saw Jennifer, Tracey and Sandy extending the limits of the bottom trench and piling the turfs near the jeep. Two other students were hunched over a drafting frame, making a plan of the uppermost wall of the building.

Ralph was nowhere to be seen. I called down to Stefan, "Are you trying to reach Australia?"

"If I was, I'd have to make a sharp turn when I'm about a mile down."

"How come?"

"The antipode of this place is somewhere in the middle of the Indian Ocean."

"I guess you're right. Anything new?"

"Yes. Sort of."

"Sort of?"

"Yes. Wait there. I'll be up in a minute."

Stefan clambered up a rather rickety ladder which was wobbling against the side of the trench, then approached me, wiping the sweat off his face with his bush hat.

"The girls—that is Tracey and Jen—have been hearing sounds."

"Sounds?"

"Yeah. In the pit. They've been down twice since yesterday and say they heard sounds."

"What kind of sounds."

"Ask them yourself. I can't make head or tail out of it. Tracey! Jen! Could you come over for a second? Marc wants to ask you something."

"Good afternoon, Mr. LeBlanc," said Jennifer. "How can we help?"

"Hi Jennifer. Stefan has been telling me about your hearing sounds in the pit."

"He doesn't believe us." Jennifer giggled. "He thinks we're teasing him."

"And are you?"

"No. Twice we heard them, didn't we, Trace?"

"Sure did," said Tracey. "No question about it."

"What were they like, these sounds?"

"They're kind of hard to describe."

"Try."

"Jen and I have a slightly different take on it. She says they remind her of furniture being moved."

"What do you say?"

"To me it's more like when the garbage men come with the truck."

"You mean a truck engine?"

"No. More like a rumbling when they push the big bins."

"But we both hear the voices," said Jennifer.

"Voices?"

"Yes. Kind of. Mumbling."

"Men or women?"

"Mostly women but some men, or maybe one man."

"What are they saying?"

"Can't tell. It's like murmuring."

"Mumbling," Jennifer corrected.

"Since we can't apply any known scientific test to this information, I regard it as fanciful if not spurious," Stefan said firmly.

"See? He thinks we made it up," Tracey said indignantly.

"You've heard nothing?" I asked Stefan.

"Indeed I have not! Marc, when you're in an enclosed space fourteen feet down, it's easy for the mind to play tricks on you. The power of suggestion increases exponentially as you go down."

"Is that scientifically proven?"

"If it hasn't been, it should be. Look, I have to go into town to get some more planks. Pretty soon we will have to shore up the lower sides because the soil is getting wetter and less stable. I'll be back in about half an hour."

We watched Stefan get in the jeep and drive off down the lane, where the wind was tossing the brambles on either side.

"Now, young Jennifer," I said sternly, "did you really hear sounds down there?"

"Cross my heart and hope to die."

"Why don't you go down yourself," said Tracey. "You might hear it."

"Can I? Am I allowed?"

"Sure. Stefan is in town and Mr. Giffin didn't show up today, so who's going to stop you?"

"Alright, I will!"

Very gingerly I swung my foot over onto the ladder, which slid unsteadily from side to side. Then I slowly descended into the pit.

It was not at all as I expected, and I was surprised by the claustrophobic effect even at that limited depth. I was also astonished at how dark it seemed. Stefan had been working with a light on the end of a cable, but had taken it up with him.

I stood quietly on the bottom. The earth had a very unpleasant, sulphurous smell to it, and momentarily I felt panic.

"Can you hear anything?" Jennifer called down.

"Not yet. I'll stay a few minutes longer.'

After a while I fancied that the eerie silence was broken by faint sounds of some sort. Maybe it was the power of suggestion, as Stefan had insisted, and I was imagining it, but I thought I could hear something. I could not have said it was like furniture being moved or people mumbling, only that it was an indeterminate series of vibrations.

I was starting to get spooked by the place, so I decided to get out quickly.

As I put my foot on the bottom rung of the ladder, something caught my eye on the ground. At first I thought it was some kind of worm emerging from the pit floor, but when I brushed it with my shoe, it fell out. I bent down, picked it up and brushed the earth off it with my sleeve. It looked like a primitive arrow head.

I do not know what prompted me to put it into my pocket and tell no one about it, but that is what I did, and hurried on up the ladder. I scrambled out onto the edge of the trench.

"Did you hear them?" Tracey asked.

"I'm not sure. I think I heard something. Very faint, but something. Maybe."

"So we're not making it up?"

"I wouldn't swear to it, but I don't think you are. I have to go, girls. Have a good day."

"See you later Mr. LeBlanc."

I am not sure why I hurried down the hill or why the arrowhead seemed to be burning a hole in my pocket, but I got home quickly and went straight to the kitchen sink.

When I washed the object under the tap it became clear that it was made of flint. When I lived in England, I once attended a seminar in Wiltshire on prehistoric flints given by *Time Team* star Phil Harding, so I was in no doubt at all about the substance. But how old was it and where did it come from?

A search on the internet told me that while there are other mineral deposits in the province, including chert, chalcedony, agate, and jasper, flint is not a primary mineral deposit in Nova Scotia. So that meant the arrowhead was somehow imported (against my will, Upward Percolation occurred to me) and now I had to determine its age. Again, the internet made it clear that it was a flint barbed and tanged arrowhead of the early Bronze Age, which meant it was made somewhere around 2300 BC.

My mind was reeling. Of course, I realized that it was quite possible that persons unknown had been in the trench before me and had pushed the arrowhead into the pit floor. And it was also possible that because it had been inserted into the soil with force, the earth could have expelled it, creating the impression of it emerging in front of my eyes.

But if the arrowhead had been—salted, is the term, I think—who would want to do such a thing? Moreover, why would they want to go to the trouble of doing likewise with the Judean coin, the facsimile of the Dispilio Tablet and a copy of the *Imago Mundi*?

When I came to reconsider the question, no matter how utterly preposterous it seemed, there was considerable appeal to the notion that all ages and all cultures were connected by an underworld river which occasionally welled up and broke out into our own world.

I remonstrated with myself for wasting time on such fantastical ideas, and set about preparing dinner. As I peeled the vegetables and put a chicken into the oven, I told myself that the most logical answer was that someone who had a stake in propounding the theory had planted the artifacts in order to reinforce and advance it.

Just how he or she would benefit from the wider acceptance of the theory remained a mystery to me.

24

About six in the morning I heard a vehicle in the yard and several blasts on the horn. Wearily, I slipped out of bed, grabbed a gown, hobbled downstairs and went out by the front door.

"There you are, sleepy head!"

It was Bill Jolly, holding a burlap bag. Behind him was his big pickup truck, the engine still running.

"Bill, what the hell are you doing? It's six o'clock in the morning."

"Six bells and all's well. It's the time every real man should be up and about."

"I guess I'm not a real man, then. What can I do for you?"

"I brought you some fish. Fresh out of the sea. We docked about twenty minutes ago."

"That's very kind of you, Bill. You should have phoned first."

"I don't know your number. In any case, you're up now."

Bill lit up a cigarette and smoked it, holding it between his thumb and forefinger and cupping his fingers around it. "Quite a place you got here, Marc. I ain't seen it before. Mind if I have a look around?"

"No, fill your boots. It's not exactly the way I would have designed it, but we like it fine."

"Who built it?"

"Old Hillier. You know, the pulp millionaire. He even had an airstrip out back, but I've let that overgrow with grass."

"You got a fantastic deck," he called from the rear of the house.

"Yes. We like it a lot."

"Jesus Look at all that glass! Don't you feel the whole world is looking at you when your walls are glass too?"

"You get used to it."

"I guess you would."

He paced on around the house. "What's this?"

"The garage. That's where we keep the Fiat and the BMW."

"And this?" Bill indicated what must have appeared to him as a small fortress.

"Ah. That's where I keep the Bugatti."

"Wow! It looks like Fort Knox."

"The old girl is still worth almost half a million, so the insurance company insists I keep her under maximum security."

I entered my code and the doors rose with a quiet hum to reveal the Bugatti snuggled into the narrow space. "You can see now how thick the walls are."

"Can I ever! What are the doors made of, aluminum?"

"No, steel."

"Cool. And I see you got a nice garden there, Marc. Needs a bit of weeding."

"They never stop growing. Would you like some radishes and lettuce to take with you?"

"I sure would. Thanks, Marc."

Having taken a sizable bunch of each vegetable and stowed them in the truck, Bill gave me a salute and drove off.

When I got inside, Rosalie was coming downstairs. "Who on earth was that?"

"Bill Jolly He brought us fish. He said it was landed about half an hour ago."

"How nice of him. Any mackerel?"

"I'll take a look."

I rummaged in the bag and brought out four small mackerel and a beautiful, medium-sized salmon. "Look at that. Breakfast and dinner right there."

"Lovely. Let's get started."

She took the salmon from me and put it into the fridge. "By the way, did you do as you promised?"

"What did I promise?"

"To tell Ralph he had to wrap up the dig in two weeks."

"No, I didn't."

"Why not?"

"Ralph wasn't there. I didn't think it would be right for Stefan to know before Ralph did."

"Fair enough. Will you do it today?"

"Sure."

Halfway through breakfast, the phone rang. It was Gerald from the book shop. Gerald had been my father's right-hand man in the shop for some years, and had assumed ownership of the business after his death.

Always dramatic and excitable, Gerald was especially over-wrought on this occasion. "Marc, oh, Marc, I need your help. Can I hire you?"

"What are you talking about?"

"You're a private detective. I want to hire you."

"Hire me? To do what?"

"I need you to find someone."

"Would you rather not discuss it on the phone? Would you prefer I come down to the shop?"

"Oh, please do."

"I'll be there in about an hour."

"Who was that?" Rosalie asked when I had hung up.

"Gerald."

"Gerald? What does he want?"

"Apparently he wants me to find somebody?"

"Do we know who?"

"Not yet. I have to go down there now. With all this other stuff going on, I would like to get it out of the way, so I may be gone all day."

"Okay, but you have to tell Ralph tomorrow."

~

The place had changed a lot since my father's time. Then it was the way most people think of book shops, rather dark and dusty, with shelves full of hundreds of mostly drab, boring volumes.

Now the store was a positive kaleidoscope of every colour in the rainbow and was randomly adorned with flowers and silk ribbons.

In Dad's day the books would have included titles such as *Historic Places of Nova Scotia, Farmhouses of the Annapolis Valley, An Encyclopedia of Insects*, Robie Tufts's *Birds of Nova Scotia*, and *Canadian Prime Ministers 1867-1968*. Now the titles I observed on display near the door were *Dark Restraint, Our Evenings, Call Me by Your Name* and *Young Mungo*.

The smell was very different too, a musty odour having given way to burning incense. Gerald had certainly stamped his character on the place and it seemed to be thriving.

"Oh, Marc, I'm so glad you could come." He greeted me effusively. "Go into the back room and I'll make some chamomile tea."

"Now then, Gerald," I said when he had set the cups on the table. "What exactly is it you want?"

"I need help and I'll pay whatever your fee is."

"No, you won't. We're old friends, besides which I don't charge for my detective services."

"Oh my! That's so very kind. So very generous."

"Now tell me who's missing."

"Stephen."

"Who's Stephen?"

"He is—or was—my significant other." He burst into tears. "I came home yesterday and he was gone."

"Did you have a fight?"

"No. Nothing like that. One minute he was here and the next he wasn't."

"Did he leave a note?"

"I couldn't find one."

"Does he have any relatives around Wolfville?"

"None. Maybe in Halifax. I don't know."

"Did you call round your mutual friends in the area?"

"No. I didn't want people to know how wretched I am."

"Alright. Can you give me names of some of his best friends in town?"

"Yes, I can do that."

"Just write them down for me, please."

"Okay. Oh God, just look at me. I'm dropping tears on the paper."

"Never mind. As long as I can read it, it'll be okay."

Gerald had written four names: Lionel Keating, Cecily Archibald, Tommy Handley, and Bingo. If Bingo had a real name Gerald did not know what it was.

Cecily and Tommy, he told me, were a couple. They were not gay, he said, but one of them (I did not ask which) was trans. Lionel, Gerald said, "might not co-operate" because they had once been an item and had not parted company amicably.

With this unpromising information I set forth into the mean streets of Wolfville.

It was noon by the time I had seen all but one of the people on Gerald's list. Bingo had left town, the others told me, and very likely with Stephen. They said that Gerald did not know it, but Stephen was a rather two-timing gadfly, it being quite in character for him to disappear without telling anyone. They told me that Bingo had a wealthy brother, a doctor in Halifax with a large house in the South End, and that was probably where I would find him and, by extension, Stephen. They were sorry they did not know the address but said the brother's name was Dr. Martin something or other.

I decided to waste no time and head to Halifax, so I called Rosalie and told her not to expect me home until late afternoon the next day. She said she did not want to be left alone, given the prevailing circumstances, so would ask Rachel Bland if she could stay with them for the night.

That gave me the idea to call Patrick to see if I could stay with him and Ruth. Patrick was away from his desk, so I called his home and Ruth, always obliging, said they would be delighted to have me.

To find out who Bingo's brother was, I thought the best place to start would be the Infirmary, so, having parked, I wandered around the corridors, engaging people in conversation, peering at door labels and examining sheets on bulletin boards.

It took me quite a while, but finally I found two doctors with the first name Martin, one Dr. MacIntyre, a vascular surgeon, and the other Dr. Penhally, a neurologist. A talkative nurse told me that Dr.

MacIntyre was in his seventies, so I deduced Bingo's brother was likely to be the other one.

At the library I was able to access the voters' list from the previous election, and from that I found a Martin Penhally on Oakland Road.

It was he who answered the door and, after I explained who I was, he finally let me in. He was a tall, well-built man in his forties with slight greying at the temples and wearing a bright blue sweater.

"Yes, you are right," he said as he showed me into a well-furnished living room. "Bingo is here and so is his boyfriend."

"My problem, Doctor, is that until yesterday he was somebody else's boyfriend."

"Ah, I see. Bingo is some ten years my junior, so I don't pretend to understand him, but I must confess that he never struck me as a particularly faithful character."

"Could I talk to Stephen please? Preferably alone."

"I'll go and get him. He's in the den."

He left the room, returning some minutes later with a young, willowy, blond man.

"I'll leave you to it," said Dr. Penhally, and closed the door behind him.

As I talked with Stephen it became apparent that, like Bingo, he was promiscuous and disliked being "tied down" to one person. He told me he had nothing against Gerald, and gave me his word that he would return to him in a few days.

"I'm not entirely sure he'll take you back," I said.

"Oh, he will," Stephen said with a smirk.

I have seldom had such an urge to hit someone as I did at that moment, so I jumped up and quickly left the room.

In the hallway I got to chatting with Dr. Penhally again, and during our conversation I happened to mention where I came from.

"Forgive my being nosy," he said, "But are you, by any chance, connected with an archaeological excavation?"

"Yes, I am. Why do you ask?"

"I suppose you know Ralph Giffin?"

"Yes, I do."

"Well, obviously I can't go into details—professional etiquette and all that—but he's one of my patients."

"Really? I didn't know he was ill."

"I can't say any more." Penhally said, reaching into his pocket. "Here's my card."

As I left I glanced at the standard professional card he had handed me. I flipped it over and saw a handwritten phone number.

~

At Patrick's house, I told him about the extraordinary coincidence I had encountered earlier. We were relaxing in his lounge after having a lovely meal of roast lamb, cooked by Ruth. We were sipping the remnants of a bottle of *Tignanello* 1971, a blend of 80% Sangiovese and 15% Cabernet Sauvignon grapes. It had aged well and was delicious giving flavours of oak, chocolate, sweet tobacco, cedar, and vanilla. The silky perfectly ripe tannins gave it a smooth finish, but still provided some backbone.

"It sounds like you have a very strange situation down there, Marc. I should be very careful, if I were you."

"It is very worrying, especially for Rosalie."

"You understand that I'll do what I can, but we can only step in if and when the law has been broken."

"Well, it was definitely broken when Balser fired through my window and then drove his truck into my wine shop."

"Wait a minute Marc. We don't know if it was the same person."

"What?"

"The shot could have been fired by someone other than Balser. No suitable weapon was found at his house."

"Why the hell didn't Lomas tell me?"

"I don't know. He should have."

"Jesus! You mean there is another maniac out there trying to kill us?"

"I'm afraid it looks like that." Patrick drained his glass. "Shall we open another bottle?"

25

The afternoon I returned from Halifax I went directly to the book shop to report to Gerald. I found him moping about the place, flicking a small feather duster along the shelves.

"Oh, Marc!" He rushed towards me, tripping on a rug. "Did you find him?"

"Yes, I did."

"Where was he? Is he alright?"

"I found him in Halifax. He seems to be fine."

"Is he...with anyone?"

"He is staying with Bingo, whose last name I discovered is Penhally. Apparently, he's the brother of a neurologist, Dr. Martin Penhally."

"How do you mean 'staying' with Bingo?"

"Do I have to spell it out for you?"

"No, you don't."

Gerald was on the verge of crying. "Is he coming back?"

"Yes, I think so. Maybe within the week."

"Ooh, good!"

"Gerald, do you think Stephen is a nice person?"

"Er...why do you ask?"

"Is he? Please answer my question first."

"I hear he is quite kind to some people..."

"But not to you?"

"I think he tries to be."

"But apparently doesn't succeed."

"Oh, Marc."

"It's none of my business, and if you hadn't involved me I wouldn't dream of interfering or voicing an opinion."

"But you're going to now, aren't you?"

"Yes, I am. Look, Gerald, I understand what loneliness is and how we sometimes think having anybody is better than having nobody, but I think you'd be well rid of Stephen."

"Oh, Marc."

"Gerald, he's a selfish, conceited little shit. If he doesn't break your heart now, he will later on."

Gerald said nothing. He looked at me in a desperately forlorn manner, then turned away and shuffled into the back room, where I could hear him tinkering about with the kettle. I decided no good would come of my trying to press him any further, so I slipped out of the door. I heard the bell ring behind me as I stepped onto the sidewalk.

As I was getting into the Bugatti, my phone buzzed. It was Rosalie.

"Marc, where are you?"

"In town."

"What town?"

"Wolfville, of course."

"What the hell are you doing there?"

"I've been to report to Gerald."

"Oh. Well, you better get back here pronto."

"Why, what is it? What's happened?"

"We've got another threatening message."

I got home in four minutes flat, jumped out of the car and ran inside.

"Show me!"

"Here," she said, thrusting it into my hand.

> Do what you're told and you won't get hurt.
>
> You've got until mid-day tomorrow. Last chance.

"I see they've dropped the pretense of semi-literacy."

"They didn't have much choice." Rosalie said. "Now that Alaric Balser is dead."

"Do you think he even wrote the other letters?"

"Who knows? But if he didn't, why did he plough into the wine store?"

"He could have had a separate and completely different griev-ance from these other bastards."

"It's possible, but what is *their* grievance, whoever the hell they are?"

"Unless it has something to do with this curse nonsense, I can't think what it could be. I guess we should call Lomas."

"I've already done it. He should be here any minute."

"Just time to have a drink of malt. You want one?"

"Ugh, no. I'll have a quick sherry."

We barely had time to down our drinks before Staff Sergeant Lo-mas' cruiser pulled into the yard. He came straight in without knocking, took off his cap, laid it on the hall table, and then put on a pair of rubber gloves.

"You've both handled this?" He asked brusquely, taking the let-ter from me.

"Obviously," I said.

Lomas gave me a stern look. "It's different from the others."

"We had noticed."

"Paper's different."

"Yes."

"And the style is quite different."

"Yes," I said, trying hard to be patient.

"I'll take this with me," he said, turning towards the door.

"What do we do?" Rosalie asked his retreating back.

"Do?" He looked round. "What do you mean?"

"You're the police. We've been threatened. What advice do you have for us? Should we just stay here like sitting ducks?"

"I hardly think you are in danger," Lomas said with obvious con-tempt. "The man who wrote the others—"

"Alaric Balser?"

"Yes, yes, that's him. He's deceased, so he's no longer a threat. This is probably a copycat. Possibly some kid or student who heard about the others and decided to have a joke—"

"A fucking Joke?!" I exclaimed.

"Marc!" Rosalie reprimanded me.

"Not likely to pose any danger," Lomas said coolly.

"How do you come to that conclusion?" I was starting to get furious. "What if you're wrong?"

"About what?"

"About there not being any danger."

"Ah, well, we can't be certain about anything. It's a question of making a probability assessment based on experience."

"A fat lot of help you are. Get the hell out of here!" I snapped. "You can be sure that there's a very high probability that Superintendent Kennedy will be hearing about this."

"I have no doubts about that," muttered Lomas as he grabbed his cap and stalked out.

Seething, I watched his cruiser going down the lane to the highway. I came in and poured myself another scotch.

"Marc, should you have lost your temper like that?" Rosalie was almost in tears.

"Son of a bitch! At least last time he left a constable on guard as protection."

"What shall we do?"

"Just keep away from windows and not go outside until it's light, I guess."

"Are you going to call Patrick?"

"You bet I am. Right now!"

In stark contrast to Staff Sergeant Lomas, Patrick was reassuringly sympathetic. As best I could, I outlined what had happened, the contents of the latter, and what Lomas' attitude had been throughout.

"You have to remember, Marc, that you're not the only one who has hard days. For all you know Lomas could have dealt with a dozen robberies, six murders and five rapes earlier in the day."

"Patrick, please don't patronize me."

"Okay. I admit I'm very unhappy with Lomas, if it happened the way you described it."

"You can ask Rosalie, if you don't believe me."

"That won't be necessary. You say he took the letter with him?"

"Yes."

"Did you make a copy?"

"No, should we have?"

"It would have been a good idea. In case the original"—he cleared his throat—"got lost, for any reason."

"Lost?"

"These things happen from time to time."

"Jesus. Now I'm really getting worried."

"Look, Marc, how are you fixed for the day after tomorrow?"

"For what?"

"For us to come down. Ruth and I could spend the night, have a nice dinner, and while I'm there I could pay a fraternal visit to the Wolfville detachment."

"That would be wonderful."

"Will that be okay with Rosalie?"

"I'm sure it will. We can go through the whole thing from start to finish. Put you fully in the picture."

"That's also what I had in mind."

Rosalie was already in bed. It was still quite early and we had not had any dinner, but somehow bed seemed the safest place to be. I undressed, put out all the lights, climbed in and took her in my arms.

"Marc, you see that it is all the more important now to stop the dig."

"I'll take a walk up tomorrow and see if Ralph is back."

"Even if he is not, will you tell Stefan? Please?"

"I don't like by-passing Ralph since he is the director, but if you want me to, I will ask Stefan to give Ralph the order."

"That's not a nice way of putting it."

"It's the same as we have been given."

"What?"

"An ultimatum."

26

In the middle of the night I had to get up to go to the bathroom. As I passed the window on my way to the washroom, I twitched the curtain a little to see what the weather was like.

Still half asleep, I thought I detected a slight glow on the hill in the vicinity of the dig. Then it disappeared, but on my way back to bed I looked and saw it again. I realized that it could well have been the lights from a car on the road beyond the hill, so I put it out of my mind and went back to bed.

The next morning I felt like something special for breakfast, so I cooked us some tamagoyaki, a delicious Japanese dish composed of thin layers of eggs cooked and rolled into a kind of log.

To make this I needed a special, rectangular tamagoyaki pan, which I found at the back of one of the kitchen cupboards, and then mixed the eggs with salt, soy sauce, oil and a tiny drop of mirin, which is tangy rice wine.

I served this with some *Fazenda Santa Ines* coffee I had received from my Toronto supplier a few days before. This is a bright, sweetish coffee with a tinge of citrus flavour which is grown at the foot of the Mantiqueira mountains in Brazil. Both Rosalie and I liked it, but not as much as our regular Blue Mountain or the Black Ivory.

"You'll do it this morning?" Rosalie asked when we were scrap-ing our plates.

"Do what?"

"Oh, Marc! You know what. Go and tell Ralph they can only dig for eleven more days."

"I thought we agreed to give them two weeks."

"That was three days ago."

"You really want them gone, don't you?"

"Yes. Before one of us is murdered!"

"Well, we can't wrap up the dig before noon today—which was the deadline in the note—so we can't stop whatever they have in their evil minds."

"Marc, darling…"

"Yes, sweetheart?"

"Just do it!"

Knowing that further reasoning would get me nowhere, I quickly left the house.

On my way to the back fence I stopped in the garden to pull up some of the ubiquitous, multitudinous weeds, crunch a few radishes and peek in a pea pod to see how big the contents were. Then I hopped over into the field and headed up the hill.

Halfway there I stopped and sat down amidst a spray of wild-flowers and Indiangrass. The latter was already four feet high, so I had to pull it aside to get a good look at the breathtaking view. In the far distance I could see the Parrsboro shore, a pale, smoky blue, then Blomidon, a blue-purple, then the deep blue-green of the Minas Basin. Closer still were Evangeline Beach, where I had first met Frank Wilberforce under mysterious circumstances, Boot Island and Avonport Beach.

It was already hot, even though it was only mid-morning, and the air was filled with the sounds of bees and a myriad other in-sects. I watched one poor little caterpillar trying to climb up a stalk of grass, but it kept falling off. Gently, I picked it up and placed it at the very top of the plant which I supposed to have been its original destination.

Then I lay back and gazed at an almost clear azure sky, barely punctuated by a few scattered, creamy-white clouds.

I must have dozed for almost an hour, because when I glanced at my watch, I saw it was almost eleven-thirty. I scrambled up, brush-ed the pollen and tiny blades from my clothes and walked up to the site through a thick sea of swaying grass.

Stefan greeted me and gave me a helping hand over the fence. I noticed at once that the facial sores, whatever they might have been, had now healed, but had left marks almost like smallpox scars. I observed the same phenomenon on the faces of the other diggers.

"You'll want to see this," he said with obvious enthusiasm.

"What is it?"

"It looks as if we've found some kind of a door."

"A door? Where?"

"In the pit."

"How is that possible?"

"I don't know, but I thought we'd come across something like that yesterday, and when I came in this morning, I saw it."

"I don't understand."

"Old Ralph must have been working here last night and finished uncovering it."

"Ralph? Where is he?"

"Don't have a clue. If he was here last night, I imagine he's sleeping in."

"Does he often work at night and not appear during the day?"

"Lately, yes."

"Strange. I thought I saw a kind of glow coming from here when I looked up in the middle of the night."

"Well, that would account for it."

"I guess it would. How's his health these days?"

"That's hard to say. I'm not a doctor, so I don't know what's going on with him, but sometimes he seems to be in really bad shape."

"Does he have a wife or girlfriend to look after him?"

"No, I'm sure not."

"How about relatives?"

"No, none of them." Stefan hitched his pants up. "He's the only member of his family left."

"How can that be?"

"He told me all about it when we were having a drink one night. His parents, who he came to Canada with, died a few years ago, and the rest of his family back in Italy were killed in an earthquake."

"All of them were killed in an earthquake?"

"Yeah. No, maybe it was a landslide. Yes, that's it, a massive land-slide."

"Wow. Do you know where this was?"

"He told me it was in Trentino Alto Adige."

"That's where he came from."

"Yeah, right. It was in 2001."

"So he's all alone in the world?"

"Literally."

"How sad."

We both stood still, thoughtfully gazing at our feet while the scraping of trowels went on around us.

At length I said, "I have a message I want you to give Ralph. I'm afraid you won't like it."

"Oh yes?"

"Yes, my wife and I would like you to wrap up the dig in eleven days."

"What? You can't be serious. We have no idea at this point how much more there is to do. Depending upon how deep it turns out to be, the pit alone could take weeks to excavate."

"I know and I'm very sorry, but that's the way it has to be."

"They're getting to you, aren't they? You're feeling the pres-sure?""

"Something like that."

"I've heard about the threats and stuff. It's not like I don't under-stand, it's just that we might have something very important here on this site. Unique, in fact."

"I'm aware of that."

"You'd be giving in to them. Letting them have their own way."

"Look, Stefan, to be frank, my inclination would be to say, 'Damn the bastards,' but Rosalie is terrified. Surely you can appreciate that?"

"Yes. I Imagine I'd do the same if I were in your situation."

I asked him to show me the pit. He took me over and we crouched on the edges and looked down. It was now about eight-een feet deep and were it not for the bulb in its cage at the end of the cable, it would have been too dark to see anything. I could just make out what could have been a door, or doors, made of metal or dark wood, bearing curiously raised strips.

"You want to go down?"

"Is it safe?"

"Sure. I'll have to shore up the bottom with more boards if it rains, but the trench sides are solid enough right now."

"In that case I would love to take a look. Thanks, Stefan."

By now the ladder was in the extension mode, so was even shakier than it had been when I had used it previously. I crept down very slowly, making doubly sure my feet were securely on each rung as I went.

At about the twelve foot point I stopped and listened intently. Sure enough, there they were: the same or similar sounds I had heard on my earlier visit. Whether or not I could actually distinguish voices and furniture being moved was doubtful, but there were definitely noises which one should not expect that far into the earth.

At the bottom I stepped off the ladder and looked up, amazed to discover that Stefan's face was so small. It seemed much deeper than the eighteen feet I had been told.

"You okay, Marc?" he called.

"Yes, fine, thanks."

"If anything happens to the light, grab the other rope and tug it."

"If anything happens to the light, I'll be up the ladder as fast as a speeding train."

I heard Stefan laughing as I cautiously moved away from the ladder and started peering about me.

In appearance the floor, or door, could have been either wood or metal, but when I knelt down and struck it with the trowel Stefan had given me, there was a dull, but marked metallic ring. I delicately scraped with the trowel, but could not determine what the metal was, only that it was not smooth, having raised parallel ridges which I guessed described a large rectangle.

Within the rectangle there was an inscription which I cleaned up with a small brush I had brought down with me. I wondered why Stefan had not told me about this, as it did not seem possible he was unaware of it.

As far as I could make out it said Αἴθουσα Διδασκαλίας which, with my rudimentary knowledge of Greek, I interpreted as "The Hall of Learning".

If my approximation of the translation was correct, I speculated on what manner of learning might have been conducted here and, moreover, why such a place would have a door horizontally located eighteen feet below the surface.

This aimless theorizing was interrupted by a slight but noticeable shaking in the earth and a deep booming sound. Then I could hear indistinct voices above me crying out in what sounded like either fear or amazement.

After a few minutes Stefan's voice came from directly above. "Marc, I think you'd better come up here."

"Right, okay," I said.

I was glad of a reason to leave this gloomy shaft, and ascended the ladder more than willingly.

When I put my head above the trench I saw all the diggers gathered at the fence, looking out over the hill. When I looked again, having hoisted myself out of the pit, they seemed to be staring at a large black cloud which was slowly moving upwards in the sky.

"What's going on, Stefan?" I called as I stumbled across the dig.

"Oh, Marc, you'd better come quickly."

The diggers parted to let me into their line, and I instantly saw the cause of their concern. It was clear that the sound I had heard in the pit was an explosion at my house.

Smoke was still rising, but from exactly what part of the house was unclear. My blood ran cold at the thought of the possible consequences of this outrage, and I immediately took out my phone and called Rosalie.

"Yes?"

"Rosalie, are you alright?"

"Fine thanks."

"Where are you?"

"At my office at the university."

"Thank God."

"What's happened?"

"I'm not exactly sure yet, but I'm going down to find out now. There was an explosion at the house."

"An explosion?? What kind of explosion?"

"I told you I don't know until I go down and take a look."

"Oh I get it. You're up at that fucking dig."

"Yes, I was delivering your message that they have to wrap up in thirteen days."

"Our message."

"Okay, our message. You'd better meet me at the house as soon as possible. Better park near the end of the lane and walk up."

"Why?"

"So you don't obstruct police and emergency vehicles."

"Oh, right. I'm on my way."

I called the fire department and was told they would be at the scene in ten minutes. Then I called Staff Sergeant Lomas.

"I don't exactly know what damage was done, but this makes your assurances that we were in no danger seem incompetent, to say the least."

"There's no need to be hostile, sir. I guess you'll be notifying Superintendent Kennedy?"

"I will. He is coming down here tomorrow to pay a visit to both of us."

"Both of us?"

"Yes, us and you."

He did not answer but hung up, whereupon I climbed the fence and hared down the hill as fast as my legs would carry me. As I came closer to the house, it appeared that all of the living quarters were untouched and that the explosion had occurred on the yard side.

As I rounded the corner, my heart almost stopped. The explosion had neatly confined itself to the garage, which had been virtually demolished, along with my precious Bugatti.

I raged, cursed and finally wept. That car was my pride and joy. It seems childish to say so, but after Rosalie there was nothing which could break my heart so much as this. There were only 92 Bugatti Veyron Grand Sport Vitesse made, and the engineering by Wolfgang Schreiber was so superb that the car was not only the fastest roadster in the world at the time, reaching an average top speed of 408.84 km/h, but was also impressively reliable.

As one would expect, the asking price for these precision vehicles was enormous so, despite my success in the money markets, I had to settle for getting mine second-hand from an Arabian sheik, Abdul Aziz. In any event, the waiting list for new Bugattis is endless and unless you had the many millions for the one-only versions, you could be old and grey by the time you acquired one.

The only consolation to this monstrous incident was that the house was untouched, except for some smoke stains on one side. Even the other garage, where we keep the BMW, was intact.

I sat down on the front step and disconsolately waited for Rosalie and the authorities to arrive.

27

I did not sleep much, and neither did Rosalie. No doubt she passed the night staring at the ceiling, wondering what might have happened if one or both of us had been home at the time of the explosion.

I was staring at the ceiling, wondering how anyone, no matter how evilly motivated, could want to destroy a Bugatti Veyron Vitesse Sports, and how little I would enjoy driving the BMW SUV for the foreseeable future.

In addition, and not for the first time, I wrestled with the question of why anyone would go to such lengths to prevent the archaeological dig from proceeding. One of the few answers I could rationally entertain was that there was something underneath the "doors" in the pit—or possibly even lower than that—which these people, whoever they were, did not want anyone else to see.

If that was indeed the answer to "why?", it did not provide the answer to "what?" What could possibly be worth the trouble of threatening, intimidating, and killing? Was some ancient artifact of astounding value thought to be down there, or was it supposed to be gold, a substance which has entranced, enriched and ruined thousands in its pursuit throughout the ages?

But if I accepted that notion, it would leave unanswered the question of how these people knew what existed at lower levels in the pit, as the archaeology did not indicate that the ground had been disturbed in hundreds, possibly thousands, of years.

The only remaining rational answer I could envisage was that one of the neighbours whose land abutted mine was highly indignant about the archaeological activity, either because they imagined it to be a disturbance and an inconvenience, or because they believed they were the real owners of the land on which it was taking place.

In my mind's eye I pictured the plans which Walter Bryson and I had reviewed in his office, and could clearly recall that there were only four points of contact between my land and that of others. First, was old Adam Nicholson, whose ancestor had been the original disputant over the little plot of land on which the dig was situated; the late Alaric Balser; John Dempster's vineyard (and mine, too, since I was a major shareholder in his winery); and a woman, completely unknown to me, Alice Archibald, of whose property a tiny stretch of no more than ten feet was contiguous with mine.

I wondered, how likely was any of them to hold a grudge so severe as to warrant outrageous vengeance? Balser was dead, and since the hostility toward Rosalie and me continued after his death, he was out of the picture. Adam Nicholson, well into his nineties, was deaf, almost blind, had very limited mobility, and in any event had not shown any dissent from the existing land arrangement. Although we had fallen out as friends, I considered John Dempster a very level-headed, business-like fellow, and I recalled, with a touch of bitterness, that our estrangement was the result of my being aggrieved by his actions, not vice versa.

So that left Alice Archibald. Her name had been scrawled, at what date I had no idea, on the map, so I did not know if she was alive or dead. I had never seen her property, but it was very small, and on the least productive, most scrubby land in the area.

I made a mental note to take a stroll in her direction very soon, spy out the land and ascertain if Ms. Archibald was a viable suspect, even though her holding was some considerable way from the dig.

When I had exhausted all the rational answers, I was compelled to consider the irrational ones. This brought me back to the nonsense about the "curse" and whether local people could believe it sufficiently strongly to take extreme action. If that was the case, what, precisely, did they fear? In what form would the "curse" manifest itself? Did they believe that if the doors of the pit were opened they would unleash a fire-breathing monster or, alternatively, a plague which would infest the region, resulting in seven years of crop failures?

This brought me perilously close to black magic, witchcraft and all the hysteria attendant upon accusations and mob rule. I had done some reading on this and recalled that the last legal case was in 1919, when Maggie Pollock, a medium from Blyth, was charged with telling fortunes. The case went all the way to the Ontario Supreme Court.

Two other Canadian women were charged in 2018 with pretending to practise witchcraft, breaking a then-little-known law in Canada's criminal code. The first charge was against Dorie Stevenson, a fortune teller from Milton, who was accused of defrauding a client of $60,000 and property, and, a week later, Toronto psychic Samantha Stevenson was also arrested in a similar but unrelated investigation. Police said she convinced a man the only way to get rid of "evil spirits" in his home would be to sell it and transfer the proceeds into her account!

Apart from those historic cases, the only local example I could recall was Pamela McInnis, a store keeper in Halifax who claimed to be a witch.

Finally we drifted off to sleep about four in the morning, but were rudely awakened at 8:30 by the RCMP bomb squad, accompanied by Staff Sergeant Lomas and his officers.

I greeted this delegation at the front door dressed only in one of Rosalie's dressing gowns (I hate pyjamas and never wear them). The chief of the bomb squad was a middle-aged woman who, when we were introduced, regarded my attire with obvious distaste. Under the circumstances, I felt I was entitled to respond in kind.

"You're about a day late," I said dryly.

"I hear that a lot. Take me over to the site of the explosion and answer my questions," she ordered, indicating that there would be no nonsense with this lady.

We stood within ten feet of the entrance to the garage, and I answered everything she asked about the way it had been constructed, how the doors usually operated, what mechanisms were employed, and what the contents had been—even down to the presence of oily rags.

"Thank you." She nodded at me, then turned to her crew. "Alright, gang, you know what to do."

I headed back to the house, but my way was blocked by Lomas.

"What do you want?" I could barely be civil.

"Just a few questions, Mr. LeBlanc."

"What questions could you possibly ask which you haven't asked before, over and over?"

"I just want to establish where you and your wife were when the accident occurred."

"*Accident?!!*"

"Incident," he corrected himself. "Just tell me where you were."

"Rosalie was at the History Department at Acadia University and I was twenty feet below the surface in a pit."

"I don't think this is the right time for joking."

I noticed that he had long since dropped the "sir" when addressing me.

"I'm not joking. I was down a pit up on the hill."

"Down a pit up on the hill," repeated Lomas, giving me a fixed steely stare.

"The dig."

"Ah, that fucking dig again!" he cursed softly.

"It would seem so. An angle, I might say, the police appear to have neglected to sufficiently investigate."

"Alright." He sighed like a man who had given up. "What time is your friend Kennedy arriving?"

"I'm not exactly sure, but I would guess around four or five, to be in time for dinner."

"For dinner, naturally., Lomas muttered. "Do you happen to know where he'll be staying?"

"Here, of course, with Rosalie and me."

"Of course. Where else?"

Lomas closed his notebook, turned on his heel and walked to his cruiser.

I heard him give orders to the driver to take him up to the archaeological site. I took a step forward, intending to warn them that the old lane was rough and likely only fit for jeeps, but I stopped myself. Sod him, I thought. Tough luck if he got stuck halfway.

I was just going back into the house when I noticed a man struggling up the driveway, carrying a large briefcase. He was out of breath and was sweltering in the heat.

"Mr. LeBlanc?"

"Yes, that's me. I don't usually look like this. I didn't have a chance to get dressed yet."

"My, there's an awful mess around here. I see you've got the experts in."

"I'm sorry, but who are you, and what do you want?"

"I'm Henry MacLeod from the International Commercial Insurance company."

"Ah, yes. It's very good of you to come in person. I telephoned yesterday as soon as I could, but I didn't expect a personal visit, at least not so soon."

"Can we go in and sit down?" asked MacLeod. "I wonder if I could trouble you for a glass of water, please."

"Certainly, Mr. MacLeod. Something stronger if you like."

"Well…" He hesitated. "That would be nice, but just a small one. It's very early in the day to be drinking."

"This won't be drinking, Mr. MacLeod, this will be medicine. Fifteen-year-old Dalmore sound okay?"

"Oh my, better than okay. Yours is a long driveway to walk up, especially on a hot day."

"Please come into my study and take a seat. I'll get your medicine."

MacLeod took the whisky from me as if I were handing him a newly-born child, gently swirled it around the glass, and then carefully sniffed it. Then he took a sip and a smile spread over his face.

"That, Mr. LeBlanc, is wonderful. Perhaps I should call you Doctor LeBlanc. Your medicine is perfect."

"May we get down to business, Mr. MacLeod? I've not had breakfast yet."

"Of course."

He put his briefcase on the table, pulled out a single sheet of paper and placed it in front of him. "There is no easy way to say this, I'm afraid."

"What?" I felt the blood freezing in my veins.

"Unfortunately, on both house and car, you are not covered for acts of terrorism."

"Terrorism?"

"Why yes, an explosion, deliberately induced by a party or parties unknown, is classified as terrorism. Was that not explained to you when you took out the policy?"

"It might have been." I was in a daze. "But who thinks they will be attacked by terrorists?"

"Alas, not many of us."

"Jesus! You mean to tell me that I've been paying more than twenty-two grand a year to insure the Bugatti with a deductible of $50,000 and I get nothing? Not one red cent?"

"I'm afraid not."

"But if this maniac had burned it down I would?"

"Um, yes, if committed by a third person it would be considered vandalism not arson or terrorism. In that case you would be paid, unless, of course, you had paid or incited the person to do it."

"Holy crap!"

"I'm sure you appreciate that my hands are tied, Mr. LeBlanc. But in view of the circumstances I had to come in person rather than send a letter or email."

"I'm grateful for that anyway. I sure hope you don't have other calls of a similar nature today."

"Yours was the only one." He paused to rub his nose. "I wonder if I could ask you something."

"Yes, go ahead."

"I see you also have your house, a Fiat and a BMW insured with us. None of them have terrorism coverage either. Would you like to adjust those policies?"

"You don't let the grass grow under your feet, do you? What would be the extra cost?"

"About 2.5% of the value."

"What would that be for the house and the two cars?"

"Er…" MacLeod pulled out a pocket calculator. He looked up grimly. "Oh dear. More bad news."

"What?"

"Twenty three thousand per annum, plus change."

"Extra?"

"Um…yes."

"Holy shit!" I shook my head in amazement. It was not as if we could not afford it, but it would have to protect us when we needed it.

"When would it go into effect?"

"Immediately upon receipt of either the first monthly premium or the entire amount."

"The figure you quoted was for payment in full, I assume. Monthly payments would cost more."

"Oh yes, of course."

If we could get our mystery wrapped up we might not need the additional insurance, but if it was prolonged and our unknown adversary struck again it might prove useful, so I did the deal with MacLeod and, after he was gone, made myself some much needed breakfast.

Rosalie had grabbed some toast and had left me to go to work. She told me there was not much she could accomplish in her state of mind, but she would be better off at the university than at home, with the place crawling with police.

28

As soon as I had washed, dressed and eaten, I started to think about our imminent guests. Patrick and Ruth would arrive late afternoon, which would give me at most six hours to plan and execute our dinner. Given that consideration, I decided upon what I thought would be relatively quick and easy to prepare.

Assuming I could find some in town that afternoon, that meant smoked salmon with salad and rack of lamb. If time permitted, I would make an almond tarte, and if not would rely on fresh fruit and ice cream, always a good stand-by for us.

I went to get the BMW out of the other garage, but the police told me it had to stay in place until their investigation was complete. Incandescent with rage, I had to call a taxi to take me to the grocery store.`

When I got to the supermarket, I found that some unknown event or festival had depleted their vegetable supplies. Since I had no car, I could not flit around the shops at will and had to make the best of a bad situation.

The only remaining vegetables which did not look like they had been dragged backwards across the Kalahari Desert were some cauliflowers. They were marred by brownish stains, but I could cut those off. There were fewer than a dozen rather misshapen Yukon Gold potatoes, looking very forlorn on an almost-empty shelf so I grabbed them. Some loose mushrooms nearby looked like refugees from the Battle of the Somme, but a lone package next to them was acceptable, so I added it to my basket.

The fruit section appeared to have been afflicted by the same frenzy as the vegetable shelves, so I had to give up on that idea and rushed around to the baking section, where I found many bags of ground almonds, but only two of whole nuts. I took the latter as my preference and several of the former in case of emergencies.

I had some trouble persuading the butcher to cut into a fresh lamb carcass to provide my rack of ribs, but after flattering and ca-joling him, I managed to acquire two healthy, but rather large, racks. What we might lose on delicacy we might gain on volume.

Having stupidly forgotten to bring my phone, I had to persuade a very irate store employee to call me a taxi. After I had waited for twenty minutes, it finally arrived and took me home.

To my disgust he refused to go up my driveway. "Sorry, but my buddy was here earlier and he said the cops are all over the place up there."

"So what? They won't bother you. Drive!"

"No way. You gotta get out. I ain't goin' up there."

"Why? Have you got something to hide from the cops? I've got all these groceries. I can't carry these all the way to the house."

"That's not my problem, buddy."

"Yes, it is your problem. I'm not leaving. What are you going to do? Call the police?"

"How's about I drive you part way up?"

"Now you're talking. Drive until you see the first of their vehicles. That alright?"

"Yeah. I guess so."

Installed once more in my kitchen, I set about preparing our evening meal. First, I finely ground the whole almonds, added some of the powdered nuts, mixed them with a lot of sugar, a lot of butter and half a cup of flour. I poured the mixture into a shallow baking pan and put it in the oven at 325 for about 45 minutes, or until an inserted knife would come out cleanly. We would eat this cold with some whipped cream.

Few would believe that this simple, plain-looking dish could taste so heavenly, and I decided that it called for a special wine, *Chateau D'Yquem* 1975, to accompany it.

I peeled and par-boiled the potatoes, first taking care to have them shaped with straight sides. Then I cut them into two inch squares and scored their surfaces, placing them in a baking tin with melted duck fat, and sprinkling them with coarse salt and pepper. I cooked them for twenty minutes at 420 in the oven. They would go back in the oven later on while the lamb was resting.

I quickly pan-fried the mushrooms until partly cooked, to be heated up just before serving. I seared all surfaces of the racks of lamb and, when they had cooled, smothered them with a mixture of Dijon mustard, salt, pepper, powdered thyme, ground rosemary and thin slices of garlic. They would wait until approximately an hour before eating.

I cut the brown bits off the cauliflowers and just put them in pots of salted water. Nothing more than quickly boiling them would be necessary. These would be served covered with the mushrooms.

I went back down to the cellar and pondered what we should have with the smoked salmon and the lamb. The latter choice was relatively easy, and I went for a *Chateau Pichon LaLande* 1982. For the first course, I wanted something with enough acidity to offset the smoke, but with richness to match the fish, so I eventually decided to go with a 2010 Leeuwin Arts Series Chardonnay from the Margaret River in Western Australia.

Rosalie got back from university at 4:30 and immediately went to shower and change. I had no such opportunity, because Patrick and Ruth were only a few minutes behind her. I took them and their baggage upstairs to their room, banging on the bathroom door to let Rosalie know they were here. Then I got towels for them and showed them where their bathroom was.

"See you downstairs in…?"

"Ten minutes," said Patrick.

"Make that twenty," Ruth countermanded.

Which gave me enough time to splash some water on my face, and slip into a clean shirt and some decent pants.

When I went down, Patrick was already in the lounge examining my display of single malts.

"I have a bubble to start with," I said, "but if you prefer malt you may have it."

"I think I will. Just a dram."

"A dram it shall be. How about some fifteen-year-old Macallan?"

"Perfect. It's great to see you again, Marc."

"You too, Patrick." I handed him his glass.

"Under the circumstances, it can't have been easy to squeeze us in."

"To be honest, we'll feel safer with you here than if you weren't. Have you been fully briefed by your people?"

"Yes, I stopped at the detachment on my way here."

"Is there any news from the bomb squad?"

"Yes."

"You'd better tell me before the women come down."

"In that case, I don't know how much we have time for. But I'll start and if they come down I'll clam up."

"Okay. Go ahead."

"There's not a lot to tell. You know that in recent years most explosives have been using commonly available materials, such as fertilizer, gunpowder, and hydrogen peroxide."

"Yes."

"Explosives must contain a fuel and an oxidizer, which provides the oxygen needed to sustain the reaction. Worry over explosives made from liquid components which can be moved and mixed at the site of attack is the reason they stopped air passengers taking liquids on board."

"I didn't know that."

"In this case, all ingredients, so to speak, were fairly easily obtainable, primarily ammonium nitrate and derivatives. I won't bore you with all the technical details, mainly because I don't understand them myself, but the difference between your bombing and others employing similar components is that some skill was required in order to limit the effects of the blast."

"You mean to confine it to the car and garage?"

"Yes."

"So that wasn't accidental?"

"No."

"Why would they want to do that?"

"I don't know. Maybe to single out the Bugatti, your most precious possession. Or maybe to tell you that your house, where you actually live, would be next if you don't give them what they want."

"God, that's not good news."

"To say the least of it."

"Is there any chance the ingredients used or the methods employed could lead you to the bomber?"

"About one in a million."

"Charming. Thanks, Patrick."

As if on cue, at that moment the wives came downstairs, I opened some Champagne and soon we were happily chatting, especially about our joint adventures in the highlands of Cape Breton on my last case, which I have described in my book *Best Served Cold*.

"My dears," said Ruth, "you've been through an absolutely terrible time. I can't imagine how you've endured it."

"Yes, we have, but we've taken steps to put a stop to it," Rosalie said.

"How do you mean?" Patrick asked with a deep frown. "I hope you're not contemplating taking the law into your own hands."

"No, of course not. How could we when we don't have a clue who is responsible for all this? What I meant was we have told the archaeologists to pack up and go home."

"Not quite," I interjected. "I've told the assistant director that we want them out in –what is it?—ten days, but I have not yet seen the director."

"You'll see him tomorrow!" This was an instruction, not an inquiry, from Rosalie.

"If he's there, yes, but I can't see him if he doesn't show up again."

"He sounds like a strange fellow," said Patrick. "I've done some checking on him and, while he doesn't have a criminal record, I understand that he is somewhat unbalanced and is a heavy drinker."

"You can say that again!" Rosalie said. "One lunchtime here he polished off two bottles of wine."

"I get the impression he is not at all well," I said. "The last time I was in Halifax I met a neurologist who said that Ralph is his patient."

"Martin Penhally," Patrick said.

"You know him? You didn't tell me."

"No, you told me about him when you stayed with us. I re-membered the name."

"Oh."

"It was rather indiscreet, wasn't it?" Patrick asked.

"That's what I thought. According to medical ethics he shouldn't have even told me that Ralph was a patient, but I got the impression it was not a slip, that he didn't tell me by accident. It was almost as if he was warning me."

"About what?" Ruth asked.

"I have no idea. Maybe it was just to let me know that Ralph is ill."

"I'll have a word with him when I go back," said Patrick.

"You won't get any more out of him."

"No, not in words."

"Ah, I see," said Rosalie. "You'll be able to tell by his manner what's going on."

"Not exactly, but I may pick up some clues."

"Let's eat," Rosalie said, rising.

The smoked salmon and salad was never going to win a Michelin star, and the Leeuwin chardonnay was somewhat disappointing, as it was a little too old. However, the racks of lamb, roast potatoes, cauliflower and mushrooms were delicious, and the *Pichon Lalande* was spectacular. The dessert was everyone's favourite and the *D'Yquem* was an utterly stunning wine.

We moved back into the lounge, carrying the remnants of the *D'Yquem* with us, and settled down into our huge soft chairs.

"Well what now?" Ruth asked nobody in particular.

"That's a good question," I said. "The only lead I have left is this woman, Alice Archibald, who, apparently, shares a ten-foot boundary with me on the other side of the wood."

"Have you mentioned this to Lomas?" Patrick asked.

"No. I only thought of it in bed this morning."

"I know you don't like him—I don't much care for him myself—but you should tell him about this woman."

"Alright, I will. But I'm going to do some poking on my own."

I saw Patrick wince. "Don't worry, I won't take any action. I'll just look."

"Well, you have a license to investigate, but I much rather you left it to Lomas, at least for the time being."

"Will he actually do anything?"

"I hope so. I am his superior by several ranks, but I can't just countermand him without a good and specific reason."

"He's useless!"

"Maybe. But I've explained the situation."

"But what about us? What about our safety?" Rosalie wailed like a trapped animal. "What are you and Lomas going to do to protect us?"

"Yes," echoed Ruth, "what will you do about Rosalie and Marc? They have a right to know."

"Yes darling, I understand completely, and I think it's unfortunate that they don't have any confidence in the local force." Patrick was picking his worlds like a man threading his way through a minefield. "So the best advice I can give them—as friends—is that they go away for a few weeks."

"What?!" Ruth, Rosalie and I exploded simultaneously.

"Patrick Kennedy, whatever do you mean?" Ruth demanded.

"Ruth, I just don't have the manpower locally to mount a round-the-clock watch on the house. Nor do I have the men to act as bodyguards and go with them wherever they go. And I am not sure I have the power to divert manpower from other areas where they have their own crimes to deal with. Even if I did have the power, I know my Chief Super would overrule me."

"So we are supposed to stay here and be sitting ducks, or run away and hide. Those're some options you're giving us, pal."

"Marc, if I can be personal…"

"Yes, go on. You may as well."

"You're a wealthy man. If you really can't bear the thought of running away—as you put it—you can afford to hire your own protection team.'

"Go private?"

"Exactly. Why not? You have an investigator's license and that al-lows you to hire assistants. So...hire some assistants."

"We shouldn't have to do that," Rosalie complained, quite justly, in my opinion.

"I know. But the reality of the situation dictates."

"Thank you Patrick," I said. "I'm sorry I lost my temper. I confess I would never have thought of it if you hadn't suggested it. Go private. Hmm. I'll have to think about that."

29

Patrick had to be back in Halifax for a conference, so we had a simple, early breakfast of bacon, scrambled eggs, toast and coffee.

"I've been thinking about what you said last night," I said. "Even if I take your advice, where would I find private protection?"

"Maybe former police officers?"

"Yes, they would be better than other private investigators, but is there a registry of such people?"

"Ah, that's a good point. I don't think there is. Various police departments would have records of their past employees, but I suspect recent information would be confidential."

"Then what are we to do if you won't protect us?" Rosalie asked bitterly.

"Can't, not won't," Patrick corrected her firmly. "You know I think you should go on trip until the smoke has settled."

"You mean run away! No we won't do that," I said.

"Then how about hiring some people from security firms?"

"You mean the immigrants who hang about malls wearing uniforms but looking as lost as sheep?" Ruth interjected. It was good to see that at least she was on our side.

"Er, no. I was thinking more of the guys who normally guard transfers of money."

"Like Brinks?"

"Yes that sort of thing. If you're determined to stay put, you might try looking into that possibility."

"Thanks Superintendent," Rosalie said dryly. "I just hope we're not on a slab the next time you see us."

After the Kennedys had gone, and Rosalie had left for the university, I spent an hour weeding in my garden. Then I decided to wander up the hill in the opposite direction from my normal approach. I seldom went this way, except to occasionally peek at the vines in John Dempster's vineyards, and it made a pleasant change despite the walking being much slower and more difficult.

Although it was part of the same large field, because of the lie of the land and the subsoil, this end of the property was quite different from the part near the archaeological dig. Here, the field sloped steeply down to a river, really a large brook, and the growth was coarser and higher, with not very many delicate wildflowers, but more tansies, thistles and ragweed.

I noticed that at this end of the field there were far fewer sparrows, yellow throats and warblers, than there were crows, jays and grackles. I thought the geology must be very different on the slope on the other side of the brook, as all the vines growing there looked healthy and vigorous.

I worked my way slowly around the edge of the field, frequently being waist-high in the rough grass, noting places where the fence needed repair.

After a few minutes I came to a short stretch where the fence was very dilapidated and there was a narrow clearing in the woods. This, I determined, must be the property of Alice Archibald, so I climbed over the remnants of the fence and ventured forward.

Within less than a thousand feet, I came into a large clearing in which stood a very old, very tiny house, taller than it was wide, suggesting no more than two rooms up and two down. The paint, now almost completely weathered away, had once been a greenish colour. So, apparently, had the drapes on the small windows, although decades of sunlight had almost bleached them white. A wisp of grey smoke lazily climbed from the single chimney.

I crept up to the window and peered in. The scene which presented itself was one I doubt had changed in seventy-five years. Furniture, appliances, pots, pans, utensils all seemed from a long-forgotten age.

Sitting in an ancient rocking chair by the stove was the smallest, oldest lady I had ever seen. I am not good at judging ages, but this woman must have been well into her nineties and, I guessed, weighed no more than ninety pounds.

I tiptoed around the house to its only door and tapped lightly. Receiving no response, I knocked loudly. Again there was no reaction, so I pushed the door and walked in.

"Mrs. Archibald?"

"That you, Albert?" she asked in a thin, reedy voice.

"I'm sorry, Mrs Archibald, it isn't."

"That must be you, Albert."

"No, it's Marc LeBlanc. I'm your neighbour from over the hill."

"Sit down, Albert," she said. "I can see a little bit of the sun today, but I can't tell one shadow from another."

From this I surmised that Miss Archibald was partially blind. Gingerly, I sat on the edge of an old, high-backed chair which creaked loudly.

"What do you want, Albert?"

"It's not Albert, Miss Archibald."

"I guess you're checking up on me again, aren't you Albert?."

Now it dawned on me that in addition to being blind, the old lady was also deaf. Under these circumstances I could see no further reason to stay.

As I made my way to the door, I heard her talking, if not to herself, to some unseen audience.

"I was born on March 16th 1925," she intoned, "in Grand Pre, in the County of Kings, in the Province of Nova Scotia, in the Dominion of Canada."

As I turned the corner of the house to go back to my field, something shiny caught my eye. About twenty yards away, its nose just poking from behind some spruce trees, was the fender of a dark blue pickup truck.

"Hello!" I called. Getting no reply, I called again. "Hello. Is that Albert?"

Again silence greeted me. I stood staring for a few more minutes but could discern no movement. However, there was the unmistakable smell of fresh cigarette smoke in the air.

As I thrashed my way back uphill through the rough grass, now shoulder deep, I wondered about what I had, and had not just seen. Obviously, nothing was to be feared from a hundred-year-old blind and deaf person. I could not be anywhere near as certain about the person or persons lurking behind the truck, but as to their identity and motives I could only speculate.

The likelihood was, I told myself, that the hidden personage was a son or nephew of Mrs. Archibald who was called Albert and was shy with strangers.

It took me another twenty minutes to skirt the rest of the wood and approach the dig. Not only was the vegetation and wildlife much nicer here, but the view was spectacular.

As I entered the site Stefan came up to me.

"Hey, Marc."

"Hey. What's new?"

"We've opened one of the 'doors' in the pit."

"And what did you find?"

"Looks as if there could be steps or stairs leading down."

"No kidding! That's fabulous."

"I know. But I can't go any further until I've cleaned off the other door and planned and photographed it."

"Yes, you have to be careful of the inscription."

"What inscription?"

"The one on the door."

"What the hell are you talking about, Marc? "

"I saw it when I went down the other day. It was Greek. It said something like 'the hall of learning.'"

"On the door? In the pit?"

"Yes."

"Well, it's not there now. You must have been deceived by the poor light."

"I don't think I was. I saw it."

"You can go down again and look if you want."

"If it's not there now, someone must have removed it."

"Why would they do that?"

"I don't know." I was very annoyed. "It's just one of the many mysteries about this whole fucking dig. One of them is where the hell is the fucking director?"

"Calm down, Marc. He's here."

"Oh, he finally decided to turn up, did he? Did you tell him he has to be out of here in ten days?"

"I tried."

"Tried?"

"He's not too well. I don't think he understood what I was telling him."

"Is he drunk?"

"No I don't think so. I'm not sure."

"Well, where is he?"

"He's in the jeep."

"The jeep! A fat lot of good he can do there!"

"You can see him, but I don't think you'll get much sense from him."

"Look, Stefan, if what you say is true, where does the university stand on the dig continuing without its director?"

"I haven't told them."

"Why not?"

"Because of what we are finding in the pit and what it could mean...to archaeology, to science."

"And you think that if they knew the state he's in, they'd pull the plug even before I'm pulling it?"

"Yes. It's really important. I have a feeling it could be a major discovery."

I snorted in disgust and started to head for the jeep, which was parked in the narrow lane.

Stefan called me back. "Marc, there's something else."

"What?"

"I'm not sure how to put this, but Ralph is like two different people."

"Different? What on earth do you mean?"

"Like Jekyll and Hyde. Sometimes he's cogent and others he's incoherent. A lot of the time he's obviously laid up and can't do anything, but I know he comes up here at night, and I get the impression he roams around."

"Roams around? Where? Doing what?"

"I wish I knew, but I suspect it's not good, whatever it is."

"Jesus." My mind was reeling. "Stefan, do you think he's actually dangerous?"

"To himself? Yeah, sure."

"No, I meant to others. Is he capable of pulling the shit I've had to put up with?"

"I don't know. I did wonder about that. But why would he want to stop his own dig? That would make no sense."

"Unless Dr. Jekyll doesn't like what Mr. Hyde is doing."

"Is that even possible? That within one person there could be two personalities fighting each other?"

"I have no idea. It sounds fantastic to me, but the way things have been going lately, I'm just about ready to believe anything. Let me take a look at him."

"Be prepared, Marc. He's a real mess."

I went to the jeep and peered through the window. Ralph was lying on the floor in the back, so I went round and opened the back door.

Stefan was right. Ralph was a mess. I was so appalled by his appearance that it made me jump backwards. He had lost weight, was filthy from head to toe and his face was twisted almost beyond recognition.

"Ralph, it's me, Marc."

I took a step forward and, with some revulsion, put a hand on his shoulder and gave him a gentle shake.

Then I stood up and called over to Stefan. "You'd better call an ambulance."

"Is he bad?"

"No, Ralph is dead."

~

I stumbled back to my house in a daze. How many more calamities had this—I almost said "curse"—wretched business claimed and who had been responsible for them? First, we had thought Alaric Balser was our primary adversary, but his death had removed him from consideration. Fleetingly, I had thought Alice Archibald might have been some sinister vixen with an axe to grind. She had now been ruled out, although there was a slight possibility the mysterious Albert might be a suspect. Now, Ralph loomed as a person who, in the throes of what seemed to be a dissociative identity disorder, might have been wreaking the havoc we had experienced.

One way to find out if Ralph was our culprit was to wait, and if no further disaster occurred we would be in the clear. But I was not prepared to wait. I was unwilling to live in fear and suspense any longer that I absolutely had to.

I decided that I would seek answers from the one man who might be able to supply them: Dr. Martin Penhally.

30

There was nothing wrong with the BMW SUV; in fact it was an excellent vehicle, but I hated it because it was not my Bugatti. Truth to tell, I actually *mourned* the loss of that car as if it had been a person, and could not get comfortable behind the wheel of its substitute. As for Rosalie's Fiat, in my view it was little better than a mobile tin can.

As I sped towards Halifax, I fidgeted awkwardly in my seat, regretting my loss as one might lament the end of a perfect love affair.

As soon as the ambulance had taken Ralph's body away, I returned to the house and searched for the card which Martin Penhally had given me, and called the number written on the back.

A woman, whom I assumed was his wife, said he was not at home but was expected around six that evening. Stressing that the matter was of extreme urgency, I asked her to get him to call me back, preferably as soon as he got in. There was a polite argument in which she recited the litany about having to be referred by a family doctor and then making an appointment.

"This is not strictly a medical matter," I said.

"What do you mean 'not strictly' a medical matter? Are you a friend of Martin's? Is this personal."

"No not personal. Not exactly."

"Look Mr. LeBlanc, I don't understand what you're trying to tell me. I think I'll hang up now."

"Please don't. If this wasn't important, how would I have your home number?"

"Yes. That's a point. How did you get it?"

"Martin, Dr. Penhally, gave it to me some days ago when I was at the house."

"Oh, you've been here, have you? Why didn't you say? Alright, I'll tell him, but I can't guarantee he'll call you."

It was after seven o'clock when Penhally did call.

"Mr. LeBlanc? I got your message. What's this all about?"

"I need to talk to you about Ralph Giffin."

"I've already said more than I should. I can't discuss a patient with you."

"I don't know whether you heard, but Ralph died this afternoon."

"Oh. No, I hadn't heard. Where was this?"

"On my property at Grand Pre."

"Oh, I see. That can't have been pleasant for you."

"It wasn't. I guess this makes a difference."

"No, I'm sorry, it doesn't. I'm obliged to maintain confidentiality even after death. The only exceptions would be to notify a coroner, which I assume has been done by the hospital in Wolfville and, under some circumstances, to speak to a legal representative. Blood relatives would be able to request access to the records to verify the existence of a genetic disease."

"I can assure you, Dr. Penhally, that Ralph had no living relatives."

"None at all?"

"His parents, with whom he came to Canada, are both dead. He has no siblings, and all his known relatives were killed in a landslide in Italy some years ago."

"That's highly unusual. But even if he had named you his heir, I couldn't breach the rules because you wouldn't be related by blood."

"I think you can sense that this is of some considerable importance to me. Could you call Superintendent Patrick Kennedy at RCMP H-Division? He will vouch for me."

"No, that won't work, either. If you have your superintendent call Doctors Nova Scotia and the office of the Minister of Health to explain the situation, they might authorize me to discuss the case with you."

"Alright. I'll try that. Thank you doctor. I'll be up to see you as soon as I get the green light."

I called Patrick at home and brought him up to date on what had happened since he and Ruth had left us that morning.

"Christ. They're dropping like flies." Patrick said. "I always said you attract trouble like a magnet attracts iron."

"Cause to step up RCMP activity?"

"No, Giffin's was a natural death. Do you have any reason to suspect it wasn't?"

"Sadly, no. But you appreciate why I need to know everything about Ralph. Can you swing it with the health authorities?"

"Not without a court order."

"You must be joking! It could be a matter of life and death. Mine and Rosalie's!"

"Ordinarily I'd have to get a warrant or a subpoena, but in this case I'll talk to my Chief to see if we can get this classed under the 'imminent risk' section."

"What the hell is that?"

"It's a public safety exception. The Supreme Court of Canada says that personal health information can be disclosed to police when there's a reason to believe there's an imminent risk of serious bodily or psychological harm, or death, to an identifiable person or group of persons."

"Well, there you are, then."

"The question here is whether the risk is imminent. I'll have to convince my Chief of that. Leave it with me. I'll call you in the morning."

Today, I confess I was expecting to wait around for hours on end for Patrick to get back to me, and was pleasantly surprised when he got back to me before nine-thirty.

"Okay, Marc. The Chief says it's okay. He'll take care of the legalities. When can you get here?"

"I don't have the Bugatti any longer, so we'd better say an hour and a half."

"Where is Dr. Penhally's office?"

"I don't know. I'll call and find out."

Alright. Call me back."

I called the office and discovered it was located in the Professional Building at the corner of Spring Garden Road and Robie Street. I phoned Patrick and advised him.

"Will you let him know we're coming?" I asked.

"I'll tell him that *I'm* coming. It might be better if he finds out you are attached to the mission when we get there."

I arrived ahead of Patrick, largely because a parking space miraculously opened up just as I turned onto Spring Garden. I found Penhally's office on the ninth floor and kicked my heels in the corridor for about fifteen minutes until he came bustling along.

"Usual rules," he said sternly.

"What?"

"Don't you remember? When you're with me, you speak only when you're spoken to."

"Oh, okay. What if you don't ask the right questions?"

"I'll pretend I didn't hear that. Let's go."

Presenting his warrant card, Patrick told the receptionist that he wished to see Dr. Penhally immediately. She was unruffled, and I admired the cool way she told him he had to wait until the doctor had finished with a patient.

Fortunately, the wait was not long, and we were ushered into Penhally's inner sanctum. Patrick handed him a number of papers, which I assumed were the necessary orders for the doctor to tell us what we wanted to know.

"Right," said Penhally. "That all seems to be in order. Before we proceed I must ask what is LeBlanc doing here? He's not a policeman."

"He is assisting me in his capacity as a licensed private investigator and as a principal who was present at the death of the deceased." Patrick was at his official best. "He also has a serious personal interest in the case as will become apparent. I can ask him to leave, if you wish. But it would mean that I would have to record our conversation and play it all back to him afterwards."

"Hmm. Very well. Please sit down, gentlemen, and tell me what you want to know."

"First of all, doctor, what did Ralph Giffin die of?"

"You must understand that I can't say he died 'of' his condition, but he certainly died, at least in part, as a result of it."

"I think I comprehend your meaning. What was the condition or disease which was substantially contributory to his death?"

"That's very well put, Superintendent. It's a very rare disease. In fact the only case of it I've ever encountered, and I've been practising for over fifteen years."

"What is it called?"

"It's called Marchiafava Bignami Disease, or MBD for short."

"I've never heard of it."

"No, you wouldn't have. It was discovered by two Italian pathologists, Ettore Marchiafava and Amico Bignami, in 1903, after observing multiple cases of seizures and coma in middle-aged men who drank large amounts of inexpensive red wine."

"I'm a wine aficionado myself, Doctor; so is Marc here. But not, I hasten to add, of inexpensive wine."

"Is that so? Well this disease was at one time associated with a wine called *Teroldego Rotaliano*."

"That's where his people came from," I interjected. Patrick glared at me.

"Sorry," said Penhally, "where is that?"

"The Valley of Rotaliano is in north-eastern Italy, up near Austria."

"What an extraordinary coincidence."

"How does this disease present, Doctor Penhally?"

"As a consequence of neurological and immunologic conditions, the patient develops a variety of symptoms, including, but not limited to, multiple pulmonary infections, irrational behaviour, decrease in short-term memory, paresthesia of the lower and upper limbs, depression, paranoia, psychosis, apathy, aggression, seizures, hemiparesis, ataxia, apraxia, dysarthria, difficulty walking, incontinence, impaired consciousness, progressive severe global dementia, visual hallucinations, and auditory delusions."

"My God! All those?"

"And sometimes more symptoms, though I gather it would be very infrequent that they would all occur simultaneously."

"What causes these symptoms?"

"Well, here I have to get technical so I doubt you will be able to follow me, but it's caused by primary degeneration of the corpus callosum associated with chronic consumption of ethanol. The disease may occasionally occur in patients who are not alcoholics but are chronically malnourished. The diagnosis of Marchiafava-Bignami disease is not always easy and is based on neuroimaging studies, especially MRI. The main hypothesis for its pathogenesis is that the disease is a result of B vitamin deficiency.

"In Giffin's case"—Penhally picked up and read from a file—"he showed signs of meningeal irritation, focal deficits and cranial nerve abnormalities. Cranial CT scan revealed a hypodensity in the corpus callosum, which was better characterized by the MRI, which showed involvement of the cortical regions and subcortical white matter of both frontal lobes, as well as small areas of the postcentral and superior temporal gyri, with signs of disruption of the blood-brain barrier. After a while, he likely would have become septic, exhibiting a fever along with worsening of his respiratory status. I can't be sure of a lot of this because I haven't seen the post mortem, assuming they have conducted one at Wolfville. Not that long ago, a diagnosis of MBD could only be made with an autopsy. Now, it's more or less a confirmatory procedure."

"I'm very sorry, Doctor, but I understood almost nothing of what you just said."

"Well, I did say it would be technical."

"You weren't wrong there!" I said.

They both frowned at me.

"Let me see, how can I put this so you will better understand? MBD is a primary degeneration of the corpus callosum usually associated with chronic consumption of ethanol."

"I'm none the wiser," said Patrick, scratching his head.

"In the crudest possible terms, Superintendent, MBD splits the brain so that one side doesn't communicate properly with the other. That's a very poor explanation, but the only one I can think of which will give you an idea of the problem."

"Jekyll and Hyde," I said.

"In a manner of speaking," said Penhally, with reluctance.

"Doctor, what concerns us is the kind of behaviour Giffin would have been capable of. Apart, that is, from drinking wine immoderately."

"It's almost impossible to say from case to case."

"Would he have been capable of violence?"

"In the right circumstances, yes, I think so."

"And if he were violent, would he remember what he had done?"

"Possibly not, but that could also be due to excessive inebriation."

"Now, here is the rub. In, for want of a better term, one condition, could he like, or be in favour of, something, but in another condition, be hostile to that same thing or person?"

"I don't recall anything in the literature dealing specifically with that possible aspect, but I couldn't rule it out."

"Let me try to pin you down—"

"Please don't."

"I'm afraid I must."

"You can try."

"Let me be very specific. Giffin headed up an archaeological excavation in which he was heavily invested in a psychological sense. He was also extremely grateful to Marc for allowing it to take place on his land."

"Yes?"

"If he were in his 'Mr. Hyde' mode, could he try to sabotage the excavation and attempt to harm Marc?"

"Oh dear. That's a tough one. You must understand that I am not an expert in this disease, so I'd have to do a lot more reading, but again I would have to say that I couldn't rule it out."

"Thank you very much, Doctor Penhally."

When we were half way through the doorway, I turned back.

"Oh, Doctor. Is Stephen still staying with Bingo?"

"No, he's moved on. Detestable creature."

"On that we are completely agreed!"

Out on the street, Patrick put his arm around my shoulders.

"I think your worries are over. You can forget about hiring protection. For my money, Giffin was your culprit. The poor guy was as mad as a March hare!"

31

Since he had no relatives, there was no funeral for Ralph Giffin, but the archaeologists stopped digging for the day as a mark of respect. Rosalie went to work at the college to read a number of doctoral theses, while I just lounged around the house, tidying up my cellar.

Early the following morning Stefan called in and told me he had spent the previous day talking to the university authorities, asking them to allow him to continue the excavation. They agreed, subject to my own permission, which I granted and, as the threat had now been removed, I said they could continue digging until the fall.

Stefan thanked me profusely, explaining that he thought that the "steps" they had discovered in the pit would lead, not to an underground chamber, but rather to a tomb. "There is no direct parallel in Canada that I know of," he said, "but many funerary traditions around the world favour concealing the dead body in an inaccessible location, so subsequent generations of grave robbers would not be able to loot the sites."

"Like the tombs of the pharaohs in the Egyptian pyramids."

"Exactly. And, to a lesser extent, like the Bronze Age megalithic tombs of Europe, where the bodies were covered with enormously large, heavy slabs of stone."

"If you're right that this is a tomb, do you have any idea what period or culture it belongs to?"

"Not really. Very little about this site makes much sense, but my money would be on some variant of the early native inhabitants, rather than some weird import for elsewhere."

"Will there be human remains?"

"I'm hoping so. If it is a tomb, we would expect to find bones. And if there are bones, we can carbon date them."

"I've heard of that. How does it work?"

"It's complicated but in any organic material carbon exists, and deteriorates over time, at a rate which is known, during which half of it decays. So, carbon dating, or radiocarbon dating or C-14 dating, is the scientific method which estimates the age of organic materials by measuring the amount of carbon which has not deteriorated. Understand?"

"Not really, no."

"Well, put it this way: Living organisms absorb carbon-14 from the atmosphere in the same proportion as it occurs naturally, and when they die, they stop absorbing carbon-14. The remaining carbon-14 begins to decay into carbon-12. So we measure the ratio of carbon-14 to carbon-12 in the sample and compare it to the ratio in a living organism. "

"I see. So the age of the organism can be estimated based on how much carbon-14 has decayed."

"You've got it."

"Is it exact?"

"Not completely. Unless the object being tested is very old, say older than 60,000 years, the margin of error can be as little as plus or minus forty years."

"When will you know if you have a tomb or something different?"

"Today. I'm going to start on it right away. Want to come?"

"You bet."

On our way up the hill to the site, I filled Stefan in about what we had learned from Martin Penhally about Ralph's condition.

He shook his head sadly. "I wasn't close to Ralph, but I respected him. He was a good archaeologist until the last few weeks. I knew something was very wrong, but I had no idea it was this—what do you call it?"

"Marchiafava Bignami disease."

"Yeah, that. I'll make sure I don't get hooked on that *Teroldego Rotaliano* wine."

"Me, too."

We reached the site and walked over to the pit. Stefan told Jennifer that I would be assisting him, and ushered me down the shaky ladder. With each step downwards it shuddered, and I was very glad when I got to the bottom, now some eighteen feet below the surface.

It was very slow work, partially because the light was poor, and because Stefan and I got in each other's way, but chiefly because whatever features were in the soil were so friable they almost disappeared when disturbed.

Working with paint brushes and knitting needles we carefully picked at the remaining "door". If I had been correct in seeing an inscription when I first descended into the pit, it had since either been removed or had degenerated beyond recognition.

As we worked, we had to take photographs of every stage in the procedure and, if something appeared to be significant, we had to plan it on graph paper. As earth was displaced, it had to be gathered in dustpans and hauled to the surface. Occasionally, if one of us stood up to stretch, we would knock our heads on the hanging light bulb. The previous, dim bulb had, I was glad to see, been replaced with one of stronger wattage, but working in that light was still a considerable strain on the eyes.

After some hours, the remaining half of the "door" had been removed and we brushed off the "steps", expecting to see a downward progression, but they simply stopped. What we had been calling "the steps" was in fact only one small, rather poor, nondescript step leading nowhere.

We had, in fact, encountered a compact, dark, almost black, layered rock which Stefan said looked like ancient lake bed sediment. We continued brushing the surface of this layer, then stood up to take more photographs.

"Look!" I grabbed Stefan's arm.

"What?"

"Are those footprints?" With my finger I outlined shapes in the soil.

"By God, I think you're right. Let's see if we can clean it up. This calls for extreme delicacy. You won't mind if I ask you to just watch this time."

"No, of course not. With my inexperienced hand I could destroy the find of the century."

Stefan continued working in silence, picking gently at the flakes of covering material, until the footprints became clearer. There were four of them, all facing in the same direction.

"Oh look here," he said, holding his hand up. There in his palm were tiny pieces of rock.

"What is it?"

"Fossilized seeds," he said excitedly. "They were in the rock between the toe prints. We can date these and that will tell us when the footprints were made."

After we had drawn more plans and taken more photographs, I looked at my watch, I was surprised to see that it was already well into the afternoon. We had been working steadily for over five hours.

In the corner of the trench, some feet away from the footprints. I noticed a small hole. Idly, I picked at it with my trowel and soon it became larger, with sections of the layered rock giving way to reveal a chamber or passage underneath.

"Holy cow!" Stefan exclaimed. "What have you found, Marc?"

"I don't know, but it looks as if it goes down quite a way."

"This is exciting! What on earth can it be? Look, we had better cover it for now. One thing at a time. We can come back to it after we have processed the footprints properly."

He shouted up for a board to be sent down.

I looked up and saw Jennifer lowering a piece of gyp rock attached to a rope. Stefan unhooked it and placed it carefully over the hole, trowelling earth over the edges to secure it in place.

"Time for me to go," I said wearily.

"Okay, Marc. Thanks for your help."

"It was a pleasure, Stefan. Thanks for allowing my clumsy efforts on the site."

"I must say, it's a relief not to be working under a black cloud of uncertainty. I find it hard to get my head around what the doctor said about Ralph, but it explains everything."

"Sad, but true."

"I won't know about the footprints until tomorrow. I have a very good relationship with the gang at the Dalhousie University lab, so I'll have them speed it up."

"I'll be intrigued to know when those footprints were made. Any preliminary ideas?"

"The youngest fossils we have found so far come from the end of the last ice age, so that would be at least 9,000 years ago."

"Wow! So, whatever is underneath them is even older?"

"Yeah. It's awesome. And a little scary."

As I rearranged the ladder to make it more stable, chunks of earth fell out of the walls of the trench. I noted that this was because the lower five feet had not been shored up with boards.

"I'll get that fixed as soon as I get some more boards from town," Stefan said. "Will you be around tomorrow?"

"Yes."

As I wandered down through the sweet-smelling grass and buttercups, I realized that for the first time in weeks I was in a very good mood.

32

Over the next few days, I had a great deal of personal paperwork to catch up on in addition to weeding and tidying my garden, so I did not get up to the dig. Nor did I hear from Stefan, which I assumed meant he had not yet received the report from the lab on the footprints, but I saw Jennifer and Tracey one evening as they were walking down to the road. They told me that the diggers were concentrating on expanding the trenches westwards and that work on the pit had been temporarily suspended.

One day, I had to go into Wolfville to see how Louise was progressing in acquiring the old burgundies I wanted. Since the workmen had completed the renovations after Alaric Balser's depredations, she was back in her regular place behind the counter.

While I was in town, I dropped by the bookshop to say hello to Gerald.

Even as I was pushing the door open, I felt a wave of revulsion coming over me, and I knew that Stephen was on the other side. He was perched cross-legged on the counter and greeted me with that horrible smirk I had found so unpleasant when last we met. He threw back his head, tossing his blond curls over his shoulders.

"If it isn't Gerald's guard dog," he said. "Gerald, honey, your guard dog is here!"

"Please don't be like that, Stephen," said Gerald, as he came through the beaded curtain which separated the shop from the back room. "Hello, Marc. It's just his way. He doesn't mean to be rude."

"Oh yes, he does," Stephen corrected. "He doesn't like guard dogs."

"I won't stay Gerald," I said quickly. "I just dropped in to see if you're alright."

"He's fine, thank you, guard dog," said Stephen. "Now just run along like a good little doggie."

When Gerald followed me out into the street, I could see that he had been crying.

"Are you sure you're okay?"

"Well, you know…"

"No I don't, Gerald. The longer you are mixed up with that toad the more you'll be hurt."

"Yes….but it's not simple."

Gerald looked so much like a wounded animal that I was compelled to ask. "Does he get violent?"

Gerald's voice dropped to a whisper, "Sometimes."

"Why don't you kick him out?"

"Ooh, I couldn't do that. He'd never allow it."

"It wouldn't be his decision, it'd be yours."

"Marc, you have no idea how powerful he is."

"He's not that big. I could take the bastard."

"You don't understand. It's not just him. He has a lot of friends."

"So what?"

"They're even meaner than he is."

"Come on Gerry." The door had been opened a few inches. "Come away from the guard dog. Come back to Stevie."

"I must go," Gerald said with a whimper.

As I turned to go, I saw Bill Jolly on the other side of the street.

"Hey, Bill."

"Hey, Marc. I hear you stopped them foolish old diggings up on the hill."

"Yes, I did, but they've started up again."

"That's too bad."

"Got any fresh fish?"

"Not today, Marc. I gotta run."

Apparently, Bill was one of the very few people about town who did not know that the dig had resumed after Ralph's death. Wherever I went I received comments, most of them favourable to the dig's resumption. Walter Bryson, whom I met in the wine store, was most enthusiastic about it.

"I think we should find out more about the people who went before us," he said, "and especially if the site proves to be an important archaeological milestone. Jennifer loves it and gives us nightly reports on the dig."

"I see her and her friend Tracey up there from time to time."

"Yes she tells us that, too. Seems you're quite a hit with those girls."

"I am?" I was genuinely surprised.

"Yes. They've never forgotten the way you straightened them out on the Father Mike affair."

Water was referring to an incident when a Catholic priest was accused of sexual assault, which I have described in my book *The Plot to Kill the Premier.*

"That's nice of them. I'm glad they enjoy the dig. Now that we're clear of these stupid threats, the excavation can carry on to September."

"Perfect timing for when they go back to college."

I was glad to hear Walter being so positive, but some others I met were of the tut-tutting and head-shaking variety. One of the latter was Gary Marshall, whom I bumped into when turning a corner.

"That's a shame it's continuing in my opinion."

"Gary, you're an educated man," I said. "A lawyer and an officer of the court. Surely, you can't believe that nonsense about the 'curse'?"

"No, not really, but I guess I feel the same way about it as I do about putting my client on the stand. If I can't be certain of what he'll say when he's up there, I won't take the risk." He glanced at his watch. "Speaking of which, I have to be in court in ten minutes. Best to Rosalie."

"Okay, Gary. Love to Jane."

As I was parking the BMW in front of the house, I saw Stefan climbing over the fence from the field.

"Hello, stranger," I called when he drew near. "I was expecting to hear from you before this. Is everything alright?"

"Yes, thanks, Marc. C-14 results on the footprints were delayed at the lab. They had to be double checked, and then checked again."

"Why was that? Was there something wrong with the sample?"

"No. The lab just couldn't believe the results, so they kept doing them."

"Come in and have a drink. You can tell me all about it."

We went into the living room, where I poured us both glasses of 15-year-old Aberlour malt. Then we sprawled on the big Chesterfield, looking out at the hill.

"So," I said, "what was the problem at the lab?"

"I'm almost embarrassed to tell you, because it makes absolutely no sense."

"How so?"

"The C-12 test showed the seeds to be about 20,000 years old."

"20,000? You're joking?"

"I wish I was. If we believe that the seeds are contemporary with the feet which made the prints—"

"And do we?"

"I don't see that we have any choice. If anything, the feet would be somewhat older than the seeds."

"Has anything like this been found elsewhere?"

"Yes, at White Sands National Park in New Mexico. There they found seeds in the sediment layers which dated to between 21,000 and 23,000 years, which is the oldest record of humans in the Americas."

"Holy cow!"

"Yeah. Until the White Sands find, the conventional thinking was that human settlement of the Americas began at the end of the last Ice Age, about 13,000 to 16,000 years ago."

"I seem to recall reading something about that. What was it called?"

"The Clovis culture theory. It's named after the town of Clovis in New Mexico, where the first evidence of their culture was discovered in the 1920s."

"Isn't this at the centre of a hot debate about whether the so-called indigenous people were actually migrants from Russia?"

"That's rather crudely expressed, but yes. It was believed that the Clovis people were the first Americans, crossing the Bering Land Bridge from Asia to North America."

"When was this supposed to have occurred?"

"Between 12,000 and 11,000 BCE. They then are alleged to have migrated south through an ice-free corridor to what is now New Mexico. Then, supposedly, they spread across North America."

"But not everyone agrees, I gather."

"No, indeed. The White Sands discovery—if accurate—means that people arrived some 8,000 years before the Clovis people."

"Why do you keep hedging?"

"Because some doubt has been cast on the White Sands C-14 results, suggesting they may have been, not exactly contaminated, but that the use of an old carbon reservoir could have compromised the accuracy of the radiocarbon dating."

"You've lost me, Stefan. Please speak in ordinary language."

"Okay." He laughed and took a sip of his whisky. "The seeds at White Sands were from plants which originally grew in water, and some scholars say that dating seeds from an aquatic plant to tell the age of the footprints is potentially problematic."

"I won't ask why because I wouldn't understand the answer. Is that the only reason it's controversial?"

"No, there's a lot of politics involving scientists and native people, some of whom want to close down any discussion which would favour the Clovis theory and boost work suggesting older origins."

"I can see why."

"I'm sure you can, in the present climate. I think the term 'indigenous' has been improperly appropriated for political reasons. All the term really means is that you are in the place where you were born. If you were born in this area, Marc. You are indigenous."

"Thanks for that."

"It all revolves around the importance people attach to being somewhere first or before other people. For example, in the Middle East debate, it is important for Israel to state that Jews were there some 1000 years before Bedouin Arabs and 2300 years before Muslims."

"Yes, my friend Rachel Bland often tells me that."

"So, in order to establish a claim to ownership of the land by prior occupation, it is important for those we used to call *Indians* to have transmogrified from that to *natives*, then to *first nations* and finally to *indigenous*, although I expect there will be another change in the future."

"That's all very interesting, but getting back to our site, do our footprints have anything else in common with White Sands?"

"Yes, another similarity is that neither show signs of footwear being used."

"You would expect them to go barefoot in those times, I guess."

"Yes."

"I sense there's something else you're not telling me. What is it?"

"It's the kicker. You might not like it."

"Why not?"

"We have C-14 results for our seeds, and hence our footprints, at approximately 20,000 years. Right?"

"Right."

"If the White Sands results are overturned at any point, for any reason it would mean—"

"That ours are the oldest footprints in the Americas!"

"Well, maybe, but yes."

"And it would mean that whatever is in the corner, under the board—"

"If there is anything."

"Yes, but if there is anything there, it will be even older."

"Stratigraphically, yes."

"Why wouldn't I like that? It's wonderful."

"That's not all."

"What else is there?"

"At White Sands they estimated that there are hundreds of thousands of fossilized footprints. It's possible the same applies here."

"I think I'm beginning to see what you are driving at."

"Yes. It would be declared a national historic suite and you'd be under considerable pressure to allow more excavation."

"How much more?"

"In theory, your whole field."

"I'm not having that! No way!"

"If it is like White Sands, you may not have a choice. The government could expropriate the land to make a park."

"Fuck!"

"Calm down, Marc. The extensions to the trenches are already a good way down and there are no signs of seeing anything like we did in the pit."

"You'll keep me informed? Let me know the minute you find another fossil, so I can start looking for somewhere else to live."

"We're nowhere near that point yet," he said, laughing. "There's a strong likelihood that we've found everything spectacular there is to find. Most archaeology deals with the commonplace, not the extraordinary."

"We live in hope," I said with great feeling.

33

It was another almost-perfect day, one of a large number we had enjoyed this year, making it the best summer I could remember since my return to Nova Scotia seven years ago.

My garden was growing well, and I was already picking many crops for our table. The leeks, tomatoes and peppers still needed some time yet, and the squash was not yet fully grown; but we were regularly getting cucumbers, French breakfast radishes, baby gem lettuce and a multitude of fresh herbs. The rosemary was particularly vigorous, and the lemon thyme was spreading like wildfire along the edges of my plots. The chives were extremely healthy, as was the mint.

The only herb not flourishing well was the basil, which seemed to be struggling.

As almost a week had passed without incident, apart from Ralph's unfortunate demise, Rosalie and I were convinced we no longer had anything to fear, so we relaxed back into our regular routine. We walked freely about our property, and stopped peering around corners to see if any rogues awaited us. It was as if a huge weight had been lifted from our shoulders.

Rosalie felt sorry for the diggers after their loss so, the day following my discussion with Stefan about the footprints, she decided to invite them all to lunch again. This time she pulled out all the stops and prepared a delicious seafood chowder, lobster rolls, and smoked salmon sandwiches. I teased her by saying that, at this rate, soon she would be on her hands and knees up at the site.

At 12:30 they trooped down and occupied all the seats on the patio, chattering and laughing as they contemplated the feed which Rosalie had laid out for them. Some sat on the steps, and one or two perched on the wall and fence separating us from the field.

Despite the tragedy of their director's death, they were obviously in good heart, something I attributed to an expectation of a considerable archaeological discovery in the near future and, from all that Stefan had told me, I did not think they would be disappointed.

Rosalie asked me to serve the bowls of chowder and as I made the rounds, I noticed Jennifer sitting by herself.

"Hi, Jennifer. All alone today? Where's Tracey? Is she sick?"

"Oh, hi, Mr. LeBlanc. No, she stayed behind to clean off her trench. She'll be right down."

"Shall I bring you an extra bowl and chowder and a lobster roll for her? The rate these ravening wolves are eating, there'll be nothing left in a few minutes."

"Yes please, Mr. LeBlanc. That'd be good."

I went to the kitchen where Rosalie was slaving away, cutting bread for more sandwiches.

"Your grub is a real hit," I said. "I think all customers are happy."

"Are you here to help or hinder?" She asked tartly.

"Help. I need another bowl of chowder and a lobster roll. Tracey hasn't arrived yet and I don't want her to miss out on the goodies."

"Oh, okay. Here you go."

I took the food out to where I had left Jennifer, and immediately noticed she was still alone.

"Still not here?" I cast my eye over the field and hill, but could see no sign of her. "She isn't on her way. Does she have a mobile with her?"

"Yes," said Jennifer. "I'll give her a call."

Several attempts to reach her were unsuccessful, so Jennifer asked a lad who just finished his lunch if he would go and fetch Tracey. He was a tall, athletic boy of about nineteen who hopped over the wall and loped off up the hill.

We watched as he attained the brow and disappeared into the site. A few minutes later he reappeared, frantically waving his arms in the air, before racing back in our direction.

Sensing something was amiss, I took Jenifer by the arm and rushed over to where Stefan was finishing his lunch.

"Something's wrong." I said, urging him towards the field.

Just as we got to the edge, the boy hurried up to us. "Stefan, Tracey's had an accident!"

"What do you mean? Where?"

"In the pit. There's been a collapse. She's buried and she's not moving."

"What hell was she doing in the pit?"

"I don't know, but you'd better come quickly."

"Alright. Jennifer, call an ambulance and tell it to go as far up the lane as it can. Keep the crew here. I'm going up to take a look. Marc, you come with me."

We moved up the hill so fast that even Stefan, who was years younger than me, was gasping for breath when we reached the top.

We rushed over to the pit and looked down on what appeared to be a lifeless Tracey. A huge section of the lower trench had come away and the earth had spilled across, covering almost half of her body.

"Marc, steady the ladder. I'm going down. We need to check if she's still alive. We don't know how long the ambulance will be."

He quickly descended the juddering ladder and felt Tracey's one exposed wrist for a pulse. Then he tried again on her neck. He looked up at me.

"I'm pretty sure she's dead." he said flatly, and slowly climbed out of the pit and sat down on the edge of the trench.

"That lower section should have been shored up days ago," he said very ruefully. "I should have seen to it when Ralph first asked me, but I got sidetracked by other stuff."

"Was Tracey supposed to be in the pit?"

"No. Her trench is up the top there." He waved his hand. "They were all told, not only to stay out, but to stay away from the pit. I made that very clear."

"Then what could she have been doing down there?"

"I can't think. She was just a beginner. She wouldn't know what to do even if I had let her go down."

At that moment, we heard the first sounds of the ambulance's siren, so we stood up. I walked back to the pit and looked again, this time more attentively.

The collapse could easily have been a natural phenomenon due to groundwater, I decided, but what I noticed on the margins of the pit was another matter entirely. There were indentations in the earth like scuff marks, the kind of marks that might have been made if someone had been pushed over the edge and their heels had dragged against the upper sides.

I was about to call Stefan over, but something—I don't know what—told me I should keep this information to myself. I was surprised to find myself surreptitiously flattening the scuff marks with my shoe.

Creating further panic would be stupid, especially when, by their own admission, the police were unlikely to do anything positive. I resolved to keep my counsel, tell no one, and especially not Rosalie...until the time was right.

I was under no illusions. This new incident meant that the threat we had thought lifted was still very much present. This was a problem I had to deal with myself. Whoever was posing the threat had to be found, faced and destroyed.

As distasteful as it might be, I came to the conclusion that what I had to do was to contact *The Times* of London and place an advertisement in their personal columns.

34

I had a very restless night. I was acutely aware that Rosalie felt badly enough about Tracey's death without my adding to her stress. If I told her what I knew, or rather suspected, she would have become almost hysterical, and would phone Patrick to demand round-the-clock protection. He would have no choice but to repeat to her that what she wanted was not possible at our location. Then, doubtless, she would have become enraged and would take it out on me.

For none of that could she be blamed, but it reinforced my determination not to inform her until I had measures in place to deal with the situation.

The problem was that, for many hours, I had not totally decided what action to take, and knew I would not be completely comfortable with the decision I was contemplating.

I waited until the police had done their work and the ambulance had taken Tracey away, then I came back to the house and locked myself in my study. I was both furious and frightened. If I had been able to accomplish the task, I would have done it instantly, but *The Times'* website was so confusing that I could not figure out how to place a personal ad. When I tried, I found that what I wanted to place fitted into no listed category. It was not a birth, death or marriage, was not a classified ad and was certainly not one seeking a romantic date. I tried at least a dozen permutations of the question on Google, but all directed me back to the original, confusing entry.

I reflected that, while to the skilful and initiated, company and government websites provided a useful service, to the uneducated, the disabled and the elderly they presented as a frustrating nightmare. No longer able to speak to a living person who could answer a simple question, many, possibly millions, simply got lost in the quagmire of conflicting directions and so-called "Frequently Asked Questions." No doubt, like myself, they discovered that none of the questions they wanted to ask were ever found in the FAQ lists.

Finally, I sent an email to *The Times* asking if a personal ad could still be placed, and if so, how I could go about it. I received an acknowledgement saying that one of their advisers would get back to me as soon as possible and that in the meantime should consult their FAQ!

This enforced wait allowed me to cool off and consider my options. But what *were* my options? Following Patrick's advice meant leaving home, something Rosalie and I were loath to do. To go away would seem like cowardice, but that was surely better than being maimed or killed.

I had made some preliminary inquiries into hiring private guards, but found that even those who supervised cash shipments and the like were not trained as personal bodyguards. Neither did hiring other private detectives seem feasible, because the ones I had met were overweight and unfit, suggesting that detection was not the same as protection.

The more I thought about it, even though it was not ideal, the more I became convinced that my original idea was the only one which made sense

Two years ago, when I was in London, I had a chance meeting with my brother Larry, who told me that if I ever needed help I should place a personal ad in *The Times*, saying *Sir Leonard, please call home*. Sir Leonard was a pseudonym Larry used when he was in London, and he was known by that name in such places at the Ritz Rivoli Bar. The time to exercise that option had come, and since I had done a favour for Larry not long ago, I was sure he would oblige me now.

When Larry arrived I could tell Rosalie why he had come. In time—and hopefully not too much time—he could find out who had been threatening us and deal with them appropriately. Beyond suspecting that Larry's methods might be questionable and not entirely within the law, I had no idea how he would go about the task, and I did not propose to ask too many questions.

Following the disaster, the dig had shut down for the day. Stefan told me they would start up again the day after, but stop yet again for Tracey's funeral the next week.

Rosalie went off to college in a very teary mood, leaving me to kick my heels at home.

It was not until noon that I heard back from *The Times*, instructing me how to proceed with my ad, so I arranged to have it run each day for a week. I had no idea how frequently Larry read the newspaper, so I did not know when I might hear from him.

35

It was two days before I received an acknowledgement that my personal ad in *The Times* had been read. Not a moment too soon, I thought, because I had been on pins and needles the entire time, worried that another attempt might be made on our lives or property.

Rosalie was in worse shape than me, constantly drawing the drapes and moving furniture away from windows. She had even borrowed a friend's dog, although as far as I could see the creature was so friendly it would likely have licked an assassin's hand rather than bitten it.

In the meantime, the dig had resumed, but the pit had been roped off, and excavating inside was suspended until the Department of Labour could investigate and rule on whether it was safe to carry on working there.

The diggers had ample other work to do, extending the trenches to the fence on the western side and to almost flush with the property line on the east. No further structures had been revealed, but Stefan told me that puzzling changes in soil colour had shown up the further they trowelled downwards. He said the primary reason for their extending the area of the excavations was to attempt to find the location of the midden, or garbage dump, in which he would expect a mass of broken pottery and other dateable items. Then he said something which struck me as odd.

"To date we haven't found a single thing we can date except for those fossilized footprints."

"You mean apart from in the pit?"

"No, anywhere on the site. The footprints—or rather the seeds —are all we have that we can date."

I was about to ask him about the anachronistic discoveries

Ralph had made, but immediately realized that he had not informed Stefan about them. Why the director of the excavation would deliberately keep knowledge of very valuable finds from the assistant director was a question I could not begin to answer.

Despite my interference to eliminate evidence after Tracey was found, I was amazed that foul play did not seem to have even crossed the RCMP's minds. After they had brought Tracey's body up, they set up the usual yellow tape around the pit, but as far I knew had asked no penetrating questions of anyone and certainly not of me.

Stefan told me that he had been asked only the most rudimentary questions, such as her identity and how long she had worked on the site. He said that when he told Staff Sergeant Lomas that Tracey was not supposed to be working in the pit, he had just nodded and said, "Thank you, sir. You've been a big help."

I felt certain that Lomas would have come to see me, slyly hinting at some irregularity or other on my part, but he did not.

It was late morning. I had intended to go directly into Wolfville to pick up a few supplies when, quite unusually, I dropped by my study and peered at the computer. There was one email from an address which was given as a twenty- eight figure configuration which meant nothing to me. The message was simple:

Get a phone

Taken by surprise, at first I thought it was part of some telecom advertising drive, but then I realized it must have been from Larry. I took it to mean that I should buy a cheap mobile phone—what is called "a burner" in the movies—for a one-time use. I presumed I might get other instructions once I had acquired the burner.

On the short drive I admitted to myself that I had no idea what kind of security precautions I should take, so, once I had done my other shopping in town, I contrived to call at the wine store a few minutes before I knew Louise would be going on her lunch break. Then, just as she was leaving, I asked her to bring me back a cheap phone. She said she would, but gave me a strange look which I hoped would not lead to an embarrassing interrogation later.

I wasted the hour talking to Delia, Louise's assistant, serving a few customers and idly scanning the shelves. I was pleased to see how, soon after Alaric Balser's violent intrusion they had managed to get the place back in some kind of order, and particularly how Louise had replenished the stocks.

"Here you go," Louise said when she came back from lunch. "That'll be fifty-two dollars. I didn't know how much time you wanted to put on it, so I opted for more rather than less."

"Thanks, Louise." I said as I pocketed the phone.

"I'll take the money now, if you have it."

"Yes of course."

I fumbled in my wallet, gave her the money and quickly made my escape onto Main Street.

Seated back in the BMW, I took out the phone and stared at it, expecting it to look somehow mysterious, but it was plain and ordinary, so I put it back in my pocket and drove home.

At the house, I closeted myself in my study, sat down and waited. In about twenty minutes another email came through, giving a London number followed by the word:

NOW

I copied the number on a scrap of paper and headed out to the field. Halfway up the hill, I sat down and called the number.

A strange voice answered, but I knew by now that it was likely to be Larry using one of his falsettos.

"Sir Leonard?" I asked.

"Hello, Little Brother! What's all the flap about?"

"It's a long story—"

"It better not be. I'm using the phone in the lobby of The Savoy."

"I need help, Larry, and you said if I did I should call you."

"Fair enough. You helped me in Bermuda. You scratch my back, I'll scratch yours. Tell me what's occurring."

"Rosalie and I have been threatened several times."

"What? Who by?"

"We don't know."

"Were these phone calls?"

"No, letters."

"Yeah, go on."

"Then her car brakes were tampered with."

"You're kidding?"

"No, and we've been shot at."

"Shot at? With a gun?"

"Yes. Then a guy drove his truck straight at me through the window of the wine store."

"Fuck me!"

"And, Larry, there have been two deaths, one of them almost certainly due to foul play."

"Jesus!" There was a long pause.

"Larry? Are you there?"

"Yeah. Sounds like you do have a problem. Is there something connecting all these dots?"

"I think so."

"What is it?"

"There's an archaeological dig going on at the top of my hill. You know where there is a little bulge in the land?"

"I know it. I remember hiding in the woods up there."

"The threats said they wanted us to stop the dig."

"And when you didn't, things escalated?"

"Exactly."

"Weren't the police any good to you?"

"Not really. The local guy is unhelpful and my friend the RCMP superintendent—"

"Whoa! You have a chum who's an RCMP super?"

"Er...yes."

"I'm not sure I want to be rubbing shoulders with the cops, Marc."

"You won't be rubbing shoulders with him, Larry. He's in Halifax and he told us he didn't have the manpower to provide proper protection. He wanted us to go away on vacation until the smoke settled."

"Sounds very sensible advice. I think you should have taken it."

"We won't be driven out of our home, Larry. Surely, you can understand that?"

"Not really having a home, I'm not sure I do."

"They also got my Bugatti."

"What do you mean, 'got'? Was it stolen?"

"No. They blew it up."

"*Blew it up*?!"

"They put some kind of explosive device in the garage and blew the whole thing up, including the car."

"The dirty, rotten bastards!"

"That's what I thought, too."

"That does it. I owe you, Little Brother, so I'll help for sure."

"Thanks."

"Any idea at all what or who we're dealing with? How many might be involved?"

"None. No idea at all."

"Hmmn. I 'd better bring a crew."

"A crew? How many is that?"

"Say half a dozen. No, more like seven. That should do it. I'll need the muscle if push comes to shove."

"You can stay with us, but I don't think Rosalie would go for boarding seven people."

"Nah, don't worry about that. Four of them will be fading into the local scenery. You'll need to accommodate myself and two others, but only one of them will be awake at any given time. They'll be your round-the-clock protection. And you won't see me that often."

"Wow. That sounds good."

"Can you square that with Rosalie?"

"I guess so. Does it matter where the sleeping man is?"

"How do you mean?"

"I mean, could they share a room? They wouldn't be sleeping in the bed at the same time."

"They better not! Sure, that'll be alright."

"Would they mind if the room is at the top of the house?"

"The top?"

"Well, the attic."

"Hell, no. I think they might like that. Where they come from, an attic would be considered the lap of luxury."

"Where's that?"

"Where's what?"

"Where do these guys come from?"

"The ones I have in mind are Bulgarians. I call them Boris and Horace."

"Oh, I see."

"No, you don't, but you will." Larry gave an evil laugh which sent chills down my spine.

"When will we see you?"

"You'll see me and the Bulgars as soon as we can get there. If all goes according to plan, if I do this right, you'll never see the other guys."

"You mean, I won't know who they are?"

"Not if I can help it."

"Oh."

"Look, I have to go. Other patrons of The Savoy want to use the phone. And, Marc?"

"Yes?"

"As soon as we say 'goodbye', take the burner for a long walk and hammer the living shit out of it."

"Will do. See you, Larry."

"See you, Little Brother. Love to Rosalie."

36

I had never seen the church so full; it was quite literally standing room only, some people even having to huddle in the porch. I recognized only a small percentage of the congregation, most of whom I assumed were Tracey's immediate and extended family. It was a sombre and tearful gathering, somehow made worse by somebody's having distributed large, wilted, white lilies around the nave.

As expected, Stefan and various other diggers were present, one of them crying so much she was almost in a state of collapse.

Outside the church, prior to the service, Stefan told me that the pit was still roped off, pending the decision by the Department of Labour on whether it would be safe to resume work there. He said they did not know when the Department would inspect the site or when the decision would be made. In the meantime their work now, he said, was chiefly devoted to extending the edges of the excavation.

Still troubled by the strong suspicion that Ralph had not told Stefan about the coin and other unique objects he had found, I decided to see if I could establish it beyond doubt. "So, only the seeds can be dated?"

"Yes, only the seeds."

"Are you sure about that? Poor Ralph didn't dig anything up on his midnight visits?"

"If he did, he never told me about it."

So, it was a fact, and a mystery which might never be solved.

The priest (not our friend Father Mike, I noticed) rather unconvincingly, at least to me, told us that Tracey had died because God loved the young and wanted them to be with Him. Again, as so often in the past, I noticed that the priest read most of the service.

He was a man in his sixties so must have performed the ceremony dozens of times. How much better it would sound, I thought, if he had memorized the words and spoke them naturally.

Jennifer, having been Tracey's oldest and best friend, was asked to deliver the eulogy, which she did extremely well. She told us how Tracey was barely nineteen and how she had been doing well in her first year at university in New Brunswick. She said she and Tracey had volunteered to work on the archaeological excavation because they were interested in history and wanted to know more about their ancestors. She said they also thought it would be great fun which they would remember for the rest of their lives.

At this there was a strangled collective gasp in the congregation.

Jenifer closed by reading a poem I always thought rather maudlin, but she did it superbly. It was Clare Harner's "Immortality":

> Do not stand
>   By my grave, and weep,
> I am not there,
>   I do not sleep—
>
> I am the thousand winds that blow,
> I am the diamond glints in snow.
> I am the sunlight on ripened grain,
> I am the gentle, autumn rain.
> As you awake with morning's hush,
> I am the swift, up-flinging rush
> Of quiet birds in circling flight.
> I am the day transcending night.
>
> Do not stand
> By my grave, and cry—
> I am not there,
> I did not die.

By the time Jennifer had finished, many mourners were loudly sob-

bing and clutching the person nearest to them. When I looked at
Rosalie, I saw that she too was crying copiously. Away to my left I
saw Walter and Joyce Bryson, clearly very proud of their daughter's performance.

In a very dignified fashion, Jennifer walked back down the aisle
and sat down next to her parents.

At the graveside, we were bunched together like human bananas, some people standing in mud, some on other graves and others half in bushes and undergrowth.

The priest, who I later learned boasted the curious name of Father
Bruder, reading from his little book, intoned the words. "O Lord,
may Tracey's soul and the souls of all the faithful departed,
through the mercy of God, rest in peace."

Various people muttered, "Amen."

"Accept the prayers we offer in sadness for your servant
Tracey, deliver her soul from death, number her among your saints
and clothe her with the robe of salvation to enjoy for ever the
delights of your kingdom. We ask this through Christ our Lord."

Now we all said, "Amen."

As we watched the family leaving the grave, I felt a prod in my
back and heard a voice whisper.

"Just to let you know I'm here, Little Brother."

"Good," I said. "Do you have a vehicle?"

"Of course, we have a vehicle."

"Go to the house and park near the trees. Make sure you're not
visible from the road."

"Right. See you there."

"Marc," Rosalie asked. "Who are you talking to?"

"Shhh. I'll tell you later."

"You'll tell me now!" She said sharply.

"Alright, but wait till we're outside."

Slowly, we extricated ourselves from the throng and edged our way
to the lychgate and finally onto the sidewalk.

"Well?"

"Larry's here."

"Larry? Larry who?"

"My brother."

"He's here?"

"Yes."

"Why?"

"To give us protection. He's the private protection I hired. You remember Patrick advised it."

"But that was when we were under threat."

"Yes."

"But we're not anymore." She stared at me intently. "We're not, are we?"

"I didn't tell you because I didn't want you to be worried and I wanted to get the protection in place first."

"What are you talking about?" She was becoming annoyed. "Tell me. Are we still under threat?"

"Maybe."

"Maybe?" she shouted, drawing attention from mourners filing out of the cemetery.

"Keep your voice down," I begged her. "Wait until we're in the car."

I took her by the arm and ushered her across the road to the BMW.

When we were seated, she turned on me. "Alright. Tell me why Larry is here. And this better be good!"

"I believe Tracey's death was not an accident."

"What?"

"I think she was pushed. A fall of eighteen feet could've killed her, or collapsing earth could have suffocated her. I don't know the details."

"My God. What do the police say?"

"They, rather Lomas, has treated it as an accident."

"Then why do you think you know better than the cops?"

"Rosalie, can we please keep the rest until later? I'm going to have to go through it all for Larry's benefit and you'll be present for that."

"Okay," she said reluctantly, "but tell me this. How does Larry propose to protect us? He's only one man."

"No, he isn't."

"What do you mean?"

"He didn't come alone."

"How many does he have with him?"

"Seven, including himself."

"Seven? That's a small army. Where are they going to stay? You know we can't put them all up at our house."

"Apparently four will find accommodation in town or surroundings. Only Boris and Horace will be at our place."

"Boris and Horace?"

"They're Bulgars."

"Burglars? We're going to house criminals?"

"Not burglars, Bulgars. From Bulgaria. Larry says they'll be happy with a bed in the attic. They'll take it in shifts to keep watch over us."

"What about Larry?"

"I told him he could have one of the spare rooms."

"I guess we have to feed them. I don't know what Bulgars eat."

"Me neither. I suspect they'll eat whatever they're given."

We got home a few minutes later and saw that Larry had acquired (I thought it wise not to ask how) a Mercedes, which he had artfully snuggled under the trees on one side of our yard. We left the BMW by the front door, did a quick visual sweep of the surrounding landscape, then beckoned Larry to come in.

When he got out of the car, so also did two enormous, sullen—I could have said 'evil'—looking men in their mid to late thirties. It was almost laughable that they were dressed all in black, as they could not have been more conspicuous if they tried.

"Just nod to them," said Larry. "They don't speak any English, so it's no good trying to communicate with them except with sign language."

"How do they know what they are doing here?" Rosalie asked.

"I speak a little Serbo-Croat, same as them. They know they have to protect you two—with their lives, if necessary."

"Hello," I said to Boris and Horace with a silly grin on my face. They just stared back, expressionless. Larry muttered a few words, presumably in Serbo-Croat, and they cracked huge smiles.

"*Da, zdravo,*" they said.

"That's enough of that," Larry said curtly. "For fuck's sake, let's get in out of sight."

When we were inside, he turned to Rosalie. "What time is dinner?"

"About seven. Is that alright? I don't yet know what it'll be."

"Let's be exact. Seven."

He said to the men, "*Večera u sedam,*" then turned back to us. "Doesn't matter what it is as long as it's edible. Now, Marc. Take us to the attic."

"Okay."

"Is there a bed already made up?"

"There's a bed there. I just need to put some sheets and blankets on it." Rosalie said.

"Okay you go and do that, but I don't want you up there with the guys. While you make up the bed, Marc will show us around. They'll want to see all the doors and windows."

"Okay, I'll let you know when I'm done."

He turned to the men. "*Stavite svoju opremu na pod i pođite s nama.*"

"*Da, šefe,*" they said in unison and hurled their kitbags on the floor. They made a loud noise when they contacted the polished pine, leading me to suspect that the bags were full of guns and ammunition.

We started in the wine cellar, then did the remainder of the basement level. Then we circulated through the ground floor, the men talking to each other about windows and doors. They stopped outside my study and gesticulated. I shook my head.

"*U čemu je problem, šefe?*" one of them said to Larry.

"What's in here, Marc?"

"It's my private study. My safe is in there. The room has no window. Nobody goes in here but me."

"Hmm." He glared at me for a second or two. "Alright. Fair enough."

As we were preparing to mount the stairs, Rosalie came down.

"All done. I hope they'll be comfortable."

"*Predivna je*," said one to the other.

"*Da*," he said with a grin.

"*Prestani!*" Larry snapped at them with surprising vehemence.

The men stopped smiling and hung their heads. I did not know what had been said, but I thought I had a good idea. Rosalie, on the other hand, just smiled happily.

"I'll get started on dinner. How about roast chicken with onion and mushroom stuffing, colcannon and cabbage?"

"That'd probably be the best feed they had since their weddings," said Larry.

"Oh, they're married?" Rosalie asked.

"Boris still is, and Horace used to be until his wife was killed."

"Oh my, what happened?"

"I'll tell you some other time. Let's get these guys to their quarters. Do you have a sheet of paper? I'll make a sign to put on the door of the only bathroom they're allowed to use."

"Surely, that's not necessary?"

"Trust me. Don't argue. This has to be done my way."

I handed Larry paper from my printer. He took it and scrawled what looked like

Sranje. Pišati. Samo ovo mjesto.

"Right, let's go up."

We ascended and showed the men their quarters. They seemed to be pleased with what they saw and both sat down on the bed, testing it by bumping up and down. Then they went to the little dormer window, looked down, pointed out with their index fingers, and made gunshot sounds.

"*Večera u sedam*," Larry repeated, and the men nodded.

"Do I need to know what any of that was about?" I asked Larry on the way downstairs.

"Nah. Those two will give their lives to protect you. They have given their oath as well as getting well paid."

"That's good to know."

"But tell Rosalie to steer clear of them."

"How do you mean?"

"I need to avoid any complications. She's a lovely-looking wo-man, and I'd rather she didn't go flouncing around the place in a way they might misunderstand."

"I surely will," I said solemnly, although I was suppressing a laugh. Rosalie would crack up at the thought of "flouncing", but it was sound advice nonetheless.

"Dinner sounds good," said Larry. "How come you're not doing the cooking?"

"I guess Rosalie felt like doing it tonight. She can cook, you know."

"Good. Are we going to have some wine with it?"

"Sure. What would you like?"

"Something good for the family. Rough plonk will be okay for Boris and Horace."

"Are their names really Boris and Horace?"

"Hell, no. One is called Damyan and the other is Branimir."

"Which is which?"

"I don't know. I never use names when I speak to them and they call me 'boss' when they speak to me."

"They would think it rude to be served a different wine from us."

"How would they know?"

"They've got eyes."

"For fuck's sake, you're not thinking of having them eat at the same table?"

"Well, yes."

"Jesus. Get it straight now and it'll stay straight. These guys are the hired help. If you get the relationships wrong at the start it could lead to problems later on. They eat in the kitchen, we eat in the dining room. Always."

"Okay Larry. I guess you know best."

"I do," he said firmly. "Now, after dinner, one of them will go to bed and the other will patrol the grounds. In twelve hours they'll do a switch. It means that breakfast for both of them will be at seven in the morning and dinner will be at seven at night."

"Okay."

"Tonight, when one has retired and the other is working you can crack open your very best single malt and tell me the whole story, from beginning to end."

"It will take some time."

"That's alright, so long as the Scotch lasts."

37

We stayed up until after three o'clock in the morning. I did most of the talking, while Larry did most of the drinking.

I started with our first meeting with Ralph Giffin up on the hill, and proceeded to the present, trying hard not to omit any detail because Larry had asked me to include everything I could bring to mind. Occasionally he would interrupt with a question to clarify a point, but for the most part he let me ramble on. Even less frequently, Rosalie would butt in if I had forgotten to mention something relevant.

At length, Larry drained his glass and sat back with his hands clasped over his stomach. "And you have no idea who has been dropping all this shit on you, or why?"

"No, no idea. At first, we thought it was local people who didn't like the a dig in their backyards."

"I can see why you might think that. But it seems to me much more likely we are dealing with a gang of criminals."

"They've committed crimes, alright!" Rosalie interjected.

"No, you misunderstand me," Larry said. "What I mean is that it's probable that these people were criminals before you got involved with them."

"Really?"

"Ask yourself why would anyone go to such lengths unless you somehow threatened their profits or were likely to expose them?"

"How would I do that?"

"That remains to be seen, Little Brother. I'm going to reserve judgment until I've checked out this Archibald woman and her mysterious Albert, but that's my current thinking."

"What now?" Rosalie asked.

"I'll be checking with my four plants later today. They will be able to tell me if I'm on the right track?"

"How will they know? They only just got here."

"For a registered private investigator you are remarkably naïve. Already, my guys have infiltrated the taverns, the coffee shops and fast food outlets here and along the Valley. If the mob is operating here, they will find out."

"The mob? Here in the Annapolis Valley?"

"Maybe. Maybe not."

"What can I do to help?" Rosalie asked.

"You should go to work as usual. Don't let on to *anyone* that I or my crew are here."

"Okay."

"And, Rosalie, when you are home, stay away from Boris and Horace except to feed them twice a day. Don't try to make friends with them. They're not here to be your friends."

"Alright."

"What can I do?" I asked.

"You can get me detailed maps of all adjoining properties and those within, say, half a mile."

"I'll ask Walter. He handles most of the properties around here."

"Why will you tell him you need them?"

"I hadn't thought of that. I'll go to Lawrencetown and see what I can find there."

"What's in Lawrencetown?"

"The Land Registry office."

"Make sure you have a good reason for asking. Oh, and I want older maps rather than younger ones."

"Right. Gerald might have some of the older ones."

"Gerald? Is that cook still around?"

"Yes, he owns the bookstore."

"I thought it belonged to Dad."

"It did, but I gave it to Gerald. It's no great loss and it makes him happy."

"Hmm. It was yours, so you could do what you like with it."

"Really it was yours, Larry." Rosalie said.

"Yeah, but I died."

Larry laughed, then craned his neck to see out of the window. "Are they still digging up there?"

"Yes, until university goes back in September."

"I need to have a look. It'll have to be at night,"

"We can do that. Although you won't see much if it's dark."

"It not what I'll see that's important, but what I'll hear."

"Hear?"

"Yes. The noises in your pit. I've got a supercardioid microphone in my kit. We'll take that with us. It may be able to pick up something that can't be heard with the ear."

"What a good idea" Rosalie said. "That sounds promising."

"We'll see. Don't get your hopes up. It's early days yet."

~

I forced myself to get up at six-thirty in order to fix breakfast for Boris and Horace, which I served them at the kitchen table. They wolfed down the bacon, eggs, sausage and toast as if their lives depended on it and swilled several pots of coffee.

Then, without a word to me, one went upstairs to sleep and the other slipped out the back door to check the grounds for signs of intruders.

I went back to bed and slept fitfully. I was vaguely aware of Rosalie getting ready for work and leaving, then drifted back into dreams of the Bulgars eating their way through every fast food place in New Minas.

I roused myself again around ten and stumbled downstairs. I passed Larry's room and peeked in, but he was not there. Nor was he in the kitchen or any other part of the house, but when I was at the sink, I glanced out of the kitchen window and saw him in the garden, sitting among the bean plants talking on his phone. I noticed that he was skilfully placed, as he could only be seen from the house, the vegetation shielding him from the field and hill.

I put on some Blue Mountain coffee, and beat some eggs with cream and a few chopped chives. Then, checking the time, I called Gerald.

"Oh, Marc. What a nice surprise, but I can't talk long because Stephen will be getting up soon."

"You're still his slave then?"

"Please don't be like that." Gerald sounded deeply hurt. "What can I do for you?"

"Sorry, Gerald. I didn't mean to be unkind. I'm looking for old property maps of the Grand Pre area. Do you have any?"

"As a matter of fact, I came across a bunch of deeds and maps only the other day. I'll never sell them in a month of Sundays, so I was going to throw them out. I can't imagine where your father got hold of them."

"Please don't throw them out. Do you know, off-hand, what area they cover?"

"Pretty much your area, if I recall correctly. From Horton Ridge down to Eye Road, I think."

"Wonderful. Do you think you could let me borrow them?"

"Take them. I have no use for them, Marc. Come and get them whenever you like."

"Is Stephen planning to be in all day?"

"Ah. No, he's going out before noon and should be gone all afternoon."

"I'll drop by at 2 pm."

"Fine."

"And Gerald..." I wasn't sure why I felt compelled to say more, but I had to add a condition.

"Yes?"

"Please don't tell Stephen anything about this. Alright?"

"If you say so, Marc. I'd rather he didn't know you were here, anyway."

I returned to the kitchen and made a batch of toast. I was scrambling the eggs when Larry walked in.

"Ah! That smells good. Any for me?"

"Sure. Sit yourself down. I just spoke with Gerald. It sounds like he has all the maps we'll need. I'm picking them up this afternoon."

"That's a stroke of luck." He sat at the table and held his knife and fork in the air. "Bring me food!"

"I saw you hiding in the bean patch. Were you talking to your plants?"

"Haha! Yes, I was. It's exactly as I thought. There's a major crime network in the area which extends from Annapolis all the way to Windsor."

"Is it...the mob?"

"No, not as far as I can tell. It's a homegrown organization. I don't yet know if it is local or run from Toronto."

"What kind of crime?"

"Drugs, of course. But also people."

"*People*?"

"Illegal immigrants. Mostly what the authorities call 'racialized' people. I've done some research on this. Until recently, the 'racialized' population in Canada has been increasing from about four million to nine million people. This was a 140% increase, compared with a 1% increase for the so-called 'White' population."

"And..."

"Well, in the last little while, apparently, the government has been pulling back on the legal side of things, which makes the illegal side more attractive to a certain type of person."

"What's 'a certain type of person'?"

"There are two types. The type from so-called racialized countries who have the money to pay the traffickers, and the type from so-called 'white' countries with no money, who are exploited for immoral purposes."

"Prostitution?"

"Yes. From what my plants are able to discover, this organization is bringing both types into the country along with illegal drugs."

"Bastards!"

"Yeah. And you know what else they are smuggling?"

"What?"

"Lobsters! Unrecorded and unreported lobsters"

"Wow. I heard about the lobster situation, but not about the other stuff."

"The people and the drugs are transferred from ocean-going ships to fishing boats out in the Gulf of Maine, and are brought back here. They catch the lobsters on the way in."

"Holy cow! They've got a lot of gall. Three for one."

"Exactly. Now we have to figure out where you and your dig fit into this sordid picture."

38

When I went to the bookstore to get the maps from Gerald, I was alarmed to see that he had bruises on his wrist and face. I could see that he had been crying, as there were red rims around his eyes. The confident, flamboyantly-dressed man of only a few months ago had been reduced to a pathetic shadow of his former self.

"My God, Gerald—"

"Please, Marc. Don't say a word."

"But—"

"There's nothing you can do. It's not really any of your business."

"Fine."

I know I sounded petulant, but I was annoyed that my sympathy for an old friend had been flung back in my face. "You have the maps?"

"Yes. Here they are." His arms were full of dusty, folded papers.

"Thank you. And remember, not a word to anyone."

"Oh, Marc..."

"What is it?" I stared at him, suddenly realizing that while fear makes some bold, it renders others ineffably weak. "You told Stephen about the maps!"

"I had to." He started to weep.

"No, you didn't! You idiot!" I was surprised at how angry I was, but I could not stop myself. "You're hopeless. You're just a doormat for Stephen to wipe his boots on!"

By now his sobbing was uncontrollable, but I was so infuriated by his violation of my confidence that I grabbed the maps, turned on heel and left him.

I looked in on Louise at the wine store and fussed around the shelves, finding fault with minor details.

"You're in a filthy mood, today," she said tartly.

"Yes, I know. I 'd better go before I do something stupid."

"Yes, I think you should," she said, pointedly, opening the door for me.

When I got home, I parked the car, noticing out of the corner of my eye that Boris (or was it Horace?) was installed high in the boughs of the large maple tree which overshadows one side of the lot. I nodded silently in approval; from up there he could command an almost unimpeded view of anyone approaching from as much as a mile away.

Larry was waiting for me, sprawled in the lounge and viewing the field with what looked like a powerful pair of binoculars.

"You've got them?"

"Yes." I poured the maps on the table, some spilling onto the floor.

"While you were gone, I checked out our friend Alice Archibald."

"Did you? And what did you find?"

"Well, she ain't going to be doing much of anything so we don't have to worry about her."

"And Albert?"

"Yep. I saw him."

"And?"

"He's her son. He's very shy, and very—how shall I put it—challenged in the brain department. He hangs around the place, helps his Ma and drives his truck down to the road to get the mail, then drives back again."

"So, that lets them out."

"Yes. Let's go into the dining room," Larry said "This table isn't nearly big enough. We need to spread out the maps."

I gathered them up again and, with my arms full of the musty, smelly documents, took them into the dining room. Larry hastily examined the covers of those which were still folded and looked at the legends of those which had opened when they flopped out.

"What are you looking for?" I asked.

'I'm not interested in anything dated later than, say, 1950. So all those issued after that, put to one side."

It did not take us long to exclude the newer maps, which we piled on one of the chairs. I noted that seven were in that pile, another twelve being of the earlier date.

"Now, let's find those within a five-mile radius," Larry instructed.

That left us with only six maps.

"What now?"

"Read me the dates on those."

"1949."

"No. Put it over there."

"1921."

"Yes."

"1924"

"Yes."

"1919"

"Yes."

"1952."

"How the hell did that get in there? Toss it."

"Larry, why are you doing this? Do you have some kind of plan?"

"Maybe. I'm not sure. What's the last one?"

"1923"

"Yes. Alright put those on this side of the table. Now, Marc, of those six, which depict this property in detail?'

"Let me look." I leafed through them and found only two. "They all show this property but only these are in detail."

I passed them to Larry, who studied them closely. Then, with a heavy sigh, he pushed them away.

"What is it?" I probed.

"I don't know. Something is niggling me. Something is starting to form in my brain but I'm not there yet."

"I hope you'll tell me when you do get there."

"Sure I will. Let's go and make a nice dinner. We need to fortify ourselves for tonight's escapade."

"Ah yes, the visit to the dig by moonlight."

"I hope that will help me unclog my mind. What do you suggest we eat?"

"Rosalie's dining with Rachel Bland, so it'll be just us. And Boris and Horace of course."

"They'll eat anything."

"Okay. For them burgers and fries, and for us duck breasts with mushrooms, green beans and fondant potatoes."

"Sounds great. Any good plonk to go with that?"

"I don't keep *plonk*. But do you think we should drink? We'll need clear heads if we're going to be scrambling over the site."

"Just one bottle between us will be alright. How about a nice Pinot Noir?"

"I have a 2017 Felton Road, Block 3. It's young but it might go well with the duck."

"Ah, Felton Road. Splendid country around there."

"You been there? To New Zealand?"

"Of course. We have several operations in Central Otago."

"What sort of operations?"

"Better you should remain in ignorance, Little Brother. But Felton Road is a fine winery."

"You haven't been to the winery, Larry?"

"Yeah. Last time I was there Nigel Greening gave me a tour around the place."

I knew that Nigel Greening was the vigneron at Felton Road, but I never knew when Larry was spinning a bunch of lies. So I decided to let it go and got on with preparing the meal.

In the event, the food was delicious but, as I suspected, the wine had not yet fully developed.

As soon as darkness gathered, Larry jumped up and went to his room to get his kit. When he returned, he was dressed in night-time fatigues and a black balaclava. Apart from his eyes, his face was covered with black. He threw a tube at me. It contained a dark green, greasy substance.

"What's this?"

"Camo face paint. Put it on. And get shot of those light coloured clothes. Have you got anything black?"

"Yes. I'll go get them."

Suitably disguised, we set off up the hill, the long grass now damp with dew. I quickly became aware that, despite the age difference between us, Larry was exceptionally fit. Even disadvantaged by carrying his microphone, equipment and batteries, he ploughed ahead of me and reached the site a few minutes before me. I was puffing heavily when I arrived. Instinctively, I pulled out a flashlight.

"No, you fool! No lights!"

Hastily, I replaced the flashlight in my pocket and climbed over the fence. Larry moved slowly around the site, occasionally knocking into a bucket or protective plastic, until he came to the tape surrounding the pit.

"How do we get down?" He whispered.

"We have to go down? You know the Department of Labour has declared it a danger zone?"

"Talk sense, Little Brother. You said the sounds were in the pit. How can we hear the sounds if we're up here? Is there a ladder somewhere around? See if you can find it and bring it here."

I stumbled around and came across a ladder on the southern edge of the excavation. I had not realized how heavy it would be and it took what seemed like an age to drag it to the pit. Carefully removing the yellow tape, we manoeuvred the shaking ladder down into the darkness until we felt it hit a soft floor.

"Down we go!" Larry said.

"Both of us?"

"Both of us. You've been before, so you go first."

"Thanks a million."

I gingerly moved down the ladder until my feet were in the mud. The floor was not level and it took me a while to get my bearings.

Feeling along the sides of the pit, I discovered where the collapse had occurred. It felt like a large, concave depression, the centre of which was about eight feet from the surface, and its original contents had piled up on one side of the pit, making the bottom very uneven.

I called up to warn Larry what to expect, then moved away from the ladder, groping my way as I went. Soon he was alongside me and took out his equipment.

"Where did these sounds come from?" he asked.

"It was hard to tell where they were coming from, but I think it was this side," I indicated. "I guess that would be the eastern side."

"Alright. I'm going to put the earphones on now, so the second you hear anything let me know by tapping me on the shoulder."

I could not see my watch so I do not know how long we waited, but it seemed like an eternity.

Just when I was on the verge of telling Larry that we should go home, I heard faint sounds. I tapped him on the shoulder and he held his microphone half an inch from the trench face, and began to very slowly move it from right to left. He did this several times until finally stopping in two places. He held those positions for at least five minutes each before removing the headphones and moving to the ladder. We climbed to the top, carefully replaced the tape around the pit, put the ladder back where it belonged and left the site.

"Well?" I asked him as we were heading through the grass to the house.

"Yep. Two sounds. One moving of some kind of tank, I should say. The other women's voices in a language I don't speak. I'm guessing Polish."

"Could you tell if these two sounds come from the same place?"

"Different. The mike is highly directional and it pinpointed two distinct areas, although they might be relatively close together— like adjoining rooms."

We went in and removed our face paint and black clothes.

"Can you get us a drink, please, Little Brother? I need to do some research on the net for a while."

I brought Larry a twelve-year-old Aberlour, and then poured myself one. He retreated to the kitchen with his laptop and I heard nothing from him for at least half an hour.

At length he came into the lounge, bringing one of the maps with him. "I've figured it out."

"Please tell me, because I'm lost."

"Alright. Look at this map. This is the 1919 one. See where the dig is now?"

""Yes."

"Go an inch or two to the left. What do you see?"

"Adam Nicholson's farm."

"It wasn't Adam Nicholson's then, but what do you see in small letters just a bit to the right of the farm?"

"Ah. It says *Depot*."

"Quite right. Now I have found out that in the First World War, that is, just prior to the date this map was made, the West Nova Scotia Regiment had two bases in this area. One was at Fort Edward near Windsor, which was the camp serving as a dispatch centre for troops heading overseas. The other, which was their headquarters, was at Aldershot. Both are within twelve miles of here."

"I think I see where you are going with this."

"Good. Where am I going?"

"You going to tell me that the spot marked Depot was some kind of storage for these two encampments."

"And what else?"

"Ah! That it was probably a storage place for explosives and munitions."

"Well done! Anything else?"

"How do you mean?"

"Where would the safest place for explosives and munitions be?"

"Er...not near dwellings?"

"But this is next door to the farmhouse, so—"

"Jesus! That means it would have been underground! Of course!"

"Exactly. What we were hearing tonight was coming through the earth from the underground depot..."

"Although not being used not for munitions, but by criminals for clandestine purposes."

"Yes. Likely what sounded like the moving of tanks was associated with the illegal lobsters—"

"And the women's voices were likely associated with enforced prostitution."

"You got it!"

"What do we do now?"

"Well, I don't think we can hand this over to your pal Kennedy until we've got a lot more evidence. So we have to mount surveillance on the Nicholson place, take notes, and photograph vehicles coming and going. You said Nicholson is old?"

"Yes, very. I think he's 96, or maybe older."

"So they could be entering and leaving through his place without him knowing what the hell was going on."

"Will you get your plants to do the surveillance?"

"Yes. And you and I will take a look from the top of the hill."

"That'll be interesting."

"I think so. And you know what?"

"What?"

"We'll have to go in there ourselves soon."

"You don't mean down into the depot?"

"Yes. I don't see we have any choice if we want to collect the evidence which will put these bastards away."

39

After the previous night's exertions, Larry and I slept late again. Rosalie, bless her, gave Boris and Horace their breakfasts before she went to the university.

When we finally stumbled downstairs, neither of us spoke. Larry buried his head in his laptop while I prepared one of my favourite hot and cold meals: ham thinly sliced off the bone, cherry tomatoes and fried potatoes. We had it with Hawaiian Kona coffee, which is said to convey hints of chocolate, jasmine and peaches. We ate in silence, except for the thunderous snoring of Horace (or was it Boris?) in the attic.

"Imagine how loud it must be if you were up there," I said, but Larry just grunted.

While I did the dishes, Larry went into the garden and installed himself in the bean patch, presumably to get reports from his men. I did some cleaning around the ground floor and, after a while, walked out into the yard to breathe the still, cool summer air, tinged with the scent of buttercups and daisies.

I looked up into the maple tree to see if a bodyguard was there, but the boughs were empty. It was only when I turned back and looked at the house that I noticed Boris (or was it Horace?) on the roof, cunningly tucked against the chimney stack, visible only from my own angle. The Bulgars were looking after us well, I thought, and not for the first time I regretted Larry's strictures about not trying to make friends with them.

I was just about to go back in when Larry came around the corner from the garden.

"Anything?" I asked.

"No, but I wouldn't expect the bastards to be making moves in daylight. I have someone at the entrance to the Nicholson property, just in case."

"So, tonight may be the night."

"I hope so. I'll continue to have someone at the entrance to take down license plate numbers, but you and I'll go up and take a look from there."

"Where did you have in mind?"

"I thought a few hundred yards east of the dig. We should be able to see the comings and goings, as well as identify the entrance to the depot."

"What then?"

"We go in."

"Us? Go in?"

"Sure, what else? We need to see what's down there and, in particular, if any of the villains are there."

"Can't we just hand it over to Patrick Kennedy?"

"Not until we have it all sewn up. We need hard evidence, especially photos, which we can't get on the surface."

"But, Larry, what if there are more than two of these villains down there. Even five or six?"

"That depends on who they are, I guess, and what kind of shape they're in. But we should be able to handle them if things get rough."

"*Get rough*? I assume these men will be armed and we won't be."

"Of course we will, Little Brother. I have a Walther PDP four inch, steel frame and a Sig Sauer P320 X10 in my kit. I'll also be bringing along a Beretta 1301 Tactical Mod 2."

"What the hell is that?"

"Best shotgun in the world for close combat."

"Close combat! Jesus, Larry, why can't we take Boris or Horace with us?"

"And leave the old homestead unprotected? I don't think so."

"How about taking your plants with us?"

"Stealth is the whole point, Marc. We wouldn't be very stealthy, thundering in there with a complete squad of heavies. We need to slip in and out like thieves in the night." Larry laughed loudly at his simile.

"Nothing you say is reassuring me, Larry. To tell you the truth, I'm scared shitless."

"Don't worry. What's the worst that can happen?"

"We could both be killed!"

"Well, I can't deny that it's a possibility," he said, rubbing his chin with his hand. "Oh, I forgot to tell you that I got a little something on your old chum, Alaric Balser."

"What was it?"

"My guys say they found out that he was an alright sort of guy until about a month or so ago, but then he got into heavy debt. Some lawyer is involved—"

"Which one?"

"They don't know."

"Could be anyone. There must be at least twenty lawyers in the Annapolis Valley."

"Well, they tell me they don't know if he or she is the creditor or is representing the creditor."

"Do we know what kind of debt? Did he borrow money, or sustain losses gambling?"

"No idea. But apparently it was very heavy, they say. This made Alaric very beholden to someone."

"Beholden enough to drive his truck at Louise and me, apparently."

"So it would seem. Look, why don't we try to get some rest this afternoon? We don't know how late we're going to be up."

~

I had been asleep for about an hour when I was awakened by the faint noises of what sounded like heavy equipment. Irritated, I stumbled out of bed and went to look out of the window, but could see nothing, so I went to one on the south side of the house and peered up at the field.

Up at the archaeological dig, I could see two huge, yellow, earth-moving machines marauding about the site like prehistoric monsters. Hurriedly, I put on my shoes and dashed out.

As I drew near the site I could see Stefan and the students gathered disconsolately at the fence, watching what, for them, must have been an act of desecration.

"Stefan, what on earth is going on?" I called out.

"The Department of Labour has closed the site. They've declared it a danger zone and ordered it backfilled."

"Everything?"

"Everything. Of course, they filled in the pit first and are now pushing the spoil heaps onto the structure."

"What about the fossilized footprints?"

"Buried. Thank God we've got some photographs, but all physical evidence is gone."

"Except the seed. You've still got the seed?"

"Not even that. The lab lost it. You can understand. It was very small."

"They won't even let you look on the outskirts for the midden?"

"No, the whole shebang is kaput!"

"I'm very sorry, Stefan. The site posed so many unanswered questions. If it's possible to restart the dig at some time in the future, you know I'll give my permission."

"Thank, Marc, but it won't be when I'm around. I'll be moving on next spring. Back to Vancouver."

"Good luck."

I shook hands with him, said goodbye to the others, then sadly sauntered back to the house.

Larry had also been awakened and was standing outside the door. When I told him what had occurred, he seemed only vaguely interested, but this did not surprise me because he had never been invested in the dig the way I had been.

"Larry," I said quietly, "now that the dig is over, the villains have got what they wanted. Shouldn't we just leave it alone and do nothing?"

"You little coward!" Larry was furious. "You can do what you want, but I'm going ahead tonight."

"You're right," I said, ashamed and embarrassed. "Let's do it!"

~

We waited until an hour after it got dark, then set out up the hill, armed to the teeth and with two cameras. We shambled across the dig, now completely backfilled, and over the eastern fence onto Nicholson's land. We gingerly approached the brow of the hill and lay down on our stomachs. From there we could clearly see the farmhouse, and the long driveway from the road.

I saw a split-second flash from that spot, letting us know that Larry's men were in place.

Larry studiously laid out his weaponry on the ground in front of him, then slowly unwrapped a Werther's Original and popped it into his mouth. The sound of his sucking and lip smacking nearly drove me mad, and I desperately tried to think of something to distract me.

I hit on trying to recite in my mind all the words of Coleridge's *The Rime of the Ancient Mariner*, and I persevered with this until Larry's candy had dissolved.

It was exactly two hours and twenty-three minutes before the first vehicle pulled into the driveway and parked behind the farmhouse. It was a dark sedan of some kind, but we could not identify the make or colour. In another seventeen minutes, a pick-up truck drove up and parked alongside the car. Then, in quick succession, a small bus and three trucks followed, parking between the other vehicles and our position. Three men got out of the car, one from the pick-up truck and one driver from each of the other vehicles. They huddled in a group for a few minutes, then moved towards what looked like a black hump at the end of the yard.

Then we saw it: A sudden blaze of light flashed into the night. It was the entrance to the depot.

The first four men to arrive went in and disappeared. Then the driver of the bus opened its door and proceeded to escort nine women into the depot. At that point the trucks backed up to the entrance and their drivers then started to lug in whatever their cargoes were. Some looked like boxes, others like bundles of some substance.

From one truck, the driver, with some difficulty, wheeled mobile bins through the entrance opening.

"Lobsters," Larry mouthed at me. I nodded.

We had been gone almost four hours and I was becoming frantic to answer a call of nature, so I put my mouth close to Larry's ear and whispered:

"Going to take a piss."

He nodded and, taking the Beretta with me, I crawled away for a few yards then stood up, walked some way to the west of the brow behind a large bush to relieve myself, even though modesty in the dead of night was silly. I was comforted by the Beretta, the gun giving me a sense of great authority, although I was not exactly sure how to use it. Several times I put it to my shoulder and pretended to shoot, then made my way back to our look-off.

When I was about ten yards away from Larry, suddenly a darkened figure stepped between us. My heart almost stopped. I was struck with terror.

The man had a handgun which he pointed at Larry's head. "You're going to die, asshole," he said quietly in a vaguely foreign accent.

I saw Larry's body go rigid as I heard the gun being cocked.

In that instant I realized that I was holding the Beretta by the wrong end, so I swung it as hard as I could at the man's head. Exhaling a grunt, he crumpled like a house of cards.

"Well done, Little Brother," Larry whispered. "Smart enough not to make any noise, too. Very clever."

I did not disabuse Larry of the notion that I had held the gun by its barrel deliberately, but took the rope I was handed and bound the man as tightly as I could, stuffing a handkerchief in his mouth as I had seen people do in the movies.

Larry took my hand in his. "I owe you my life, Marc. Many thanks. I won't forget this."

"You're welcome," I said, weak now that the adrenaline rush was over.

"Right, let's go in. Follow me."

When we got to the level of the entrance I noticed there was only one truck remaining, the bus and the other two trucks having driven off. Stock still, we waited until the driver came out, climbed into his cab and left.

Then I followed Larry into the depot, my heart pounding so loudly I was worried it could be heard by our enemies.

I later discovered that what happened next consumed no more than thirty minutes, but it felt as if hours had passed and, to be honest, it is still something of a blur. I was so frightened and so appalled by what I saw that I would be hard-pressed to set down all the details.

Suffice it to say that Larry's speculations had been correct, in that we found room after room of live lobsters in mobile tanks; a few rooms piled high with brown, plastic-covered bundles which Larry said were certainly drugs; and one room in which the women we had seen leave the bus were sitting forlornly on bunks, looking totally lost. All the while, Larry was taking photographs so we would have a concrete record of what we encountered.

The biggest shock for me was when we tiptoed around a corner to see four men conferring some forty feet away from us. We shrunk back into the shadows and froze.

One man, the youngest of the four, was clearly the leader as he was giving orders to the other three. They had their backs to us so we could not see their faces, until the leader turned around to spit on the floor. It was *Stephen*!

As he moved away, the other two also turned in our direction and revealed their faces to us. *I was utterly astounded to be looking at Bill Jolly, Staff Sergeant Lomas, and Gary Marshall!*

Silently, Larry took more photographs, then nudged me, indicating that we should back away and make our escape.

Never have I been so glad to get out of any place as much as I was to leave that depot, and I ran up and over the hill as fast as my legs would carry me.

When we were well into my property again, we both breathlessly collapsed.

"You knew those guys, didn't you?" Larry said. "I could tell by the look on your face."

"Yes. I've known Gary Marshall since we were at school together. The son of a bitch! Obviously he's the lawyer Alaric Balser was indebted to."

"No doubt about it. What about the others?"

"Bill Jolly—who I also thought was my friend—is a captain. He has a small fleet of fishing boats. And the last one is a dirty cop."

"Ah! It all starts to make sense."

"What now, Larry?"

"I have enough pictures to seal the fate of those bastards, but you'd better get them to your friend Kennedy before they find that guy you tied up."

"But if I do that tonight—"

"It must be tonight."

"But Patrick'll be down here in a flash."

"That's okay. Boris and Horace are already gone. I'll be gone as soon as you have these photos on your computer."

"I won't say it's been an unalloyed pleasure, Larry, but there's never a dull moment when I'm with you."

"Not a bad night's work, Little Brother. Only one person got hurt, and you didn't even have to fire a gun."

40

As I expected, when I rose in the morning there was no sign in the house of Larry or Boris and Horace. Their work done, they had disappeared into the night. I did not even hear them leave, I was so glued to my computer in the study, busily transmitting the photographs to Patrick Kennedy.

I had to phone him first to get him to get out of bed and go to his computer. It was one of the most difficult conversations I have ever had.

A very sleepy Ruth answered the call. "Ruth, it's Marc. I'm so sorry to wake you, but I must speak to Patrick."

"Good God, Marc, it's two-thirty in the morning."

"I know, but it is very important. Tell Patrick it's an emergency."

"Oh, alright. I'll wake him. Pat, wake up. Marc's on the phone."

"What the fuck does he want?" It was more of a growl than a question.

"Patrick. Please go to your computer now," I urged.

"What the hell! Do you know what time it is?"

"Yes, but I can't help that. Time is of the essence. Please do what I say."

"This had better be good or I'll have you arrested and throw away the fucking key!"

I heard grunts and wheezes as Patrick padded his way downstairs, and then I heard him switching on his computer.

"I'm there," he announced. "What now?"

"Please look at the photographs I sent you first, and then we'll talk."

A few minutes of silence passed then I heard him blaspheme very loudly.

"Where do these come from?"

"From an underground depot on the next property to mine."

"Jesus! When were they taken?"

"About an hour ago."

"Surely, that isn't Lomas I see?"

"Yes, it is."

"Christ, I'll have his guts for garters, the bent bastard. Who are the others?"

I gave him their names and what I knew about their occupations and backgrounds, and did not fail to mention the man we had left tied up on the hill.

Then came the question I had been dreading. "Where did you get these, Marc?"

"You have to act fast, Patrick. Likely, they're all still there so you could nail them tonight."

"Answer my question! Where did you get them?"

"I put two and two together," I lied, "and followed a hunch that led me to the depot, then I took the photographs and came back here."

"What is this list of numbers you have appended?"

"Those are the registrations of all the vehicles which came to the depot."

"Very useful indeed. And you did all this on your own? What are you, some kind of fucking Superman?"

"Er...yes... no."

'Yes, no?"

"Er... I had some help from a guy I hired as a private bodyguard."

"I'll need to speak to him, for sure."

"You can't. He's already gone back...to the U.S."

"And I guess you can't even remember his name?"

"Patrick, please move. Forget about my bodyguard. He came up with the goods didn't he? Just go get these bastards."

"Okay. But you stay exactly where you are. There's going to be a lot of noise and activity over your hill before the sun comes up. I'll be there within the hour, but you won't be seeing me."

"You won't drop by for breakfast?"

"Marc, listen to me carefully. You have had nothing whatever to do with exposing this depot, you understand? These photographs came from a confidential police informer."

"Ah. I hear you."

"And the next time we meet, you will not let on that you have intimate knowledge of the details of that place. Right?"

"Right."

I did not go to bed, despite Rosalie's pleading, because I knew I would not be able to sleep. I sat in the window, nursing a glass of 15-year-old Aberfeldy, and waited.

After about forty-five of the quietest minutes I had ever known, I saw myriad lights sweeping across the top of the hill, and cars, sirens blaring, racing past our property, presumably on their way to detain the owners of the bus and trucks I had seen at the farm earlier. I estimated that at least six police vehicles were involved in the operation, which, as far as I could tell, lasted about an hour. Then the lights disappeared and all was quiet.

I longed for an update from Patrick, but knew I would have to learn what occurred from the news later in the day.

There was nothing on the eight o'clock news, but at nine there was what I think is called a "special bulletin." Patrick and his Chief Superintendent held a press conference during which they announced that millions of dollars' worth of drugs and illegal lobsters had been discovered in a pre-dawn raid. They said the biggest crime ring east of Montreal had been brought to book, and that several local men had been arrested and charged with attempted murder, drug smuggling, people trafficking, and various other crimes. The men's names were not mentioned, but I knew they would be known on the street before the day was out.

With slight regret that my part in the exposure could not be known outside my family and two Bulgars, I felt some celebration was in order. So, after checking with Rosalie, I decided to hold a splendid dinner party the following evening. Walter and Joyce Bryson, Ray and Rachel Bland and Stefan, if available, would be our guests.

Definitely *not* invited were Gary and Jane Marshall.

41

At the dinner party the following evening, it did not take long for the assembled company to get around to discussing the news of the day.

"Whoever would have thought it?" Joyce Bryson said, shaking her head. "Gary Marshall a crook! We've known him—how long is it Walter?"

"About thirty years," her husband said. "Marc, you went to school with him, didn't you?"

"Yes, you could almost say we grew up together. John Dempster, Gary and I were like the Three Musketeers. I was astounded when I heard this news on the radio."

"Did you ever suspect anything, Walter?" asked Rachel Bland, twirling her glass of *Château Rieussec* 1982.

"I often wondered how he and Jane managed to live so well, considering that his law practice didn't seem to be particularly flourishing. But beyond that, I had no idea, Rachel."

"How about that Jolly fellow?" Ray interjected. "Did anyone know him?"

"We did," said Rosalie quietly. "We used to get all our fresh fish from him."

"Really? What was he like?" Stefan asked.

"He seemed—well, jolly." Everyone laughed. "He was a nice, kind guy."

"Just goes to show that we don't really know anyone."

After Stefan said this, people looked at each other and a silence descended.

I wondered what my friends would think of me if they knew about my escapades, and that my brother was not only alive, but was himself a crook. I gave Rosalie a sideways glance and our eyes met.

I was glad when Rachel jumped in again. "Does anyone know Sergeant Lomas?"

"I did, slightly, through my practice," said Walter. "I used to see him in court from time to time. I imagine they will throw the book at him. Police corruption is not well tolerated these days."

"Rosalie and I met him a few times in connection with the explosion in the garage," I said.

"I didn't like him one bit," my wife said bitterly. "We got the impression that he wasn't really trying to help at all."

"And now you know why!" Ray said.

"Indeed we do!" I said with great feeling.

It was a good dinner party. Having friends around us again after so much stress and strain felt wonderful. I experienced a combination of relief and elation, tinged with a tiny touch of regret that my life would return to a pedestrian pattern of cooking and tending the garden. Of course, I might get another case; but even if I did, compared with what I had just been through, it would likely seem commonplace and boring.

While the others chattered on, I reflected that I had been extremely fortunate, not only with financial wealth, but also because I had attracted some exciting and intriguing cases since I began as a private investigator some six years ago. Patrick Kennedy always said that I attracted trouble like metal to a magnet. Looking back on those past cases, I had to confess there seemed to be more than a grain of truth in what he said.

It had all begun with the quest for the Holy Grail, a fascinating romp with extraordinary historical connections. Then there was the exciting, but chilling, investigation into Ray Bland's ancestors, a search which had surprising results. After that was a race on two continents to discover who was threatening the life of the premier of Nova Scotia. Most recently, had been a most frustrating exploration into a series of apparently unconnected murders, in which an abundance of red herrings kept Patrick and me in a state of perpetual consternation.

I was drawn out of my reverie by a question from Ray, which was directed to Stefan. "So, now that your dig has been closed down by the government, are you able to tell us what you found?"

"That's a damn good question. All we know for sure is that at some time, somebody—probably the Mi'kmaq—built a form of platform house at the top of the hill, overlooking the Minas Basin."

"Is that the reason they put it there—because of the dominant position?" Joyce asked.

"I don't think so, although that may have been what originally drew them to the spot."

"Then what was it?" Asked Rachel.

"I realize that this is a bit of a stretch, but I think the house was located there to protect the fossilized footprints at the bottom of the pit."

"That's why the house was built with the pit in the middle of it?" Rosalie asked.

"Exactly. We've established that the footprints were made about 20,000 years ago. If they weren't actually made by ancestors of the Mi'kmaq, the natives must have thought they were, and consequently revered them and protected them."

"Sound like a reasonable hypothesis to me," said Walter. "Now, answer me this. Marc has told me about various layers above the footprints. How do you account for them?"

"And for the horrible stench which made you sick as dogs for days?" Rosalie asked.

"I don't account for them because I can't."

"Just like Marc's discovery of the door with Greek lettering on it?"

"Yes. If we had been allowed to continue to dig, especially in the pit, I believe many of our questions would have been answered."

"And now they never will be," Joyce said sadly.

"At some stage in the future, maybe, but it would be a hell of a thankless job re-excavating that mess."

"I want to say something about the Greek inscription," I said. "It was very dark down in that pit—remember this was before the higher power lamp was put in—and the surroundings made you very susceptible to suggestion, so it is conceivable that I imagined it. Or I saw a configuration in the earth, in the half-light, which looked like writing."

"It's possible," Stefan said. "It was awfully spooky in the pit, especially when we were hearing sounds which were then unidentified."

"You know, the Greek inscription was not the only majorly anachronistic discovery on the site." It was out of my mouth before I could stop it.

They all looked at me. Stefan was frowning deeply.

"What on earth do you mean, Marc?"

"Ralph told me on a number of occasions that he had found items which, logically, could not have been there. He said these supported the Upward Percolation theory."

"That nonsense!" Stefan said.

"Ralph said he'd only recently been converted to believing in the theory because he had found these artifacts."

"Poor Ralph." Rosalie said sorrowfully.

"What were these items, Marc?" Stefan demanded.

"One was an ancient Jewish coin. Another was a copy of the *Imago Mundi*—"

"What?" Stefan exploded.

"Wait, I'm not finished. There was some kind of vitrified stone which Ralph said was from Scotland. Then a copy of something called the Dispilio Tablet. He said it was from Neolithic Greece and was about 7,000 years old—"

"Good God! You should have told me, Marc."

"He told me not to tell anyone about these finds," I said. "I'm not exactly sure why, but he was very insistent."

They all stared at me, some with curiosity, some with incredulity and some with what looked rather like pity.

Rosalie broke the silence. "Marc, did Ralph ever show these artifacts to you?"

"Well, he didn't have them with him at the time."

"Did you ever actually *see* any of them?"

"No. I didn't, but I couldn't see why he would be lying to me."

"So, no visual proof of their existence?"

"No."

"That's a relief," said Stefan. "Otherwise I wouldn't have a clue how to explain them."

"Except by the Upward Percolation theory," Walter said.

"I thought we had already dismissed that as bullshit," Stefan said.

"There are a lot of otherwise-intelligent people who subscribe to the theory," Rachel said quietly.

"Not here, I hope." Stefan was indignant.

"Ralph must have been hallucinating as a result of the illness which finally killed him," said Joyce. "What was it called, Marc?"

"Marchiafava-Bignami Disease."

"Yes, that's it. Let's face it, Ralph was really screwed up at the end," said Stefan.

"That has to be the explanation," I said. "Poor Ralph."

I said no more, but when I put my hand in my pocket to get a handkerchief, my fingers closed around something hard, something sharp. A flint, Bronze Age arrowhead.

42

It was mid-October, six or seven weeks after the archaeological dig was closed down. Rosalie was busy at the university, where she had been offered a full professorship. Stefan had returned to his home in Vancouver. Jennifer was away, in her second year at college.

I was now at a loose end.

The air was cooling rapidly and the trees were already richly coloured. The leaves on the vines in John Dempster's vineyard were various shades of copper. The grapes were plump and healthy, the white varieties a gleaming lime, and the red ones a deep purple with a misty sheen. The harvest would be any day now.

Everywhere, on country lanes, driveways, town streets, leaves gathered, fluttered and, when the wind was up, swirled like mini cyclones. Shorts and t-shirts had been abandoned in favour of pants and sweaters, and in the stores tourist items gave way to parkas and hunting hats.

Gary, Bill, and Stephen had appeared for a Primary Hearing in Kentville, and were remanded for trial sometime in the next year. For some reason I did not understand, Lomas was being charged separately at a later date. Walter had been approached by Gary to represent him at the trial, but, despite their long friendship, had declined.

"I just couldn't do it," he told me. "I know the innocent and guilty alike are entitled to representation, but I regard Gary as being Tracey's murderer, even if he didn't do it himself."

"We still don't know who did kill her."

"And we may never know. It's pure guesswork, but my money's

on Lomas."

"That poor girl. Will they be jointly charged with killing her?

"I doubt it. There's no evidence which can directly link any of them to her death."

"What about the other crimes? If they're convicted, how much prison time could they get?"

"I'd say up to six years for the drugs, another two for the lobsters."

"And the trafficking in those poor women?"

"That's when they'll really get nailed. If they have any money, they could be fined $1 million and get anything up to life imprisonment."

"Good. I hope they go away for a long time. What will happen to Jane, I wonder? Does she have independent means?"

"I'm not sure. But any accounts and property in Gary's name will be forfeit to the Crown, because they will be deemed to be the proceeds of crime. As far as I know, Jane has no relatives in the area who can help her."

"She wouldn't be able to work around here. It'd be too uncomfortable."

"Yes. I feel sorry for her. I very much doubt if she ever knew anything about Gary's criminal activities."

On the morning in question, I indulged my passion for smoked haddock with poached eggs. With this I had some lovely, freshly-baked sourdough bread, lashings of farm butter and Kona coffee. Rosalie, who thinks such a meal is so disgusting that she has to eat in another room, took her omelette and toast into the dining room while I remained in the kitchen.

Our eating was interrupted by the phone ringing. Since Rosalie had taken it with her she answered.

"Marc. It's for you."

"Damned early for people to be calling. Who is it?"

"It's Ray Bland."

Puzzled as to why Ray would be calling at this time of day, I wandered in and took the phone from my wife.

"Good morning, Ray."

"'Morning, Marc. Get your ass over here right away."

"Why? Nothing wrong, I hope?"

"Not a thing. I'll see you in about fifteen minutes."

"What's going on, Ray?"

"See you."

"Ray, tell me—"

But he had hung up. I told Rosalie what had occurred and she was as mystified as I was.

I hurriedly finished my breakfast, grabbed my leather jacket, and went out. As I was hopping into the BMW, I noticed with approval that the workmen were putting the finishing touches to my new garage. The bomb had torn the place to pieces, so it had taken a long time to get it back into serviceable order.

When I was driving along the Harvest Highway to Ray's dealership in New Minas, it occurred to me that Ray must have a new case for me and, knowing Ray as I did, I was sure it would be an interesting one.

I pulled into his forecourt, jumped out and went into the office. Ray was grinning from ear to ear.

"You are one very lucky son of a bitch!" he said.

"Why? What are you talking about?"

"Follow me."

He led me through into the large showroom. At first I thought I was dreaming.

"Isn't she a beauty?" Ray was beaming.

There, shimmering in white with cobalt blue lines, was the Bugatti L'Or Blanc. The gorgeous, 1,000-horsepower car of my dreams, which was an engineering masterpiece capable of 407 kph.

In a daze, I drifted around it, running my hands over the unique, porcelain fixtures and peering in at the sumptuous white-leather seats.

"How did you get it? What is it doing here?" I stammered.

"It's yours."

"*Mine*?"

"Sure. All yours."

"But—"

"It was shipped to you from some guy in Saudi Arabia called Sheik Abdul Aziz. With his compliments."

"Holy cow!"

"He must have heard about your other Bugatti being blown up."

Gently, I opened the driver's door and slid behind the wheel. I ran my hand over the dashboard, noticing that the glove box was porcelain with a diamond-cut finish.

I flipped it open and saw a tiny slip of paper.

Making sure Ray was not watching, I straightened it and read the message, which could only have come from Larry.

Am I my brother's keeper?
You bet.
Now we are even.

Image courtesy of mad4wheels.com

Acknowledgement

I would like to express my thanks to Dr. David B. King for first introducing me to Marchifava Bignami Disease, when we were drinking *Teroldego Rotaliano*.

About the author

Jeremy Akerman is an adoptive Nova Scotian who has lived in the province since 1964. In that time he has been an archaeologist, a radio announcer, a politician, a senior civil servant, a newspaper editor and a film actor.

He is painter of landscapes and portraits, a singer of Irish folk songs, a lover of wine, and a devotee of history, especially of the British Labour Party.

Jeremy's first novel, *Black Around the Eyes*, was published in 1981. Other projects required his intention until recently, when he was able to take up fiction again. During 2023-24 he wrote and published eight novels.

See: moosehousepress.com/authors/jeremy-akerman